# THE BONE SHARPS

*For Karonne,
With hopes that you're doing
well, and in anticipation
of seeing you again soon.
Love,
Tim
May 2007*

# The
# Bone Sharps

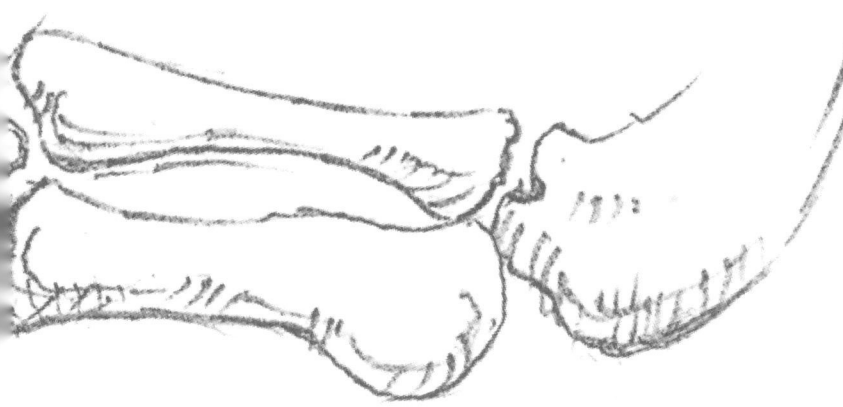

## A Novel by

# TIM BOWLING

GASPEREAU PRESS LIMITED
PRINTERS & PUBLISHERS
*Beati Anni Decimi*
MMVII

*For Bob and Renie Gross
whose generosity introduced me
to the badlands and to the story
of Charles Sternberg.*

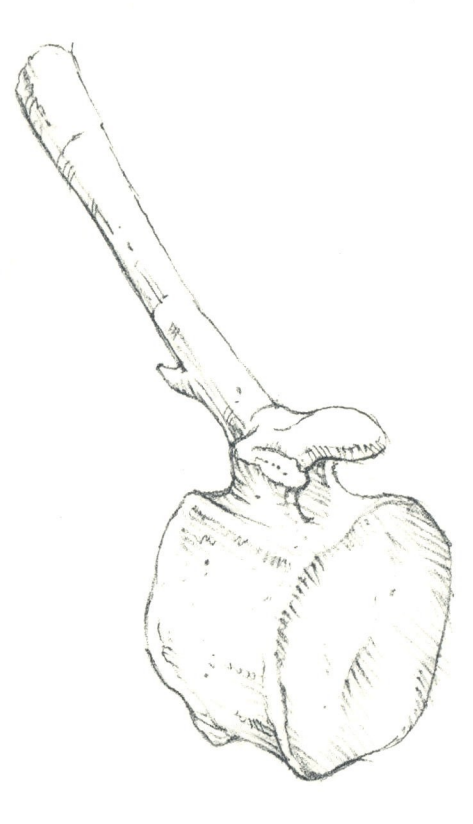

Sometimes dreams are wiser than waking.

BLACK ELK

The iron throats nearby crashed forth their message of death
to the Germans, and from three thousand guns the tempest
of death swept through the air. It was a wonderful sound. The
flashes of guns in all directions made lightning in the dawn ...
In an instant the enemy's artillery replied, and against the
morning clouds the bursting shrapnel flashed. I knelt on the
ground and prayed to the god of battles to guard our noble
men ... There was such splendour of human character being
manifested in that far-flung line where smoke and flame
mocked the calm of the morning sky that the watcher
felt he was gazing upon eternal things.

CANON FREDERICK SCOTT
SENIOR CHAPLAIN, 1ST CANADIAN DIVISION

And the theologian applauds the philosopher, and says of
the scientist in his prayers, "I thank Thee that I am not as this
section cutter, this bug hunter nor even as this bone sharp."

EDWARD DRINKER COPE

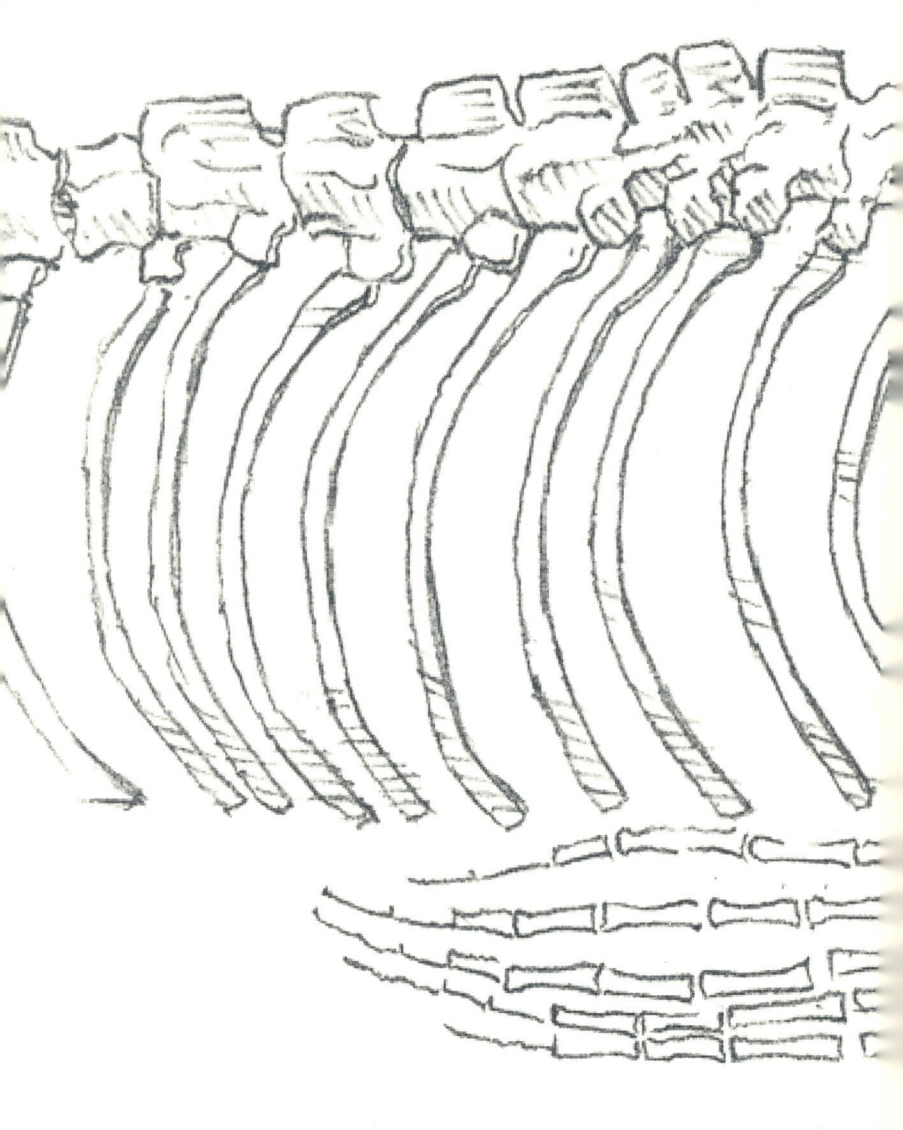

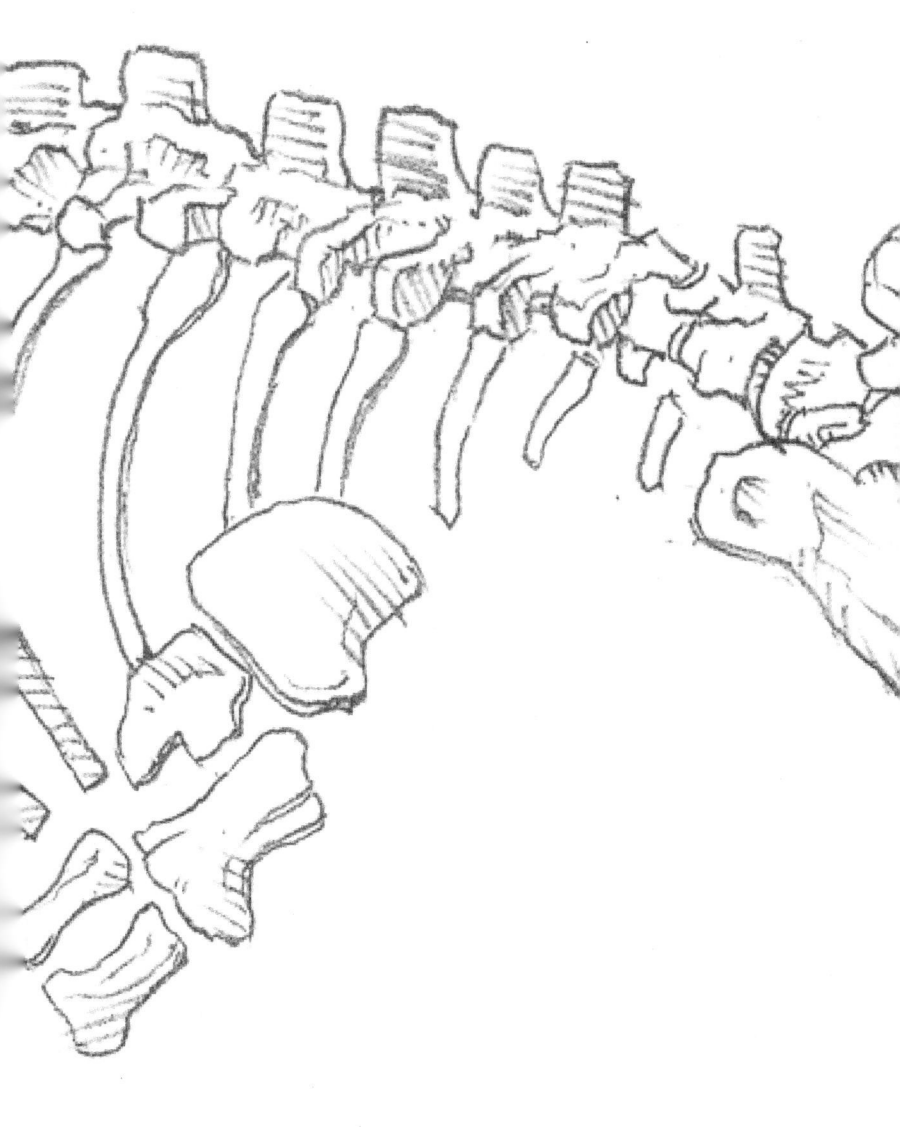

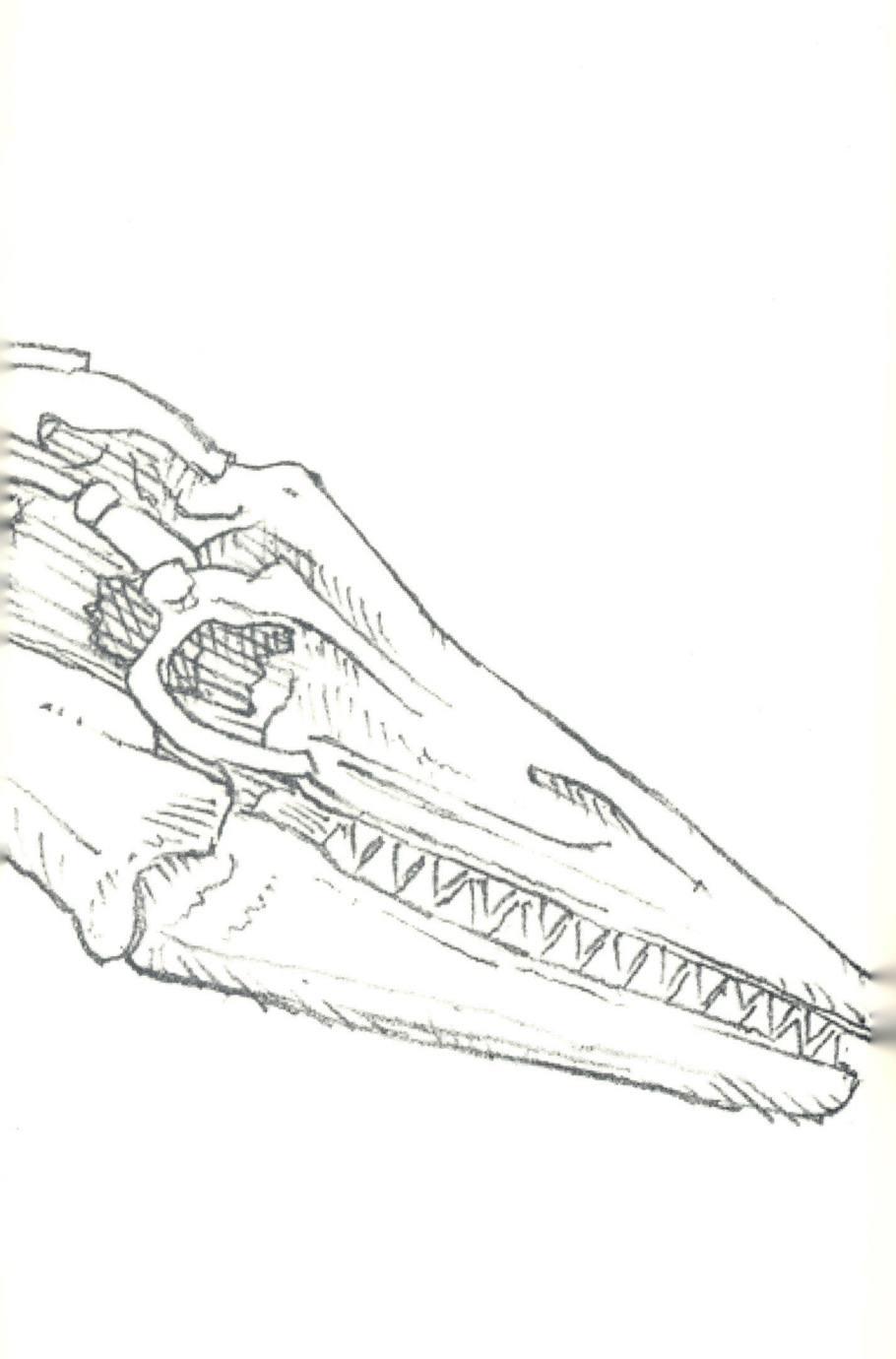

# 1916

CHARLES HAZELIUS STERNBERG, SIXTY-SEVEN YEARS OLD, game-legged, deaf in one ear, could not sleep. But it wasn't age or the body's aches and ills accumulated from over forty years of hunting fossils in the vast stretches of the west that disturbed him where he lay, on a rickety cot in a canvas tent in the badlands of the Red Deer River Valley, in the Queen's Land, the Province of Alberta, Dominion of Canada. He had long since learned to live with pain of the physical kind. What, after all, was that to the pain of the heart's loss?

He slowly pulled back the blankets, then lifted and turned his body until he had his feet on the earth and was facing the closed flap of the tent. He sat this way for several minutes, his narrow, large-browed skull held like a too-familiar fossil in his calloused hands. The silence around him, that stretched for hundreds of miles across the prairie in all directions but lay heaviest here amongst the towering, misshapen hoodoos and sandstone buttes of the badlands, was the silence of another trying summer—mosquitoes by the millions, their endless drone. He felt that his head was a jar filled with them, that he was holding his brain out as a sweetmeat for their unceasing blood lust. This thought, and the companion idea that he was being ungenerous to one of the Lord's creations, roused him. He stood, pushed through the virtually useless mosquito mesh that hung around his cot, and stepped outside.

The stars were as many as the unseen insects, but oddly dim. Even so, their numbers filled him with a familiar mixture of calm and awe. It was the kind of night he had known only in the West—vast, more God's possession than Man's. Such a dripping cluster of stars, yet the earth itself lay black. Another of the Creator's great mysteries.

Sternberg stared into the immensity, the richest bone bed of all, the nightly visible proof of God's glory and power. He opened his mouth to utter a quiet prayer of praise. But true to recent experience, he could not find the words. A tremor shook him, a whole body shiver reminiscent of the terrible grippe he had suffered as a young man in the Oregon desert. Only this was worse; it came from the spirit, not the body. He bowed his head and concentrated harder on the lost prayers, but the burnt-ash smell of the just-doused campfire distracted him. He looked up and breathed deeply of the scents of sagebrush and cottonwood leaves which lay just outside the small ring of tents, held off slightly by the lingering fire smoke. But the breath he sought, like the words of praise, did not come.

He looked down the bank to the still, barely star-glazed river. He could see the scow where Levi and Charlie had moored it, just under a huge, overhanging cottonwood. One crate full of fossils, a month's labour, bulked darkly through the filigree of leaf-work. What lay inside those hammered boards? Millions of years, God's grandeur, the treasured remains of the great lost beasts of Creation. Bones. Of the foot, the skull, the spine, of the terrible carnivores of the Cretaceous and the smaller prey they feasted on. Denizens of the tropical sea whose tides Sternberg had felt in his own blood for decades, until all of the earth was a shore he knelt on to hear the rhythms of huge bodies pushing through water.

Not now. Now he heard only the nattering whine of the mosquitoes and, behind it, fading almost to nothing, and then when he could not bear the final loss, rising until it broke him from his restless sleep—Maud's voice. He could taste the salt of his tears flowing through the tangled chaff of his mustache; he couldn't believe there was any water in them at all, just salt. It would be no surprise, given the water he'd been forced to drink in his long wanderings: alkali water, thick as Epsom salts. When a man is thirsty, he drinks and tastes the water afterwards. But when a man is lost, he turns to God for sustenance.

He recalled the angry words of the letter he'd received a week before, forwarded in a large package from his wife in New York. The correspondent chose to be anonymous, but the contents were direct and bold enough:

*Why do you persist in celebrating a villain? Cope was one of the wickedest, foulest humans ever to draw breath—you must know this. Why should you lie, a man of your character and reputation? To deliver a speech such as you did last winter at the Academy of Natural Sciences gathering! Lies! All lies! Do you choose not to believe that he stole fossils from museums, skulking around in a shabby coat like a common criminal, stuffing into his pockets what he lacked the talent and intelligence to find for himself?*

And so on, for three pages. Clearly, the writer was hysterical and supremely biased against the professor. Perhaps he was even an old enemy of Cope's, one of the many for whom the professor, witty as always, had given the Latin name *Cophater*.

No doubt he'd been some associate of Professor Marsh, Cope's great rival. Well, what did it matter now? Cope had been dead for nearly two decades, Marsh almost as long.

So why, he asked himself, did this letter so trouble him? And why, upon reading it, did his troubled thoughts turn to his daughter with an intensity he'd not known since her death twenty years before? He shouldn't have to bear this, not at his age—the past should have stayed the past. But even thinking this, he knew God could be wrathful, and he knew as well that no one escaped the hard truths of mankind. There was no sustenance even in God now. The world reflected back only Maud's suffering.

Sternberg looked heavenward, willing his heart to open as easily as a parched mouth, willing it to do what it had always done by nature, without conscious effort. But it opened only as his daughter's grave opened, to take in the light and close it with darkness forever.

He wept silently so as not to waken his three sleeping sons and two assistants, who would have been shocked by the sudden re-emergence of his grief. More shocked than he himself, who at least knew that he'd been low in spirit even before the letter's arrival. What was the affliction, then, if not some prophecy of the struggle he'd be forced to endure now, as he looked back at a past that should have stayed buried? It's all in His design, he comforted himself hollowly, unable to believe that God concerned himself with every instance of shaken faith. No, it was his own weakness; there was no divinity in it. At this stage of life, to be failing at a man's most important task, at the glorious work of praise! He was ashamed. He stood at the edges of the burnt ash, with the ancient, towering cemeteries of creation behind him, and heard Maud crying inside his crying, her tears fossilized in each living tear that carved its path down his leathery skin.

A faint footfall broke his sorrowful reverie. He exhaled brokenly, quickly wiped his eyes with a rough sleeve, and waited for someone to emerge from the darkness. But he did not hear another footfall. He squinted into the thick black beyond the tents, where the trails of loose scree spoked away into the hoodoos. The mosquito drone intensified to a crazed whine. Sternberg waved angrily at his good ear, but kept his eyes focussed ahead. After so many years in the bone fields, he did not need the evidence of his five common senses to tell him whether there was a presence in the night. But what others regarded as an uncanny, almost mystical, knack for locating fossils, he knew was simply the fine-tuning of an extra sense, one that most people lacked the patience or inclination to develop. This same instinct, that found the slightest protuberance of bone in a rocky overhang hundreds of feet above him, easily picked up the motions of any creature with blood coursing through it.

Nothing moved. But something or someone was definitely there. Normally, in the bone yards, Sternberg would have felt threatened by the presence of rival bone sharps. However, in the valley of the Red Deer, relations with Barnum Brown and his team from the American Museum of Natural History had been amicable from the start, three years before. Some minor disagreements over claims to prospecting territory, but no outright thievery or violence, nothing like the old days when whole boxcars of fossils were hijacked on their way east. And Indians were certainly not a threat here as they had been forty years earlier in the western states. Yet Sternberg knew it was folly not to take precautions.

He walked towards his tent to get a rifle. Before he'd gone ten steps, however, he sensed the presence in the night shifting again. Suddenly, the precautions seemed a burden.

Dispensing with them, he moved almost silently to the edge of the campground and stood at the foot of a scree trail which rose slightly alongside the dark shoulder of a bluff.

"Who's there?" he called out.

Seconds later, a figure emerged only feet away, faintly visible in the starlight. Sternberg's mouth opened, his hand flew to his throat.

"Good evening, Mr. Sternberg."

No, it was not Maud. Of course not. It was one of his crew. Lily, the blacksmith's daughter—only ... only ... was she not the very age Maud had been at death, barely into her eighteenth year? Had he not nursed her through the same illness that had killed his own cherished girl, as well as Lily's own father a few days before she was out of danger? A mere two years ago. Yes. He had sat beside Lily day and night, hardly sleeping, feeling as if the Lord had given him this second chance because, when Maud had been ill, he had been far away, in the field, working for Cope, where telegrams alone could not find him. In the Texas badlands. The secrecy of the fossil trade in those days, the professor's fierce distrust of other bone hunters, especially those in the employ of Professor Marsh of Yale, made communication with the outside world a dangerous matter. Yet Cope had tried, he had sent word at once, he had prayed for speed. But Maud had died mere days before Sternberg had reached home. Mere days ... the ache of that memory never dulled.

"Mr. Sternberg?"

"Yes, Lily." He sighed deeply, forced a smile. It was too dark to read the concern on the girl's face, so he understood his own smile meant nothing. "It is age, that's all. Sometimes sleep does not come so easily. You will not understand this yet, of course." As soon as he'd said this, Sternberg considered the hour. What *was* the girl doing awake and outside when, in a few hours, she'd be starting work, helping Charlie excavate his chasmosaur?

"But you, Lily? It is late, far too late ..."

Sternberg felt, rather than saw, her hesitation and curious energy. It surprised him. Lily was not a moody young woman. If she had been, he could never have employed her. Working in the bone yards demanded a physical and emotional steadiness few men even possessed. Lily had been no disappointment in this regard. His sons had been doubtful of her usefulness in the field, yet she soon proved to have a keen eye and strong constitution—no doubt coming so close to death had given her a rare strength of body and spirit. It was not like her to hesitate.

The sharp, clean smell of sage poured over her shoulders. Off in the hoodoos an owl hooted. Just at the edge of his vision, Sternberg noticed the streak of a falling star. Why could she not be his daughter, he wondered, almost desperately. Why could he not act as if she were? Perhaps, if he could make himself do so ...

The girl's energy unnerved him. Something in her flashed to the same suffering that kept him awake.

Ach! Old fool! He laboured to shut the image of Maud from his mind, to shut out the bitterness in the letter attacking Cope. His daughter and his mentor were long dead; Lily was living. If he could be of any help to her ...

"Lily, child, what is it?"

Her voice came softly, though he could not read her expression. "Have you had a letter from Scott lately?"

Sternberg stared at her. Stunned, he suddenly understood

what she was enduring, why sleep would come no easier for her. But how had he not noticed this before? And immediately he knew the hard answer: all season he'd looked at the world as a drowning man looks at the stars; the astonishing glimpses could not take him out of his peril. He tried to rally, for the girl's sake.

"Yes. Only yesterday. You will like this, I think, Lily. He writes to ask me for a reference to the chief paleontologist of the British Museum. Does that not sound like a bone sharp? Such gifts. I would not be surprised to find him continuing our work even in the midst of battle."

She flinched noticeably at the last word, as if she'd been struck. Sternberg hurried to soften his careless use of language. Lily might have been a blacksmith's daughter, but war was no fit subject for any woman.

"He is well. Excited, as always. Lily, one who is chosen by God to do His work will not be taken before he can make a proper start. Of this, I am certain."

Sternberg's voice trailed off. Convictions he'd held all his life suddenly seemed fragile as bone exposed too long to the elements. All he knew of the war in Europe was that it took funding away from fossil exploration. The Canadian government had already informed him that this would be the last season it could afford to employ the entire Sternberg family. As for the killing—the savagery of man towards man was no shock to one who had travelled through the west in the time of the Indian wars. A thought occurred to him.

"Lily, I will read his letter to you. Such excitement. Such strength. It will ease your worries. And then sleep, yes? Charlie is not so great a taskmaster as his papa, I think, but he will expect your contribution all the same."

Again Sternberg felt, rather than saw, the girl's response. The sage now seemed to flow off her like a large embrace. Yes, the letter. He turned and limped quickly to his tent.

But the first letter he picked up after lighting the coal-oil lantern was the one attacking Professor Cope. Sternberg dropped it quickly, afraid it would blight his hand. He should burn it, he thought, and immediately an image of the young Cope, the Cope he'd never known, rose before him. The twenty-year-old genius who wandered Europe for two years during the Civil War, taking voluminous notes on the exhibits in grand museums, preparing his essays, making sketches by the thousands of fossils and their imagined living forms, then, his noble, intense face blazing red in fire glow as he consigned everything he'd written and sketched to the flames, two years' worth of brilliance destroyed because, as Cope himself told the story, he had begun to view himself as a rival to God, and that folly had had to be crushed.

Sternberg stood listening, as rapt as he'd been forty years earlier in Montana, in the treacherous badlands of the Judith River. His mentor might have been standing right beside him, his voice was that clear.

"We are not greater than we know. We are smaller. This silence, this western silence that surrounds and awes, is but the faintest echo of God's heartbeat. We lean towards it, almost hear words in a tongue we recognize. Gentlemen, it is not the crow's caw at birth I speak of, it is not the crow's caw at death—though these are verily the handclaps of the Holy, nature's supreme joy at our great privilege to know the pulse of creation. Nay, I speak of the meadowlark's song between, piping up from these ancient bones around us—it is this joy, this power to discover, this science, that presses us for a few precious seconds to the bosom of our Father, and we hear the Truth, the only Truth; it beats so loudly that the starlight pours in our eyes and the blood knows other worlds. Are we so clever, are we so deadened, that the life in us does not hunger ceaselessly for more life? Are we soulless men bent over desks, waiting until the crow calls us out? Nay, nay! Joy is the knowledge of God's greatness."

The letter was gross slander. This devout man, this great scientist, who had named and described over two thousand species of God's creative glory, a villain? No. Greatness breeds envy, that was all. So why did the letter disturb him so? And why did Maud's face float wraithlike behind the words?

Ach, foolishness. He found Scott Cameron's letter, picked up the lantern and returned to Lily, who now stood on level ground, closer to the tents.

The dim yellow light puddled at her boots, then rose in a paler essence. In her dun trousers and shirt, she looked like any other bone hunter—even her slight figure was no suggestion of her sex, for fossil work reduced every frame to the very bareness of flesh and muscle. Even so, Sternberg drew in his breath. The girl was fine-featured, pretty, fair where his Maud had been dark. But not beautiful. Her skin was yet touched in places by the disease that had almost taken her; there was a sallow tinge to her face and her large eyes carried a suggestion of fear, as though the grave she'd almost found was somehow reflected in them. But what struck Sternberg most forcefully was her hair. Normally it was tucked up under her slouch hat and hidden even further by the mesh veils necessary to keep off the relentless mosquitoes. Now, however, it hung wildly down her back, over her shoulders, half covering her face. Shimmering, full, honey-coloured, it made the girl's presence at once a revelation and—Sternberg's eyes widened as the thought came on—a horror. What was she doing here, this young woman, in this hard place, her hands roughened by chiselling sandstone away from the bones of terrifying beasts? It was a judgement on him. His hands trembled as he removed the letter from its envelope. He'd always believed he'd taken Lily on as an assistant out of charity, out of respect for her father. But he knew as well it had been convenient for his own ambition. The war had severely reduced the number of able men willing to labour in the badlands for so little money. Even Scott Cameron—so gifted, a bone sharp in fact, radiant with the gift for finding fossils—had felt it necessary to leave his work to join the fighting in Europe.

Before he started to read, Sternberg met Lily's eyes again. Unusually large and faintly-lashed, they appeared even larger now, and shone without fear or dark knowledge; they were wide open. And her lips moved almost imperceptibly, as if anticipating the words of the letter.

Sternberg looked down and cleared his throat. The words shimmered on the page, but he spoke them clearly.

*Dear Mr. Sternberg,*

*I am writing to you from France. But, at some time in the next few months, I expect to go on leave to England and plan to visit again the great British Museum in London where so much of your valuable work is displayed. If it is not asking too much, might you write me a brief letter of introduction to the chief paleontologist there? I realize this is a large request, and I do not make it lightly. Some information regarding carnivorous dinosaurs of the late Cretaceous period has come into my possession, and I am eager to seek the advice of the most learned man of that wonderful museum. I will explain further at some future date. But please understand that this letter of introduction would mean a great deal to me, as much as your own first letter to Professor Cope once meant to you (thank you again for the copy of your book, which I have been returning to often with much pleasure).*

*If you are willing and able to grant me this request, Lily or Charlie can direct you where to send the letter.*

*Respectfully,*
*Scott Cameron*

Sternberg shuddered. Cope. Again. His presence was almost a haunting, twinned to his daughter's suffering. With an effort, he fought the idea off.

"Is it not just like Scott," he said with a smile, "to find fossils wherever he goes? Lily, I would not be surprised to learn he had shipped a crate full to Ottawa from France."

She did not smile. In a low voice she asked when the letter was dated.

"July 10th."

She nodded, but looked beyond him.

"Not so long," he said reassuringly. "If he has found fossils, he would put all of his energies towards that instead of writing ..." Sternberg caught the insensitivity of his words before he finished the sentence. Had he gone numb as well as deaf and lame?

The lamp hissed between them. Lily was still as the surrounding stone. Two mosquitoes rested below one eye like dark tears. Sternberg struggled to find words of comfort.

"This Lord's Day, when we go to town—child, I am sure there will be a letter for you."

Her shoulders shook slightly, moving her hair as if a breeze had caught it. Sternberg longed to brush the two mosquitoes away. The idea of her blood being taken without resistance was suddenly an accusation. The haloing darkness tinged her face and hair until Sternberg had to blink rapidly not to see Maud before him.

It was Lily's voice, however, that came out of the stillness. "I've found something that ..." She leaned forward, lips parted, a searching look in her eyes.

Sternberg almost gasped. The girl did or said nothing lightly. He noticed for the first time the state of her clothes and hands; they were dusty, dark, as if she'd been ...

"It's a little skull. At least I think it is. Only an inch of the bone is showing. But when I touched it ..." Her eyes threatened to burst. "I knew, as if someone was whispering in my ear, what I had to do."

Despite himself, Sternberg narrowed his gaze. A muscle in his lower jaw twitched. No one, not even his boys, decided what to do with fossils before discussing the matter with him. And yet something raw and pulsing in Lily diminished his old hunger for discovery. Stunned, he heard Cope's voice again, cursing, as always, the damnable Marsh. He saw Cope's eyes blaze, his nostrils flare, at the very thought of his arch-enemy.

Lily's face was inches from his. "I've never had such a feeling before. It was as if, as if ..." She lowered her head briefly. When she looked up again, her jaw was fixed. "As if I'd received instruction from God."

A great hush followed. Sternberg watched, pained, as the two tears on the girl's face became a series of long stitches. A chill touched him on the neck.

"To do what, child?" he whispered.

"To send it to Scott."

He neither spoke nor moved. The girl's eyes roamed his face hungrily.

"I've never been so sure of anything. Mr. Sternberg!" She gripped his arm. "There are so many. And after every storm, so many more. One fossil. One small bone. If I didn't know how much you think of Scott's talent ..."

She stopped short, released her grip. Then her eyes appeared to clutch the air. "If you come to the place with me, you will feel what I felt, hear what I heard."

"Lily," he said quietly. "I cannot promise this. The fossil might be rare, new to science. Or part of a fully articulated specimen. We will have to see."

She turned quickly, rattling the lamp. The light wavered.

"You will feel it too, I know it. You must!"

Sternberg flinched. Her excited conviction only magnified his despair. A sudden weariness threatened to drag him down.

"It is why I did not die, why you were here to help me. Don't you see?"

His mind whirled. Who was speaking? What was he meant to see? Maud's face, Cope's face—bones beneath skin, beneath stone. He understood only that he needed time to himself.

"Tomorrow, child. It is so late. Dawn will come soon, and we have a full day of work in the heat." He spoke out of a kind of guarded reflex which Lily appeared to recognize.

She held his gaze for several seconds, then relented. "Yes. Tomorrow. Goodnight, then." She stepped off into the dark, leaving a hollow in the light where she'd been standing.

Sternberg did not turn to watch her go. He touched the blood-throb in his own heavy brow and breathed in the ashes of the doused fire. In his hand, the letter from the young bone sharp was yellowish, the colour of a telegram, a telegram that had come too late.

# 1916

THE FRONT-LINE TRENCHES SNAKED THROUGH AN EXTEN-
sive brickfield. Two dozen massive four-square brick stacks,
dark as char, thrust up into the drear sky, half on the German
side, half on the Canadian. Scott Cameron hunched on the fire
step of a narrow clay trench; it was viscous and slippery. The
bombardment had moved off. Now only the dull thud of distant
shells sounded in the gloom. He shivered under the macintosh
sheet draped over his head to keep out the drizzle. Periodically,
he angled the sheet up and peered out at the nearby looming
brick stack. One edge of it was smashed and the rain guttered so
slowly off that edge it was as if the structure was bleeding. How
strange to be fighting amongst these partly broken towers. Images of the Red Deer Valley came to him in sharp pangs, as if the
present were nothing but a perverse mockery of the past. Even
down to the bones, Scott noted gloomily, though he knew he'd
find no ancient bones in these trenches, unless the skeletons of
the dead of 1914 and 1915 could be called ancient.

The minutes dragged by. He wondered what had happened
to Wheeler, who had left for the Y canteen to find some food
about an hour before.

From his kit, Scott removed a medium-sized book, rather

cheaply produced, but all the more valuable because of that. He knew the book had been privately printed at the author's expense, yet its cheaper paper and occasional typesetting errors were not bothersome; they simply gave the book a richer, personal quality, a quality enhanced by an inscription in the author's neat, slanted hand:

*For Scott. With Many Fond Hopes that your work in our Science will be a further Glory to the Creator. May He Bless you and always Keep you from Harm.*

*Yours in faith,*
*Charles Hazelius Sternberg*
*Steveville, Alberta 1915*

Mr. Sternberg had inscribed the book as a parting gift the day Scott had left for Calgary to sign up. It was a complete surprise, because his employer, though kindly, was not a man prone to such open gestures of affection. To write a personal inscription in his memoirs of the early bone-collecting days was akin to an embrace. Scott had basked in the glow of the gesture all the way to England.

Even now, hunched in a foul-smelling section of trench, he immediately felt that warmth again, rising off every page along with the Kansas heat and the smell of the prairie grasses and the sight of great clouds rumbling like buffalo herds over the badlands of Montana, New Mexico and the Dakotas. Scott had already read the book dozens of times, could even recite favourite passages from memory. And even though *My Life in the Bone Yards of the West* followed Mr. Sternberg's life only up to 1906, before he came to the Red Deer Valley, Scott could taste the Alberta badlands in it, smell the sweet sage, see himself straining to lever some blasted rock down into the canyon, clearing the way to some new and exciting specimen. But more than that, rising above it all, he saw the sweat glistening on Lily's top lip, pooling in the little hollow at her throat, saw her cheeks flushed with the labour of digging, her large, blue eyes widening. "You were here before?" she asked, but as he answered again, the story no longer seemed a part of him, seemed to belong to another life, even another world. He remembered with an almost clinical dispassion.

THE SUMMER OF 1903, HIS TENTH YEAR. HE WANDERED ranch to ranch, careful to close the section gates when he used them. He'd keep to the riverbank for a while, heading always, though indirectly, towards the badlands. Throwing stones over the water, or just sitting with his legs dangling in as a line of goslings took a wide berth around, he liked to feel the sun on his skin and think of nothing except what he could see or hear or feel. His chores were done early, and his aunt and uncle, strict as any in this landscape had to be who were trying to earn a living, nonetheless indulged him when they could. "Loving the land," his uncle said kindly, "is the best way to know it." So he learned early on that there was no waste, nothing trivial, in an afternoon's wandering. At some level, deeper than what he knew at the time, close attention to the coyote's broken lope or the quality of a coulee's trickle meant survival. If you paid enough attention to your surroundings, you could save your life—that's what he was learning.

He didn't even know what he preferred, the flat prairie above or the flood plain. So he followed an up-and-down route, just listening to the thrum of bugs and nothing else in the grasses at his feet, then looking up to see a sudden cloud shadow move across the river like a giant fish. In between, as a sort of secret tunnel, there was the coulee with its hidden creatures, surprising waters and delicious shade. Sometimes he spent so many hours along the river and in the coulees that he never made it to the prairie. He was always sorry for this because he loved that uncluttered, open, gently waving space—he could sometimes feel his body melt into the grass and wind as he moved forward. But he was too much of a boy to appreciate the prairie then. Mostly, he just walked home up there, its difference with the badlands almost what he needed to come down from the exhilaration of losing himself in the hoodoos.

One day in June he noted the dropped position of the sun and turned back to the east, out of the badlands. Finding a path upward to the prairie, he followed the new route and began the long walk home.

He knew many of the ranchers by name and sight, though he didn't presume to speak to them until spoken to (and many were, as his aunt put it, "quiet as the grave"). There were some whose solitude was legendary.

This day, as the sun lost its yellow fierceness and began to bloody, he saw in the distance, near the top edge of the valley, a building he'd not seen before. It was getting late, and he didn't have much time to stop, but he didn't know when he'd have another chance to investigate. Something about that small shape, growing larger as he advanced, urged him on, though he knew this was only because the horizon held no other significant mark. It was natural for anyone to walk towards it.

When he reached the building, he was neither pleased nor disappointed.

It was a small outbuilding, low and rectangular, its planks dull-black and weathered, like railroad ties. There was one door at the end. Moving around to it, he saw that the building must have once housed chickens, for the chicken door remained, along with some remnants of wire, rusted and entangled with wild grass. The main door had a sliding wooden bolt to keep it shut, but the bolt was not in place. Just slightly, on the breeze, the door creaked inward, revealing a slice of darkness.

He looked nervously behind him. The ranch house was on lower ground, a hundred yards away—small, ordinary and silent. He sniffed the air. Last heat in the grass, faint rise of sage. If there had been chickens here, they'd been gone a long time. Maybe the rancher was gone with them. He went and stood at the corner of the outbuilding and saw the western horizon spread with crimson. A meadowlark's trill followed the sloping contours of the land, then dropped abruptly into the badlands. The sound was like the trickle in a coulee, running down to the same bottom place; everything beautiful fell that way, even the climbing hawk. He understood, without living here, what the real map was; he seemed to carry it with him. Now, standing in the sunset, he felt the X in his blood again, and returned to the creaking door.

Pushing it in, he found only thick darkness and silence. Then, as his eyes adjusted and the dimming light slanted in, his heartbeat quickened and something fluttered in his throat, as if he'd disturbed a bird of prey in some corner of himself and it was beating its wings against the ceiling beams.

He knew what the long shapes were, the strange, misshapen bones, even before he moved close enough to touch them. Some were hooked up along the walls like farm tools, others sat on a low shelf projecting from the back wall about three feet, and still others lay heaped in one corner like the broken pieces of some machine. Except, he noticed, the pieces were all the colour of the badlands, so, put together, they might have been a hoodoo that someone had dismantled and carried away, like so many railroad ties. But what practical use did all these bones have?

For he identified them as such, even though he'd never seen their like before. Grainy to the touch, heavy yet brittle, they made the walls of the building fall away and the light from outside dissolve. Their dark was something new and powerful, a dark that had nothing to do with the world. Yet it was oddly familiar to him; he had walked through it even in the full sun, had stooped to pick up a fragment of what now surrounded him in a kind of incomplete wholeness, all the spokes of a great wheel but one that no longer turned. There was a bone long as a paddle with a huge knob at the end, and smaller bones like flutes, and, most startling of all, skulls with great gaping eye-sockets and … horns! Mixed in among these more obvious shocks were many skulls of varying sizes, some like clams, others like the backs of turtles, and pieces of what resembled wood, except these were also stone. He tried to calm himself. He said, looking at some of the smaller, thinner items, "These are what's left of the chickens that were here." But the others, the horned skull the size of a large rock, the bones longer than himself—what were they, and why did they tremble and seem to cry out for his touch?

The door creaked shut behind him, but he didn't notice that most of the light had gone. He was bent over in a black corner, picking up what looked like nuggets of coal. One crumbled in his hand, and he smiled; it was coal. He knew the feel of that dust, the weight of that dark. There was fire in it, warmth. But these bones were the same; they held an equal warmth. What rose off the baked stone and bronzed his skin as he wandered the summer hours away came out of these strange shapes. He

30

felt the heat inside. It was as though he was moving over the land and yet was the land too, sinking, rising, the sun and the dark coursing over him. Where had he gone? Would he ever be able to find his way back? His skin prickled. A second later, the door was kicked in with a flood of grey light.

"What do you want here?" The rasping voice came from a tall, thin figure in the doorway. It held a shotgun, pointed straight out.

He crouched into the pile of coal. He could not find enough moisture in his mouth to speak.

"Who sent you, dammit?"

He stared up. The figure belonged to that of an old man, bald, patchy-bearded, with a hewn face that seemed to consist of sinews loosely banded together.

Suddenly, the face softened. The full mouth breathed a sigh of words. "Come on, boy, get on up out of that coal."

"I'm sorry," he said, picking himself up quickly. "I only wanted to look. I was walking by and …"

The old man nodded, his head looking light as a scarecrow's. He now held the gun limply at his waist. "It don't matter much. I reckoned you was an older feller, though. My eyes ain't so good. Leastways, if you are a chicken thief, you're sorely disappointed, I'll bet!" And he cackled like he'd been waiting years to make the joke.

He scrambled past the old man into the dusk, then turned to look up, still frightened. The old man's eyes were wet and pale, as if he were constantly fighting back tears. Though tall and sinewy, he seemed as brittle as one of the bones hooked up on the wall. He wore trousers, boots that flapped when he walked, and a greyish shirt with suspenders like two long bloodstains.

"Don't know why I expect 'em to come, but they will, they

will. I keep telling folks hereabouts, I say, this here's gold to somebody. You just watch. Somebody's gonna come asking after it. Or ..." And here his look darkened and he looked back over his shoulder. "Or they won't be asking. They'll just be taking. But not what I've got here. They want this, they'll have to pay for it." He narrowed his eyes suspiciously. "You sure you're not working for somebody?"

He shook his head rapidly. "No, sir. I was just walking home. To my uncle's place. My Uncle Walter." He pointed vaguely to the east.

The old man clenched his jaw hard on one side, then un-clenched it. "Walter? Walter who?"

"Cameron."

"Hmmm." The old man grunted with a kind of satisfaction. "Heard tell of him. Don't know him. But I reckon that's all right." With the speed of a flash storm, he grinned and said, "What do you think of my keelection? Ever seen bones like these before?"

"No, sir. Never." He felt more relaxed by the minute.

"I don't spec so, boy." The old man slapped his thigh. Dust rose and mixed with the grains of twilight. "You can count yer-self lucky. Yer one of the few who has seen 'em. I don't show 'em to nobody, and nobody bothers with the ones they come across out there." He gestured in the general direction of the badlands. "Oh, they might pick up a piece out of curiosity, you know, but if I hear tell of it, they'll give it to me straightaway, and look at me like I'm a poor, pitiful creetur. Ha! Blamed fools! I hope I live long enough to make suckers out of 'em."

While the old man spoke, he could feel himself being pulled by the strange force in the outbuilding. He was no longer afraid, just curious.

32

"What are they?" he asked.

"Bones, boy! What did you reckon they were?"

"Yes, sir. I took them for bones. But what are they the bones of?"

The old man's eyes blazed as he leaned forward. "Ah well, now, that's just it. That's the gold part of the business. I don't know zactly what they are, but I know there ain't animals like that, leastways none that I ever seen. And somebody's gotta be curious enough to find out what they are. And I reckon they'll be willin' to pay for the knowledge."

He felt the air darkening, felt the absence of the meadowlark's song. Only a smear of red remained in the west. He'd have to run.

The old man noted his eagerness, and sent him away with a last warning and a flourish of his gun. "Don't you be bringin' nobody around, you hear? And don't you come back yerself. Next time, I figure you'll be lookin' to fill yer pockets, ain't that so? Now go on, before I get tired of being so polite."

Then he was running with the contours of the land, as if on the slow rolling waves of some hidden ocean, running with the black coming down in dust over his shoulders and the earth swelling with its stored heat, running as if his bones were flickers of fire.

SCOTT'S HAND, FLAT ON THE COVER OF THE BOOK, ORIented him. That west of long, deep silences and prehistoric grandeur was a long way off. And Lily, who had been amazed that he'd spent a boyhood summer in the Red Deer Valley … he did not want to think of his distance from her.

To distract himself, he opened the book at random. The life on the pages was the life he planned to follow, the black words were the prints of something he was tracking, something as mysterious and wonderful as the dead beasts of the Cretaceous. Even when the howitzers resumed their rumbling, Scott did not look up, but incorporated the sound into what he read, the past that was his future, until the sound of the guns became the immense silent rhythm of millennia:

> *I remember how, one day, I found a beautiful specimen of a Kansas mosasaur. Clidastes Tortor, Cope named it, because an additional set of articulations in the backbone enabled it to coil. Its head lay in the centre, with the column around it, and the four paddles stretched out on either side. It was covered by only a few inches of disintegrated chalk.*
>
> *Forgetting myself, I shouted to the surrounding wilderness, "Thank God! Thank God!" And I did well to thank the Creator, as I slowly brushed away the powdered chalk and revealed the beauties of this reptile of the Age of Reptiles.*

Scott saw the high forehead, the deep and wide black eyes, the thin-lipped mouth hardly moving beneath the full moustache. And the words that he heard came out of that face, that could have been the face of God, came out calmly but with iron conviction: "No man can say he loves us, when he wantonly destroys our work; no man loves God who wantonly destroys His creatures."

It was no good. Scott could not keep the badlands from being sullied by his present grim work. Even handling his trenching tool, he thought of how useful it would be for bone hunting. And the Germans, the Hun, the Boche: whenever he peered into no man's land, he remembered that Mr. Sternberg was of German origin and that hundreds of his greatest specimens were displayed in the museums of Munich and Bavaria.

Scott carefully placed the book back in his kit, knowing he could not keep his worlds separate. What he needed to do was to will his former life into the current one. Mr. Sternberg's book helped. But writing to Lily was best of all. He rummaged in his kit again for his notebook, and then, glancing out from under the sheet from time to time for Wheeler, he began another letter. The heaviness of the day and his mood, however, soon stopped him. What, after all, could he write?

His hand felt like lead. He blinked slowly. His head snapped back. Filling the daylight hours was proving more and more tortuous; he had not been prepared for so much inactivity in a war. He looked down at the blank page, knowing he couldn't write the truth, even if the censors allowed it. Besides, whatever the truth was, it was too terrible to send home.

The guns still boomed up the line in a kind of nightmare melody. The air was acrid with lingering smoke and chemicals. To stay awake, Scott forgot about writing and simply let himself gather the frayed threads of experience. The steady drizzle afforded a light rhythm to his thoughts.

THE WAR WAS BOREDOM. IN AND OUT OF THE LINE. WAITing for leave. Miserable cold. Lice crawling in your underwear. They looked like little translucent lobsters. You tried to crack them between your thumb and forefinger, exploding the blood, or burn them at the seams with a candle. There was a real knack to that; you had to burn them but not catch the material on fire. But boredom made that game. Reserve. Supports. Firing line. Week after week until there weren't any weeks. Then march through the same mud-slogged grey-black world of shriven buildings and trees, craters everywhere, rough crosses with the helmets stuck on, to some new part of the front. Zigzagging by night up the endless communications trench, heads down, through gun-ripped woods, shells crashing all around, rainbow bursts, showers of pale light, the smoking honeycomb of the earth flashing vividly for a few seconds, then dark and curses and crump of mortars and phew-phew-phew of rifle fire and typewriter clack of machine guns. Huddled against the trench, shivering in a funk, never really sleeping, one ear cocked for danger—the whiz-bang's approach, the whump of a rum-jar, somebody shouting, Jerry coming over (but he hardly came over)—the brazen rats, chemical water out of old gas cans, the same stew when it was available at all (hardtack for days, and whatever could be gleaned out of packages sent from home), and always work detail, filling sandbags, burial parties, going back for rations, repairing wire, packing sheet metal and lumber, then waiting, waiting, waiting, fighting sleep, watching the grainy fog of no man's land for the crawling enemy, and, finally, stand-to at daybreak, tot of rum, cleaning the rifle, more work detail, more burning of lice, praying for mail, getting to know your trench-mates better than you wanted or needed to know any other human, yourself included, refusing to see the corpses in their bodies, their brains slopped on your tunic, their blood spattering the parapet, their flesh in shrapnel-sized pieces, walking out in a dream of exhaustion, staggering, walking a beam where there was no beam, more work in billets, digging, always digging, trenches, graves, latrines, no difference among them, rain dripping off the waterproof sheets, then resting in an old barn full of loosely built bunks, a whole unit crammed in, stink of animals, stink of men, drinking at the estaminet, egg and chips, smoke haze, writing letters, reading, trying to get clean, shaving at the edge of a shell hole, waiting to march, waiting for night, somewhere in France, Belgium—was it Poperinghe, Neuville St. Vast, Kemmel?—marching, singing, packs always heavier, then quiet, then silence, then shells, bodies at the roadside, disembowelled, stinking horses, old bones sticking out of old trenches, caught briefly in a Verey flash, French bones, bits of blue cloth stuck to them, and newer dead, stink, slime, the relieved wounded crying, moaning, the unwounded blank-eyed, staggering out, and always the question—is it my turn, is my number up?—not me, it won't be me, and the long, held stare at the dead men as if to hear them answer the question you haven't asked about death because you don't really know it, muscles tensed at the parapet, in the listening posts, on sentry, head down, lice in your fingers, their blood your blood, crack crack, like a tiny shell just invented, cold beef, gas water, stench, black smoke, tea, rum, cutting wire, zing of bullets, rats at your sleep, rats at your mouth, shiver, long shiver, flares bursting down in fountains, the Germans over there coughing, somewhere in France, Belgium, rain and mud and snow, sometimes sun, nightingales, the grey, muttering locals, ragged children crying "Canada! Canada!," their chicken hands out, old women in black shawls, carts loaded down with junk, passing them on another shelled road to another shelled town, shell-burst behind the lines, eighteen killed in a dugout, the moans, Oh Christ please shoot me shoot me I'm blinded oh Jesus Christ!, the mandatory religious service, the padres and their patriotic prattle, for the glory of God the just cause the loved ones, hiding back of their cloths just like the brass hats, and always dreaming of a Blighty wound, a trip to England, clean clothes, no shells, no mud, a real bath, real food, the cramped cold billets again, broken sleep, rats at the corpses, rats as big as rabbits, the itch of lice at the waist and wrists, digging, digging, the rain, the pounding of the big guns, slipping off the duckboards, a fireside at the estaminet, the curve of her hip, sage and woodsmoke in her hair, whale oil on your feet to fight trench foot, stand-to, stand-down, new drafts sobbing, that boy on the stretcher crying for his mother, both legs gone, staring through snowflakes, the helmeted bush moving, blinking, blinking, nothing there, marching out, the ruined town, shells landing in a graveyard, bones tossed up, mixed up, a church ragged and black as a hoodoo, Wheeler asking how do you find them anyway? How old are they? But the Bible says Creation was six thousand years ago where did they go what happened to them why are you so interested is that what you're going to do when it's all over read me something out of that book you're always looking at no don't worry I won't expect you to listen to me read from the Bible though it won't hurt you any might help you okay I won't I promise but how do you know how old they are you can't know and where did they go, and the grey dawn over the German trenches and a boy soldier waving in a flare-flash, his body crumpling as a sniper hits his mark, the tot of rum, the brief heat of it, Macpherson writing to his little girl the world is cruel but study your algebra I miss you I hope to be home soon, cold, so cold, the estaminet empty the estaminet full, red crackle and light, almost a campfire, smoke and sage in her hair, coyote cry, that hollow at her throat slick with sweat, Jenkins sent out useless mind gone blubbering shaking, Lunn volunteering for night patrol never came back his poor wife the damned fool can't win can't get angry the little wooden crosses thousands and thousands years now France Belgium his poor children no father, Jesus here's Wheeler now why is he grinning, what has he done, something besides this boredom, of stink and

death and noise and waiting, the dead boredom the rats boredom the lice boredom the mud boredom waiting to die to go
home to get a letter yes Wheeler yes yes your damned wide eyes
boredom red face get down Jesus Christ firelight the Sioux on
their horses behind it the whole west Mr. Sternberg and Cope
alone on the wave of it the black wave dreaming the flesh back
on the bones of the dead Wheeler's face his lips moving what?
okay okay Vic tell me what is it? what have you done? Lily Lily

# 1975

AT EIGHTY YEARS OLD, LILY DID NOT FIND IT SO EASY TO order the house after her husband's death. Apart from the emotional strain, there was the physical challenge of putting away a life. Clothes drawers needed to be emptied, there were suits and shoes and jackets, many in very good condition, to be boxed up for charity, there were books—mostly large scientific tomes—to be donated to the library, and there were papers, the meaningless ephemera of paycheque stubs and tax documents and old receipts and bill statements that accumulate over decades.

On her knees, smelling the surprising cedar of an emptied drawer, she thought gratefully, "Idle hands are the Devil's workshop," and struggled to her feet. It had been a month since his death, and at last she felt able to face this dreary task, one that to her mild surprise did ease her grief a little. She had always been a self-described "do-er," after all, never one for dwelling on what couldn't be changed.

Well, she thought now, pushing back her still-long, smoke grey hair and looking around at the full boxes, I'd best make a start on my own things while I'm at it. The awareness of her age and looming death did not depress her; in fact, she felt ready to go, and arranging her possessions seemed an act of love to the two daughters she'd leave behind. Lily knew too many elderly people who put off the practical points of their coming deaths, leaving those who survived them with an unpleasant and often confusing job. She did not wish to do the same.

Almost as soon as she opened her cedar hope chest, however, and reached her hand in, she stopped. A chill passed along her spine. It had been so long since she'd looked at the object wrapped in blue tissue paper that she'd almost forgotten it was there. But then, how could she forget? The quiet of the house became the very quiet of memory. This was no accident. From touching her husband's clothes to touching this cherished object of the past, of the more-than-past, was not without design. With a thrill of joy, Lily felt the presence of God enter the room.

She picked up the tissue-wrapped object very gently and went downstairs.

With small, careful steps, she moved along the dark, narrow front hallway until she reached the living room. Sunlight flooded in the large, south-facing window. The shadows of maple branches and flitting songbirds darkened the worn hardwood floor between the crimson throw-rugs, but this darkness had the effect of light, seemed, in fact, like thicker tresses of the sun. Only the chatter of the finches and sparrows, and the loud tick of a mantel clock, disturbed the quiet.

She sat at one end of her faded horsehair chesterfield and placed the object gently on the coffee table. Slowly, carefully, with quickening senses, she removed the tissue. Even though she knew what lay inside, the skull was still a shock. She had not remembered how beautiful it was.

It was riddled with dot-like perforations over its sandy-white sides. The eyeholes were not much larger than the other perforations, and the whole bone was shaped like an anvil. Lily stared at it for a moment, feeling a strange weightlessness that frightened her, made her wonder if this was how it felt when the spirit left the body. Not a swoon exactly, but a kind of rising, as though someone were tenderly picking up her own bones. Taking a cue from this tenderness, which she interpreted as divine, Lily cupped the tiny skull in the palm of one hand. It was light as balsa wood, but solid. How many years had it been since she had touched it? Too many, too many. Yet, sitting there in the lambent sunshine, amongst the caper of bird and leaf shadow, she thought suddenly that no time had passed at all. Sixty years, was it? And what was that in God's great schedule but less than a blink?

She held the skull close to her face as though it were a mirror in which she could find the young woman she had been. But the eye sockets yawed black and mocking, as they had done for millennia, and she had to listen for the chirping of the songbirds outside to bring her back from that abyss and settle her nerves.

The presence of the skull was one thing, was surprising enough simply as a leash leading her down the narrowing passage of years. But with the surprise and the movement back came the particular faces, words, sensations, touches, pain. Lily closed her eyes, saw again the winding stretch of river, the banks of gothic prairie cottonwoods with their black-iron branches. Then, abruptly, the scoured sides of the valley appeared, the layered formations visible only in lighter or darker shades of the same dullness. She saw the refreshing green of the leaves, the blue of the sky that went on forever, the moon-blue shadows and the olive and ochre stones of the hoodoos, felt the strangeness and loneliness of the shimmering landscape. Or did she already find herself shading the images with memory? No matter—the earth fell away, time reeled back, the world became again a confusion of hidden caves and culverts, of trails so faint they might have been made by the breath of coyotes, of fossilized treasure waiting for a glance, a fingertip, a boot sole, to know the full, human sun. She looked up from below as a hoodoo with a large mushroom cap loomed over and a hawk sliced across the background. Suddenly there she was, on her knees, her face obscured by mosquito netting. Two men, their heads abnormally enlarged by the same headgear, stood above her, directing her labours. Lily could almost feel the blister from the chisel break through her skin. The heat, the dryness; it swarmed into the room even as the recaptured landscape knocked out all walls, all enclosures.

She put her hand lightly to her throat, afraid the girl she'd been would look up and stare at her across a lifetime. But the scene shifted again. She looked down on a close-up of a chasmosaurus fossil half-exposed in a cliff, George Sternberg seated in front of it, preparing a mixture of plaster of Paris. She could smell the glue.

For a few minutes more, the images whirled on—the ring of canvas tents along the riverbank, the horse-drawn wagons heaped with excavated bones in their stone matrices, Mr. Sternberg, calm and serious and looking older than she remembered him, walking towards a pillar until he vanished behind it.

But one image, one face, did not appear. It was elsewhere. It was an ocean away. Lily lowered her hand, tried to breathe evenly, wetted her lips. The room, her mouth: everything felt as dry as she remembered that summer and that landscape, as dry as his summer had been wet. The question came to her again: why should she find this now? Why should it—among all the accumulated memories in her possession—be the one to make a claim on her diminishing time?

Lord, she prayed, bowing her head until her face was almost touching the cupped skull, whatever it is you have called me to do, give me strength for the effort.

The room was quieter. The birds had moved away, as though aware in their blood cells of the strange presence nearby. Even the clock, ticking heavily with the throb of a badlands sun, seemed to slow down. Lily kept her head bowed for several minutes, her hands motionless. Despite her faith, she was afraid to put the skull down, sensing that her hold on it was like a finger in some dyke behind which a terrifying sea was pounding.

So long ago, so much time … She leaned back and closed her eyes, thinking, I know what I must do, for Scott's sake, what he would want me to do. She sat up. But would he? She looked around the room; it was empty of him, of all life. Filtered light caught the dust motes which, like the Red Deer's muds and silts, were steadily burying the material, beginning again the slow process of fossilization. Soon, all of her memories would be bone. With a start, Lily realized that what she must do, she must do for her sake, no one else's, not even Scott's. Of course, it was for love of him that she would act, to honour what they had meant to one another. When was a woman's sake, she thought proudly and a little ruefully, ever separate from her love?

AN HOUR LATER, WITH HIS LETTERS REMOVED FROM THE bottom of the same chest and placed on her nightstand, and with the skull cold as moonlight in her palm, Lily prayed for courage and strength. And as she prayed, the blood in her veins was already moving the images, as the river moved the bodies

and the bones, as the days moved the years, and the years the
millennia, swiftly in their courses but with the unchanging purpose of all things born of God.

# 1916

AN HOUR AFTER THE GIRL HAD LEFT HIM IN THE DARK-
ness and ashes, Sternberg finally drifted off to sleep. Again, in
his dreaming, Maud came to him. How much she had loved to
hear him talk about his life! Each winter, she had begged him
for stories. Papa, tell me again about Professor Cope's response
to your letter. Papa, were you really in Montana when General
Custer was killed? Papa, when did you know you were a bone
sharp, when did you *really* know?

Asleep, the decades evaporated, the border between the living and the dead gave way. Sternberg's inner voice, softened
and rhapsodic at once, widened his daughter's eyes again.

OH THE VALLEY AS IT WAS, CHILD. THE SUSQUEHANNA,
lovely as its name. Maud, dear, if I could but show it to you, if
you could be one of my companions in the majestic forests of
maples and hickories, pines and hemlocks. We lived at the time
with your grandpapa and great grandpapa, those devout men
of Our Lord, at dear old Hartwick Seminary in Otsego County.
You know your Fenimore Cooper, dear? We lived only five miles
below Cooperstown, the place of his birth. Think of it, the Walter Scott of our country. I played as a boy among scenes that he

47

made famous. So often my companions and I went picnicking on Otsego Lake, shouting to hear the echo, and spreading our tablecloth on shore perhaps beneath the very tree in which the catamount waited to spring upon poor terrified Elizabeth Temple. What a romantic country it was, and how I loved to be out in it. Daughter, there was never a child—no, not even you, nor your brothers—who loved nature so much as I. Don't smile so. I am not exaggerating. Why, your grandmama used to say she wondered that she even had a son named Charles, she saw so little of me.

It is odd to think, now, how little time I have spent among the great trees of the earth. They were my audience then. All of my boyhood orations were made beneath them. I remember we used to build sylvan retreats in the woods, weaving willow twigs in and out of the poles I cut for support. Who? Oh, Esme dear. Of course. I thought I had said. My beloved cousin, your Great Aunt Hildie's child. She died a young woman, of the influenza. We were inseparable.

*Papa. Papa. Softly through the bone that houses dreams.*

Yes, yes, I'm sorry. Esme and I, we had our special place. I often wonder if it's not still there. Perhaps. I have never gone back. On a hill, across the river. Moss Pond we called it. The woods around were hemlock, I remember, and the branches so large and close together that hardly any light broke through, even at midday. We always whispered on our way, though I don't think we ever decided to do so. It was just natural, as though the trees expected it of us, in return for the stillness and darkness and coolness. Daughter, I have never known such a worshipful place. Not even the church of the rectory trembled so with the living presence of the Lord. Esme and I—oh she was a beautiful, darling girl, all golden locks in ringlets and big saucer-shaped

48

blue eyes—we would go hand in hand through that heaven-made church, our voices hushed, or often silent altogether, until we came out of the darkness of the hemlocks and into the full blazing light of Moss Pond. How can I describe it to you? Like walking on a cloud. Yes, a greenish-gold cloud. Though—no, of course, we had to make our way across on logs, the moss was not firm enough to bear our weight. But on the shores we tread that softness, softer than the forest floor had been. And always it was the birds who broke the day's whispering, their pure, clear celebrations even clearer in the sudden brightness. Yes, you're right to smile, my dear. It's only my fancy that the days were always fine when Esme and I … but so I remember it. Isn't that strange? I cannot see rain or snow; it doesn't fall, there are no clouds, Esme is laughing in the sun, we are leaping gently, log to log, careful not to slip, for we do not know the depths below the moss, except deep it must be, for we have fished and caught the blind bullheads there.

Finally, we are at the middle of the pond, which is also the summit of the hill, and truly it is like being on a cloud. There are the woods stretching away, there are the farms, even, faintly, the grounds of the rectory. There are the shadows of the people who have come for the honouring of the body in the parlour, cold shadows, long, black shadows. Walking between them is the same as walking between the tall figures of the men.

*Shadows, Papa?*

Oh Maud, forgive me. I am tired. The work of my life has been hard. You and your mama little know how hard. The valley of the Red Deer is no fair measure, child. Texas, Montana, the Oregon desert—how many times I thanked the Creator that I did not have my wife and daughter with me, though I longed for the solace. Don't shake your head, no, no. You would have been

49

a balm to my spirit, but at too great a cost for my nerves. The troubles ... no, there are things that don't bear repeating.

Let me speak of the flowers instead. Have I told you of the flowers? How Esme and I loved to gather them! But I was especially fond. Your grandmama delighted in them so. Heaven's candles, she called them. And I lived to please her, she was my everything as a boy, I am not ashamed to admit. In the spring, I always found the first crocus for her. I have seen the crocus here in these badlands too, a different type, a prairie flower. But coming upon one in this place of stone and muted colour, I am always shocked, almost to the point of falling on my knees in prayer.

There were no crocuses, no flowers at all. The parlour was dark, a few guttering candles. Uncle's face, it was cleaned up and calm, he almost smiled. I had to look away. I loved him, though I did not see him often. There was something between us, we both felt it, something more than I felt for Esme, though in truth, I could not look at him without seeing her, the same blue in the eyes, the same curve to the mouth. And now was I never to look at her with peace again, because I had seen the twist of pain and the false calm beneath the undertaker's powder?

Oh Maud, don't ask me! I never knew. I believe Mama and Papa told the neighbours it was money. But their voices: I could tell it wasn't money. I heard another uncle say, in a whisper above those cold shadows, "Better this than to have disgraced us further." Poor Uncle Wilhelm. What a soft face he had, and eyes that always seemed brimming with tears. He told me, that last time—how was I to know I could never ask another question of him?—what it was I had found in the limestone. Ancient shells, he said. Millions of years old. But Charlie, it's best not to speak of this to others. He smiled, I remember how sad a smile. The earth is only six thousand years old.

And then he was swinging in our barn, and Papa and Grandpapa cut him down, and I saw his face hardened for the only time, his eyes bulged out, his tongue ... Oh my child, forgive me. It is too painful for you. I should know better. Your Papa is tired. He does not know his proper conduct any longer. Too many years in the wilderness.

Esme? Oh, she did not come anymore. Auntie went home to Germany, took her away. How I cried! My dearest companion gone from me! Oh it is foolish. A boy's tears on an old man's face. The times I have thought of her, prayed for her happiness, even dreamed of seeing her again. But Mama and Papa did not stay in contact. They were ashamed of Uncle Wilhelm.

That was all. I went back to the hemlocks and Moss Pond, but her ghost—and that was, forgive me, Lord, how I thought of her, as dead—was restless beside me. I couldn't bear it. I chose other sanctuaries. And Esme faded, as all things fade in the minor span of a man's life. But Uncle Wilhelm, I knew he was not dead to me, I knew he was speaking and I was not hearing. Was it the devil's voice? Grandpapa would have said so, but how could the devil speak like Uncle Wilhelm? How could I not feel the devil if he was truly there?

Daughter, everything is planned and ordered by the Creator. Never doubt it. What happens is meant to happen, is for the best. Do you think we would be here, in this valley, finding the bones of His great ancient creations if He had not ordained it so? Child, you know the infirmity in my leg? I tell you, as I have told no one before, it is not my weakness, it is my strength. The very pain that others believe must impede me in my work is the sole cause of my work. And I am grateful for it. Only man, my child, is vain enough to determine what is an affliction and what is a blessing. Ah, but the wisdom of man is foolishness to God. I have heard learned men, on the basis of almost no evidence, make claims about these bones lying around us. I once heard four different men, each convinced of his own theory, explain the mysteries of Creation. Foolishness. But I pray to know that God works in mysterious ways, His wonders to perform. This leg—yes, touch it—is a wonder, and the pain it has caused is as nothing to the life of praise and labour it has carried me to.

You are right to look puzzled. I have not spoken of that time in this way, not to anyone. Perhaps, yes, I have never spoken of it even to myself, at least not so plainly. But now … ah, Maud, it is your interest in me, so tender, you have little idea of how it lifts my heart. I have been too little in the company of the gentler sex. A man loses something, a kind of grace, and he must give himself over to God even more, with a greater humility, to smooth the roughness of his spirit, for it needs be rough at times, in this work, in this country.

I still see the chaff whirling in the barn. You have seen this effect? How the chaff and the dust dance in the fractured light breaking through the chinks, like a windblown meadow in full seed. I often thought that angels, when they appeared, must choose this special light of old barns. It is so calm and peaceful, but of this earth too, of the grasses of this world. Christ Himself might choose to return to us in such a light; it is both Heaven and Heaven's creation, as the saviour is both a man and the Son of God.

It was in Ames, New York. I had gone to visit Uncle James and Aunt Gerda, to stay for a few days and help out with the harvest, also to play with my cousins. Ach, I remember almost nothing but that day, that moment. No, it is not precisely so. The mind … were they two separate visits, or was it really, as I have always believed, the same day, even perhaps the same brief hour? Yes, yes, it must have been so. I was in the attic, alone, treasure-hunting in old trunks as children do, when I found—how my pulse still quickens to speak of it!—a cradle filled with fossil shells and crystals of quartz. And I knew, without asking, that it was Uncle Wilhelm's collection, perhaps from his own boyhood! Maud, I stood over that cradle as if it contained … what? The very light of Heaven. It was a beacon calling me to my life. I hardly breathed. I trembled as I touched those ancient works of the great craftsman. And I could hear Uncle Wilhelm's voice, encouraging me, saying, "Charlie, what I could not do is left for your hands to do, your heart."

I was old enough to know it would be unwise to show too great an enthusiasm to my aunt and uncle. Coming down into the kitchen, I only said I thought the shells were pretty and Mama might like them for her garden borders. And they were mine. Uncle did say they had belonged to my aunt's brother, and perhaps it was a good thing he died instead of spending his life wandering over the hills picking up old stones. Yes, it is funny, isn't it? To think of what Uncle James would say to me now! But what he said, it thrilled me too, because it meant that Uncle Wilhelm had not stopped his collecting once he'd left boyhood behind. So, I thought, that is how he knew so much about my limestone shells, why he was so interested. It broke my heart to hear Uncle James say that all the larger specimens had been thrown away. What could they have been? But I was grateful for the cradle of small specimens. Back at home, I labelled them all, "From Uncle James," just so I would not draw attention to my great fondness for Uncle Wilhelm. And when we moved west, to Kansas, I gave them, all but one which I have always kept, to dear Aunt Gladys. How she must have been shocked to find in the collection a lot of baculites I had labelled "Worms from Uncle James."

The barn? Yes, of course, I had forgotten.

I believe Cousin Frederick ran into the kitchen where I was speaking with Aunt and Uncle about the cradle of shells. And I was enticed out to play, feeling my reluctance would show a too great fondness for what I had discovered in the attic. And then—this is all I remember—I was running in the barn, chasing Frederick, the chaff swirling around us, a threshing machine screeching terribly inside the shadows. I ran over the haymows and piles of shocked grain, alive with the excitement of finding the shells. My cousin climbed a shock of oats on the scaffold in the peak of the barn, and I set out madly to follow him.

I went up the scaffolding. There was a hole at the top completely covered over with settling oats. The thresher screamed and screamed like a beast in agony. My cousin's face was laughing widely. I blinked into the swirling chaff and rose into the fractured light coming through the chinks in the roof. And then my blood, my heart, plunged. I shouted but the thresher swallowed the sound.

I fell twenty feet, and my cousin carried me insensible into the house. I am certain, now, that that period before I woke again was the most important of my life. I am certain I was in direct communion with the voices of my future. Perhaps Uncle Wilhelm, perhaps an angel—who am I to say? But I know this: I woke in the full conviction that I would one day give over my life to the science of fossils. I little knew, then, how or where this conviction would develop, but I felt it as strongly as I felt the pain in my leg. And through it all, the months on crutches, the rheumatism that settled into the leg years later after I was forced out into a sleet storm to water some cattle, the ankylosing of the joint so that I lay in the hospital at Fort Riley for three months, all alone in a great ward, while the army surgeon—God bless his skill—straightened the limb with a special machine: through it all, Maud, I knew that somehow I would achieve my goal of working as a bone hunter. I had only to be patient, to wait for my opportunity. Why should the leg give me trouble again, at a time when I had almost given up my dream? Daughter, it was the Lord's way of speaking to me. And it is still the Lord's way. Even now, even here, an old man, I know my God through my body as much as through my spirit. It is a rare gift. There have been times when two fit legs seemed such a wonderment that I almost wept for my misfortune, I cannot deny it. But always, no matter where I was, no matter the hardship, I grew thankful in time, and I prayed in gratitude and for forgiveness that I should fail to recognize this blessing.

Enough. It is late. The fire has almost died. I am tired. We will talk again, Maud. Tomorrow? Perhaps. Many times before you leave again, I promise. But your mama, think how she must miss you. It is still a marvel to me that she let you come alone. New York is so far. Sometimes it seems another planet to me. These badlands—the great Cretaceous Sea that once was here seems more real. Ah, enough. Good night, child. Sleep well. Remember your papa in your prayers. Dear Maud. Precious daughter. My only ...

STERNBERG WOKE TO TEARS ON HIS CHEEKS AND AN OWL hooting somewhere in the cottonwoods. It was still dark, the middle of the night. He wondered if he'd even slept at all. Perhaps this was sleep, this painful awareness that he was not, and never would be again, sitting across from his daughter over a campfire, telling her what he had never told anyone so explicitly before; the joys and sorrows of his youth. He felt very old, very heavy. The words rapidly fading from his consciousness lingered just enough to mock him with their devoutness. What had happened to the spirit that gave them breath? He had never been so aware of the weight of his body. It was as if the blood of his three living children, at sleep in the darkness around him, guyed him to the earth. And the thought was not so fanciful. Of late, he sensed that only his duty as a husband and father kept him working. The oddly hollow echo of the owl's cry repeated like a heartbeat above the blood of his sons. Good boys, good men, but when a man grows old, he needs what a daughter can provide. And he was growing old, there was no denying that. Was it simply age, then, that had weakened his faith? Once there had been his work to take solace in, work that had always been an expression of his love for the Creator. But if a genius the likes of Edward Drinker Cope could be reviled for a villain, what did any man's work amount to in the end? Cope was a true giant of science, and a benefactor to so many. Without him, Sternberg knew, he'd have spent his life unhappily herding cattle on the Kansas plains, never touching the hidden treasures of the Lord's glory. No one since Adam had named so many of the earth's creatures as had Professor Cope. Scandalous gossip! Who dared to sully such a man's reputation only sullied his own—to call a genius a villain was to spit inside a church. But then, Sternberg reasoned with a sigh, look at the world now, look at all that is being destroyed. It is an age of violence, not praise. Even the dead are not safe. His daughter, the great Cope ... how could he shelter them from a world intent on destruction and lies?

He turned over on the cot, curled into himself, and tried without apology to return again to his daughter's loving attention.

# 1916

*Dear Lily,*

*Your little skull sounds wonderful. I can't imagine what it is. But I have to tell you how much it means to me to be thinking of the badlands and its treasures in this place. It's funny, how thinking of a petrified skull makes me homesick. It's almost as if, when I imagine those black eyeholes, I can stare right into them and find the stars and breathe the sage and feel the heat of the stone. I've been daydreaming like this all day, whenever I can find the privacy. Of course, I can't tell anyone here how the idea of a skull delights me so much; it would seem ghoulish, under the circumstances. Bone is a common enough sight, I'm sad to say. And it's best not to dwell on it. Yet strange things happen, despite the war. Maybe even because of it. You'll not believe this—I can hardly believe it myself—but yours is likely the first of two prehistoric specimens I will see here. I can't say much more than this, but if I tell you that we have engineering companies fighting a different kind of war underground, and that Northern Europe, at the time of the Cretaceous, was not unlike Alberta at the same time, you'll understand what I mean. Excitement is rare here. That might surprise you, but a soldier's life is mostly routine. It's almost like a bone hunter's. Lots of walking, in the mud and the rain and the heat, and keeping your head down. And every once in a while some real excitement. Though there's no real knowledge to be gained fighting. The vandal hand of Man, Mr. Sternberg says. But it's the whole body in a war, and the spirit too, at least what you can keep of it.*

*Your gift, Lily, just the idea of it, is helping me to keep my spirit. But do you really think Mr. Sternberg will let you send it? This seems impossible, especially if you've read his book. The trials that man has been through, the great risks he's taken, to save fossils from destruction. Well, I suppose I'm being selfish, but I hope you can convince him. Of course, if I were a proper scientist, I'd mail it right back, or, better yet, take it to the British Museum on my next leave. Wouldn't they be surprised! But I suppose I'm not a proper scientist. Already, even before I've seen it, I can't bear to part with it. Already, I feel safer having it with me. It's hard to imagine that something that has survived so long could be destroyed in one of our wars, though there seems no end to the ingenuity of the destruction here. It's a hard struggle, but I'm doing fine, even better now with your package to look forward to. When do you think you'll be ready to send it?*

*By the way, how is the old man? I haven't had a letter from him in ages. His last one sounded weary. Maybe all the hard years of collecting are finally taking …*

THE DOOR OF THE ESTAMINET KICKED OPEN AND WHEELER came in, dripping wet. With him were a pair of Tommies, thick-set, snout-faced men who'd have resembled pigs if not for their almost black skin. They winced as they walked slowly forward, as if the light of day pained them.

Wheeler led them across the cobbled floor, past the empty tables, to the fireside where Scott sat, pad and pen lightly balanced on his knee.

"As promised," Wheeler grinned widely, his boyishness even more pronounced beside the almost-black Englishmen.

Scott stood, extended his hand, and introductions commenced quickly.

The Madame of the establishment, a frowsy-haired, blocky Frenchwoman nicknamed "Cheery," emerged from behind the counter somewhere back in the stone bowels of the building and asked what they wanted. With a guttural rejoinder to their attempted levity, she turned away with a clomp.

"Sweet lass," the older of the Tommies said, then broke into a cough. His name was Reg. He spoke with a Northern accent (mining country, Scott assumed) and did most of the talking. The other soldier, Will, was much younger, and oddly resembled a Victorian chimney-sweep. He glanced around nervously.

"It's all right, lad," Reg patted him on the shoulder. "Ter's naught wrong wi' it."

The younger man just frowned.

Reg grinned, showing teeth that were just white enough to stand out in his black face. "They won't shoot ee for it, don't you fret. Even if they did find out. And they won't. Nobody looks at old Rattler that close. A bone is a bone."

At the mention of shooting, the young Tommy groaned.

"A fag'd calm him," Reg hinted.

Scott offered them both a cigarette. Reg took the whole pack, then raised his eyebrows at Wheeler.

"I promised three," Wheeler said sheepishly.

"Three?"

"And some socks too."

The young Tommy brightened at the mention of socks. "Docs ee have them? Me toes are about falling off."

Wheeler produced a pair of thick woollen socks from his pack.

"That's enough," Scott said impatiently, knowing the high value of both items. He was flattered, though felt a little guilty, that Wheeler was so eager to please him.

Reg scowled and muttered as Cheery put down the drinks. "It is a risk we're taking, after all."

"Yes, of course," Scott said placatingly. Then, "So, have you got it?"

Both Tommies grinned.

"Aye, a piece of him, anyhow," Reg said. "Ee's a big chap, is old Rattler."

"Cap figures ee's a bloody big cow," Will said softly.

"Cow? Elephant's more like!" Reg tossed the drink down his throat, then stealthily undid the canvas sack beside his chair and produced a two-foot fragment of what could have been a long leg bone.

Cow. Elephant. Scott smiled and touched the greyish bone, still dabbed here and there with remants of blue clay.

"More'n forty feet down, it were," Reg whispered, sounding like a junk-shop owner convinced he'd come into possession of a rare antique. "In the clay. A whole mess of bones, whole ones, just like it."

"Skull?" Scott asked.

Reg was offended. "What do you need a skull for? Your mate here says you'd be happy looking at any big bones."

Scott nodded, running his hand along the rough edge of

the bone. A land creature. Not as big as some of the predators of the Red Deer Valley, but big enough. He'd have to write Mr. Sternberg, give him an accurate description. He started to take notes on the only paper he had, the back of his letter to Lily. He wished he knew exactly where the miners had found the bones.

"What part of the country?"

Reg's answer didn't surprise him. "Can't tell ee that."

"No, no," Will joined in quickly, swivelling around, as if expecting an officer to walk out of a dark corner and put him in detention. "Can't tell ee that. Come on, Reg, let's go."

"The lad's right. It's more of a risk than I'm saying."

Wheeler cut in as the Tommies prepared to leave. "Another pack for another bone. A whole one. Smaller." He grinned at Scott.

Will had already started to scurry away. Reg shrugged, explaining. "Nervous ee is. Well, ee's more to lose. Lass at home, ma and da. Naught for me. I'd just as soon have the fags."

They arranged to meet again the next day, provided they weren't moved out by then. Once the Englishmen had gone, Wheeler slapped Scott on the back, unable to contain his glee at the transaction. His smooth, moon-wide face was more flushed than usual in the fire glow.

"I told you they were big. Cows!" He guffawed, then intently watched Scott as he studied the bone. Moved by his friend's excited concentration, he blurted out, "Is it a good one, Scott? Do you think it's very old? When I knew those Tommies were miners, I figured they'd be getting bones from a long way down."

Scott smiled at the younger man's excitement, touched by it though troubled at the same time. He was becoming too fond of Wheeler. And too great a fondness for other soldiers enhanced the chances of being killed; he'd already seen the evidence of that rule more than he wanted to. Besides, Wheeler was doubly dangerous, as he still held onto the romance of war, unwilling to believe that it was meaningless; he took greater risks. Wheeler's earnest innocence relative to other soldiers sometimes irritated, sometimes comforted, his older trenchmate.

For now, Scott allowed Wheeler's enthusiasm for the fossil to wash over him. More than anything else, including Lily's mention of her gift, the heavy bone relaxed his nerves and brightened his future. If only the silence of the badlands came with it, replacing the ceaseless pounding of the guns, which, as Scott knew from his first leave, could be heard all the way in England.

"Yes, it's old," he said, holding the bone out in both hands for Wheeler to get a closer look. "If a million or so years is old."

Wheeler whistled lowly. "A million years. No kidding?"

"Feel it. It's stone. It's been in the earth so long that stone has replaced the minerals of the bone."

Tenderly, Wheeler reached out a hand. "How about that?" His eyes widened, cast back the fire glow. He moved his fingers slowly over the bone, as if afraid it would snap.

Scott became aware of a sudden silence. The distant guns had either paused or he had shut them out. Only the occasional crackle from the hearth broke over his shoulders. He felt that he was holding a wheel behind which the whole of the earth's history lay in his care. His arms didn't move. Orange light flickered along the bone, like burning fingers on a flute. Wheeler, too, seemed transfixed by the moment, which, like the bone, had been taken out of its mysterious grave and placed like a held breath amongst the chaos. Neither man spoke until the moment, extending, grew uncomfortable. The wonder emanated from a bone, after all, and they could not look at it indefinitely without thinking of other, more common bones they'd seen scattered over the scarred fields or floating in the mud. Scott felt Wheeler's hand vibrate on the fossil, and saw the flesh melt away, up the arm to the chest and shoulder, finally to the face now stricken with fear instead of wonder. He looked away quickly, pulling the bone down like a bar.

A burst of noise entered the estaminet. Aussies, judging by their shouted accents. A dozen of them. Scott quickly arranged the bone fragment in his pack. He well knew that a fondness for bones, even prehistoric, non-human ones, would draw unwanted attention from trenchmates and superiors alike. Bad luck, they'd likely think, everything in a war being quickly turned into superstition. And Scott himself, anticipating the arrival of the tiny badlands skull, already believed that its fate and his own were linked. But he was damned if he was going to let the superstitions of others deprive him of the protection he needed.

He smiled at Wheeler. "Thanks," he said. "This is more important to me than you know."

Wheeler couldn't stop grinning. "Aw, that's all right. You'd do the same for me."

Scott laughed, tickled by what he could do for his friend that might possibly be "the same." Then, lapsing into a comfortable silence, Wheeler picked up his drink while Scott returned to his letter. The room had become bristly with talk, musky with the smell of men, like a dugout beyond shelling range. Scott settled the pad on his knee and scratched out a few more lines.

> ... *their toll on him. I hope not. There's so much more to learn, and there's no better teacher in the world than Mr. Sternberg. And I'm not just talking about science either.*

Scott paused, overwhelmed again with the desire to be home, to be away from this misery of boredom, tedious work details, and sudden horror. The tiny skull, the fragment of leg bone: what were they except messages from his own future as well as the earth's past? It was as if they spoke to him, whispering, "Here is your life's work. Return to it." He wrote a few closing lines.

*Lily, there's so much work to be done. I can't tell you how eager I am to be home to start it. Something has just happened here that is, in its way, as surprising and marvellous as your gift. But I'll save that for next time. Now I'd better get back to the company. With any luck, the next time won't be long in coming. Give my regards to Kim and all the Sternbergs.*

*Affectionately,*
*Scott*

# 1916

LILY PAUSED, THE CHISEL INCHES ABOVE THE TINY SEC-
tion of stone she was working. For the tenth time in an hour,
she'd imagined another human presence nearby, close enough
to be peering over her shoulder. And she knew who that presence was, even saw his face hover for a few seconds in the shadows outside the coal-oil light, just as it had hovered in the sick
room when she slipped in and out of consciousness. But that
face had been soft and tender. This face appearing and disap-
pearing around her, always just at the edges of her vision, was
fixed in a scowl. No one, not even Charlie, the eldest son, had
the authority to remove a specimen completely on their own initiative. If Mr. Sternberg had caught her doing so, Lily knew the
consequences: she'd be told to leave the camp immediately.

She turned slowly again, her eyes scanning the bulky shadows of the hoodoos. Normally, she found the strange stone
structures comforting. They reminded her of the still, powerful
bodies of the horses in her father's blacksmith shop, bodies she
had stood among as a small child, holding her father's hand,
clutching it in the sudden and mysterious knowledge of her
mother's absence. The smell of leather and manure then, of
stone and shellac now, usually calmed her. But both smells were

accompanied by the difficult task of holding onto faces: her mother's, her father's, and now Scott's. It seemed cruel that Mr. Sternberg's disapproving face should be the one that remained so vivid.

At least, returning to her work, carefully chipping the dry dust away from the skull, she could hear her employer's sage advice: "The greater your excitement at uncovering a find, the greater caution you should use. After a million years in the earth, another hour, day, or week is of little consequence." But was that true in this case? The hard stone pressed into her chest, as if urging her to work faster, as if telling her, as she had told herself repeatedly since finding the specimen, that Scott's survival depended on his possession of the unusual fossil.

Lily tilted the lamp so that she could better see the partly-exposed bone. From the curvature and tiny eye sockets, she realized it was a skull. But what were these other, even tinier holes all over the surface of the bone? She had never seen anything like it before. She felt another pang of guilt. What if it *was* a specimen entirely new to science? Mr. Sternberg would feel betrayed. But then, she had urged him to come, she had made it clear how important this find was to her, she had spoken to him with more emotion than she had ever showed anyone, including Scott. It was not her fault that the badlands storms made patience a dangerous luxury, not her fault that Mr. Sternberg was too old, and perhaps now even too ill, to understand why she needed to excavate the skull quickly.

On her knees, she straightened her back and gazed into the surrounding darkness. Camp was about two miles away. She'd have to start back soon. The Sternbergs were early risers, and Kim Lu had to get up before they did in order to prepare breakfast. She looked at the skull again, and the same strange feeling

68

came over her, that the earth itself was making her a gift of this one jewel. How else to explain her finding it, her eyes catching the minutest bump in the surrounding surface of the stone? She might have walked the path a thousand years and never noticed the skull. After all, she didn't have Mr. Sternberg's expertise. Yet something had made her stop and look harder. And as the eye sockets had slowly emerged beneath her chisel, she couldn't help feeling that there was some especial sympathy in the earth, in the bones of the earth, that reached out to her because she was reaching so hard for Scott's safe return. Lily knew she was not foolish in the ways of other young women, the privileged daughters of railway bosses or ranchers who occasionally stopped off at Steveville for business reasons. Finery was as alien to her as leisure. But was she foolish about this skull? The Sternbergs, even though they understood the magic of the badlands and its fossils, would think so. They were coldly practical men, for the most part.

The thought suddenly made her painfully aware of her isolation. She had no one to confide in except Scott, and that was something she was only now finding the courage to do, now that he was overseas, at war. The bone called again, but the hour was too late. She had a full day's work in the bone fields ahead of her.

She gathered her few tools, doused the lamp, and pushed some loose rock over the skull. Then, walking towards the hoodoos, their stone as alive to her as horse flesh, she made her way to camp.

AN HOUR LATER, JUST BEFORE DAYBREAK, LILY APPROACH-ed her tent. It was fifty feet away from her employer's, across a level, burnt-grass portion of the floodplain. Relieved to find the other tents dark and still, she prepared to slip inside her own. But she heard someone call to her.

Only it wasn't her name.

"Maud," the voice said brokenly in the darkness. And again, "Maud."

Lily froze. The voice was familiar but not the tone. She had never heard a single word spoken with such longing. She peered across the camp.

"Maud." The voice came softer now.

Lily heard a cough from another tent. She did not know why, but she wanted to walk across the burnt grass and say, "Yes, it's me, it's Maud." Instead, she stepped towards her tent.

The voice did not come again.

A late feeding nighthawk folded its wings with the sound of a muffled drumbeat as the dark began to lift from the earth.

# 1916

THE WEATHER HAD BEEN FOUL, COLD, WET AND GREY. THE trench was slippery, mud up over the duckboards. They passed the huddled, dark shapes of other men, rising up like ruins collapsed off the walls. None of them spoke. It began to drizzle. Every minute, flares burst overhead, briefly creating a hollow, greenish day out of the dusk, a watery vividness sometimes, then a scorching one, like the striking of a translucent match.

Scott crouched lower. He could hardly swallow. The stench of decay and slime had been strong since they'd reached the front lines, but now it was much heavier. Clotted. He imagined that each breath he drew took in something material. It was a challenge not to gag.

They slogged a few hundred yards along the trench, away from the German lines, as far as Scott could tell. Finally, the corporal ordered him and Wheeler up over a low section.

Wheeler did not hesitate. He pulled himself over the parapet, then reached back to give Scott his hand. Scott took it, but kept his head low, helmet tilted forward.

The corporal, a bearded, bleary-eyed man with thick lips and a broken front tooth, followed. "Come on," he said, striding along parallel to the trench for another thirty yards before stopping.

Scott kept his head down, straining for the sound of rifle fire or shells.

"You can lift your head, Private. Jerry's having a rest."

But Scott kept breathing in the mud and lingering chemicals of the churned ground. The distant guns threatened to shift position and sweep closer at any second.

"That's an order, Private! You've got work to do!"

Slowly, Scott raised his head. The corporal was pointing into the trench. Behind the spot he pointed to lay a heap of shattered wooden beams, cement rubble and smoking earth. They must have had to go above-ground to get around to the other side of it.

Scott and Wheeler climbed down into a clear section of the blackening trench, then awaited further orders. The sky darkened above them, dusk moving to dark so heavily that it was like dirt mixing with water to become mud. A peculiar new odour made Scott gag as the corporal marched them around a bend to another, smaller ruin of stone, wood and earth. The rankness was the same that had hung over them since they headed to the front, but it was heavier now. The three soldiers pushed into the dark like wasps burrowing through the rotting flesh of a pear.

At a narrow, slanted entrance to this smaller ruin, the corporal removed some empty sandbags from his kit and divided them between Scott and Wheeler. Then he pointed to the gap in the ruin.

"Go in there and gather up all you can find. Then we'll bury it back of the trench. Get a move on!"

Scott and Wheeler blinked dumbly at each other.

With no change in his voice, the corporal explained that the ruin had been an emplacement for one of the big mortars, that one had exploded as it left the gun and three men had been shredded to fragments.

"Hurry it up," he finished. "It'll be too dark soon."

The two bent into the gap, stepped through the rubble slippery with mud, and looked around. The stench was overwhelming, worse now that they knew what it was.

Wheeler whispered, "Let's do it and get out," then grabbed what looked like the bottom half of a leg by its torn puttee and stuffed it in his bag.

Scott couldn't bring himself to help. He couldn't even look around. The stench was enough—he didn't want to see what it emanated from. But there was no way not to see, short of shutting his eyes. The mud, the rubble, the beams, the twisted metal, the air—it had all become soft and rotting. Poor Vic, he thought, I ought to help. He looked up.

Wheeler, bent at the waist, moved like an old peasant woman gleaning in a grain field. His bag sloshed at his hip. Scott stepped forward, but the squelching underfoot unhinged his jaws in another gag. Wheeler approached and took the empty bag from Scott's hand.

"Just stay there," he said calmly. "I'll fill this one and say that's all we could find."

Scott nodded, keeping his hand over his nose. Out of the corner of his eye, he saw a fragment of bone.

He moaned lowly, closing both eyes. He could hear Wheeler's sloshing, sucking progress. From somewhere behind him came the corporal's order to hurry.

"Here," Wheeler said, handing Scott two heavy bags. "You'd better carry them out."

His hands closed on the rough canvas as he turned back to

the narrow entrance. Almost low enough to crawl, he passed under the angled beam and burst out, pushing the air violently from his lungs.

"Come on," the corporal ordered, and led them back to the low section of the trench.

In a few minutes they stood in the open again, on a field shredded into uneven furrows and rent with craters of varying depths. There wasn't a building in sight. A few charred stumps broke the rapidly darkening western horizon.

Scott and Wheeler dug a shallow grave in a relatively untouched square of ground while the corporal stood a few feet away.

"That's deep enough," he finally said. Then, once the diggers had paused, their breathing heavy even against the thud of the roaming guns, he added, "Bags and all."

Scott was ashamed to be so relieved, ashamed to turn away from the hole so quickly and plunge his shovel back into the recently-dug pile of mud.

Wheeler grabbed his elbow. "Wait, Scott." He turned to the corporal. "I want to pray for them."

The corporal scowled at the sky, then, with a backward glance towards the sound of the heavy artillery, said, "Be quick about it."

Wheeler removed his helmet and waited for Scott to follow. He didn't want to, but felt he owed it to his friend. The corporal remained where he was, his helmet on.

Wheeler held his hands clasped at his belt, spoke lowly into his chest. "Our Father, who art in Heaven, accept these souls into your merciful embrace. Forgive them their trespasses and their sins. Your ways are all-powerful, and in your shadow we wander, joyous in your protection, till you bring us to the temple. Dear Lord …"

"That's enough, Private."

"With all due respect, sir, I'd like to finish. If it was me, I'd want it done properly."

The corporal snapped. "I said that's enough. This isn't Sunday school. Besides, if you stand there any longer, it'll be you. It'll be the three of us. Now come on!"

Scott tugged at Wheeler's sleeve. Wheeler was shaking his head, his large eyes brimming. "It's not right," he muttered. "It's not right."

But he came at Scott's repeated pressure. Together, they fell in behind the corporal and returned to the trench.

At the entrance to their chalk-cellar dugout, the corporal told them to await further orders, then disappeared. The dugout was one of hundreds the soldiers occupied, all that was left of the village that had long since been shelled to rubble.

Inside, candle-flame shivered and cast a faint, breaking light over the muddied chalk walls and floor. There was a rhythmic motion to the shadow edges, as if they moved to the far-off, subsiding artillery.

Scott dropped onto his bunk. Wheeler did the same. No one spoke to them.

"You'll need some tea," Macpherson finally said gently, and began to make it.

More than anything, Scott wanted a wash, but he knew there wasn't enough water to get the stench out of his skin.

The heavy guns pounded on. Scott fumbled for a cigarette, wondering how in hell Wheeler could keep from smoking. Maybe it was time for him to try it. He pushed the tin towards him.

"It'll help settle you," he said.

"No. No thanks." Wheeler's flushed face was even redder than usual. It seemed he was drawing all the blood in his body upwards. "I'm all right. I just wish he'd have let me finish, that's all."

Scott changed the subject quickly. The others didn't need to hear what it was they'd done, and he was in no mood to discuss it.

"Finish your letter yet, Mac?" he asked wearily, leaning back and shutting his eyes. "I'd love to hear a bit of it."

Macpherson, who must have been nearly fifty, wrote unceasingly to his daughter, a girl only a few years younger than Lily. Scott, like the others, found the letters, in their assumption of a calmer, civilized world, comforting. And then, Mac's voice was sonorous, sane. It could have been the voice of Mr. Sternberg.

As Scott listened, he shifted his weight and felt the fossils he'd traded for clack together in his kit. That sound, too, was comforting, but he let Macpherson's words wash over him instead.

> *Give Mother a good big kiss for me. And tell her at the same time that she must pet you a little every day. She is not very spooney, I know. But I think the war will change this. It's a cold world, dearest, but no colder than we make it. The trouble with older people is we allow ourselves to grow too material in our outlook and consider a little spooning and love-making a waste of time—and all the time our hearts are craving for something we know not what. Then when the clouds do come and overshadow everything, we have nothing that will dissipate them. The best motto is: Make the best of everything, think the best of everybody and hope the best for yourself.*

*God gave us Love, and the desire for Love, and He knows how necessary it is to keep life soft and pliable instead of cold and calculating. It is here, in this place, where one realizes the need of the softening influence. Just you pet Mother all you can.*

Macpherson kept his head bowed, and the silence that followed his reading was uncomfortable. Then Wheeler, with unnerving gusto, said "Amen!" and added, as always, in his efforts to be humorous, "Is she a peach, Mac? I could use some loving when I get home."

The older man was happy for the teasing and returned it warmly. "Oh, she's not for the likes of you. I'd rather she be an old maid than get hooked up with a hayseed from down around Lethbridge."

"Oho! You don't say! Well, I'll just have to look her up when the war's over and prove you wrong."

The hopeful mention of the future was genuine, unforced, but Scott was stung by it. "When the war's over." It had been going on for years already. And besides, he realized, sinking further into his stinking, sodden clothes, for them it had only just begun.

# 1975

LILY SHIFTED UNCOMFORTABLY IN HER SEAT NEAR THE front of the Greyhound bus. She needed a harder surface for such a long trip—over thirteen hours to Calgary, and then another two to Brooks. Repeatedly, she doubted the wisdom of what she was doing, but eventually came back to the one inescapable truth: it was not her business to question something in which God's design shone so vividly.

Rain dimpled the windshield and side-windows, but Lily could see quite clearly the shabby neighbourhoods of East Vancouver the bus lurched through. The houses were small, porched and peak-roofed, mostly grey as rock or brown as dirt. And all were dripping from the morning's storm, as if they'd just been lifted from the bottom of the ocean and plunked down in neat rows. Lily saw an old woman step carefully down some crooked porch-steps, and felt a pang of sympathy, then a sudden burst of gratitude. The poor soul, she thought, is off to the shops, or maybe to play bingo at some old folks home—what a gift it was to be on a different sort of journey. Lily stared out the windows until the rain smeared the glass and the few people on the sidewalks or in the tiny front yards wavered like seaweed.

She turned to the large, black purse on her lap. It contained, along with a folded wad of money (all she thought she'd need for the trip) and the usual hairpins, napkins and wrapped candies, a neatly stringed bundle of Scott's letters from the front. She'd not looked at them for many years. It wasn't that she couldn't face what they contained—after all, she could remember the emotion of them and what was unspoken between the lines, or even what the military censors had blacked out—but that the sight of his handwriting, tall, straight, and sure as the young man she had loved, always pained her. She hated to think of his suffering, even knowing he was past all suffering.

Undoing the string, she selected a letter at random, opened it carefully and, with a leaden heart, began to read the tall, slightly angled script.

*Dear Lily,*

*Your little skull sounds wonderful. I can't imagine what it is. But I have to tell you how much it means to me to be thinking of the badlands and its treasures in this place. It's funny, how thinking of a petrified skull makes me homesick. It's almost as if, when I imagine those black eyeholes, I can stare right into them and find the stars and breathe the sage and feel the heat of the stone.*

Lily read on a while, then raised her eyes from the page and stared out the bus window. Farm fields, somewhere in the Fraser Valley. Rich earth, black rows budded with the first green of potato plants, and tea-coloured puddles between the rows, reflecting the heavy sky. Old barns of flaking, faded paint, a tractor crawling around the edge of a field near a brimful ditch, and to the northeast the Coast Range Mountains, their eye-powder blue darkening to the muted greens and browns of trees and greys of stone as the bus sped closer.

What was the other specimen he referred to? Lily felt bad that she could not remember, disloyal somehow to his memory. Sixty years shouldn't make such a difference, considering the spans of time she and Scott had once discussed. What was marvellous to him should retain its freshness always. She could still feel his excitement pounding between the words, drawing her back. It frightened her a little, this passion, made her strangely elated in a way that threatened her grasp on the present. Did her face unwrinkle as she read his words, did her eyes shine again? Silliness. Yet she couldn't deny that she felt different than she had before finding the skull.

She turned the letter over. Other words in the same handwriting, but hastily scribbled, shimmered in their suddenness on the paper. She could decipher only a few words and phrases: "blue clay," "leg fragment, lower," "smaller than chasmosaur." After so much time, the fervour of the jottings still lifted off the page.

Lily turned away from the window and placed the letters neatly back in her purse. It was all so long ago, yet somehow the emotions of that time were coming back to her, more vividly than she would have imagined. Scott had possessed such passion for life, for science. Beyond all that, she reflected with a fresh and piercing sadness, he had loved her. Lily's eyes returned to the window.

One valley had become another. She saw herself as a young woman moving cautiously down a slope of crumbled bentonite clay (like walking on popped corn) to stand at last above the find. An owl hooted not far off. The "tat-tat-tat" of a partridge drummed out of the sage-rich dark. The skull seemed to glow like fire; it might as well have cast sparks.

Lily watched herself bend to the work, the lamp puddling the stone around her knees, the awl in her hand. Again the skull's tiny size amazed her. How unlikely it was that even one person had ever noticed it in all that wilderness of stone. Its miniature beauty stunned her into a wondering pause. Smaller than my heart, my hand, she thought. The mosquitoes took the blood from her veins silently. She scraped the stone almost as silently from the tiny holes near the jaw of the skull. The coal light hissed and spilled and made her small circle of working a minor sun. The sage-sweet air pressed her bones harder into the ground. Then the drenched, green fields of the Fraser Valley returned.

The bus climbed the mountains and the world outside suddenly darkened, as if a giant hand had closed around the sun.

# 1916

THE HEAT INTENSIFIED AND THE MOSQUITOES GREW FIERCE.
Charles Sternberg had known many forms of hell on the earth,
and but for the bugs he would have regarded his summer of toil
in the Red Deer badlands as soft. They weren't far from fresh
water or human company, and almost every day was profession-
ally rewarding—he had never been in a richer field of more dramatic specimens. Moreover, he had his three sons to help him,
and the other members of his team (the girl, Lily, and Kim Lu,
the cook) were dependable, hard workers. Heat and bugs: these
were irritants he could deal with, had dealt with, equably. But
the mind and the spirit could make a hell out of the most ver-
dant paradise, and Sternberg had begun to fear his most inner
sanctuaries where once he had relied on them for sustenance.

Maud is dead. Cope is dead. Maud is dead. The words
pounded out of the sun together, joined like the bones of a
fossil. The swarming mosquitoes murmured them all day in
his good ear. And, at night, he remained awake to the absence,
resisting the dream world that he knew, in the end, would only
magnify his loss, though the temporary relief of his daughter's
company was so sweet as to overwhelm even his work for the
Creator. The past—how capacious it was, swallowing the bones

of the great extinct beasts in a number of barren cemeteries like the one of this valley, and yet the fine bones of his precious child too. How could it be? That the earth could hold the beasts' gaping skulls of stone along with the softness of her hands that once soothed and cooled his calluses—it was absurd, he could not see the connection. Perhaps if he had been able to touch her before the end ... the thought was too painful and he shook it off.

Yet he was enough of a man of God, despite his new burden of fear and doubt, to recognize his thinking as a dangerous affront to truth. He knew his soul—any man's most cherished possession—was in danger. He could not even be sure of how its wounds had already affected his faculties. So he forced himself, that night around the campfire, to tell the stories that charmed his team, the stories that had once so delighted his living daughter. Speaking, he could look up and see in Lily's eyes Maud's tender interest, as he had once, so painfully, seen the sickbed suffering there, the suffering he had not been able to soothe for his own flesh and blood because he had failed to make it home in time. One day! If he had taken a different route, not slept at all ... agh, it was no good. To unburden himself of the memory, he directed his voice to the living eyes in the fire glow.

"You owe your lives to Professor Cope," he began again, his voice quiet, as level as he could keep it. "And I owe mine to ignorance. But that wasn't the first time and likely won't be the last. We are all of us ignorant before His eyes." He dropped his gaze from the girl, watched the shadowy figures in the fire. With his head down, his voice seemed to flow out of the air, the rocks, anywhere but his mouth.

"If not for the generosity of that great man, I'd never have had my start in the Kansas chalk. And my path would have been much harder without it, might never have led off my brother's ranch, away from those stubborn cattle. How often I followed those strays, how much, God forgive me, I cursed them and that life. But if it had been the Lord's will for me to tend His living creatures, I'd have accepted that, of course. But His plan for me involved finding the bones of his long-dead creations. There is no other way for me to understand how I found the nerve to write that letter. God's hand was on my hand. Everything I believed, my love for Creation and for service in that name, I put into my appeal. You see, I'd heard there was a fossil party being put together at the Kansas State Agricultural College. I'd been a student there briefly, to learn more about ranching, if that was to be my form of service. When I heard about the expedition, bound for western Kansas, which was a wilderness in those years, I took it as a sign—it was the design of providence that I join the team. And to think it was being led by Professor Marsh of Yale College. His efforts, I well knew, had secured for that noble institution the largest collection of American fossil vertebrates in the world. It was too much to ask for. Up to that time—this was 1876, I was in my twenty-sixth year—I had spent all my spare energies away from the ranch collecting leaf specimens in the Dakota Group. Magnolia, sassafras, all the remarkable beauties of the late Cretaceous. But you have seen these, you know their beauty. I don't have to explain."

Sternberg raised his head to look at his three sons in turn. They were listening, as always, respectfully. They claimed—and he had no reason to disbelieve them—to never tire of his stories, for he always added something new and surprising to what always remained interesting. In unison now, they nodded slowly, as if prodded by the same gentle hand at the back of their weathered necks. But they weren't as rapt as Scott Cameron had been. No, he had the gift. It was a tragedy he could not use it now.

Sternberg thought shiveringly of his daughter wedded to Scott Cameron. Ah, if only she had lived, if only they had met ... what pride to give her hand into his, what joy! Her hand ...

Then Sternberg met the girl's eyes. She was staring hard at him, the fire glow flickering vividly over her skin, clutching at it. But had she not been pale and sickly the last time he'd looked at her? He turned his eyes heavenward, took in the thick clusters of stars, then resumed, forgetting exactly where he'd left off. But it didn't matter. The important thing was to keep talking, filling the silence.

"I failed to secure a place, no matter how much I pleaded and pointed to my fruitful labours in the Dakota. The expedition was already full. My disappointment was great. I was lost as I never had been. To have come so close. Ah, but if a stone is put in your path, go around it or labour harder. I have always said so. It is the word of the Good Book. I have tried—no, I have succeeded—in passing that lesson on to my children."

He caught himself, noted the defensiveness in his voice. These were his children, not some angelic jury convened to assess the state of his faith. "Have I not?" he asked quietly, expecting no answer. This time, he did not look at them. A log collapsed in the fire, sent out a whoosh of light and heat. He took direction from it.

"So I wrote to Professor Cope at Philadelphia. I put all my soul into the letter, for I truly believed this was my last chance. I told him of my great love for science and of my earnest longing to enter the chalk beds of western Kansas to make a collection of its wonderful fossils, no matter what the discomfort and danger. And I mentioned my poverty, that I could not afford to go at my own cost. Here it was that the Lord's hand pushed mine on beyond reticence and pride. I asked the Professor to send me three hundred dollars to buy a team of ponies, a wagon and a camp outfit, and to hire an assistant, someone to help with the driving and cooking. I did not even send any recommendations from well-known men as to my honesty or ability. I mentioned only my work in the Dakota Group.

You can imagine the state I was in once I had despatched the letter. I couldn't sleep, couldn't eat, I gave little attention to my studies. Fortunately, for my health, the Professor responded promptly. Trembling, I opened his letter. A draft for three hundred dollars fell at my feet! The note enclosed with it was brief and to the point. The words are etched in my memory. "I like the style of your letter. Enclose draft. Go to work."

Sternberg smiled. Forty years later, Cope's words could still warm him. The warmth faded quickly, however. He couldn't reignite the excitement of that first expedition to the chalk, but perhaps, if he kept talking, he would think less on his losses.

The girl coughed. For a moment, he thought he would falter, reminded of the illness that had ... Oh, Maud must have coughed her thin frame to pieces before the end. Was it a blessing to have missed that? No, for missing that he had missed looking into her eyes one last time, missed hearing her voice, touching her cheek. He had missed the opportunity to return consolation. His jaw hung slack, his eyes watered.

"Mr. Sternberg?" a soft voice queried anxiously, reviving him.

"And so," he sighed heavily, "I went to work. And I've been working ever since, for the greater glory."

Sternberg broke off, noticed the girl looming in the flickers and shadows. The sight shook him. Risen, risen, he thought desperately. Then the place, the time, the girl's name, sank into him. He didn't want to put memory in the wrong form, the cherished voice on the wrong lips. Oh Lord, Lord, he moaned inwardly, let me keep her now, do not add that loss to the other. She is not this girl. This is Lily, the blacksmith's daughter, I know this. Let me speak of the past to Lily.

But not now. Not tonight. Tomorrow would be soon enough.

He rose unsteadily to his feet. "Goodnight," he said weakly, and as if in a dream laboured towards his tent.

"Mr. Sternberg. Wait! Please!"

Lily's face seemed to have less skin than eyes now, as if the sky was eating her from within. Sternberg shrank from the sight. In the morning, he had managed to put her off, citing the need for a good day's work. At supper, he had listened to her pleas and asked again for her patience. All along he knew he only wanted not to accompany her to the little skull. To do so would be to risk not hearing the voice she'd heard, not feeling what she'd felt. And if that happened, it would be the chilling, final proof of what he'd lost.

"Have you decided when to come with me?"

Sternberg shook his head. "Lily, the bone has been in the rock a long time. A few more days will not …"

She frowned. Again her jaw went rigid. "Days might not matter to the bone, but to Scott …"

Sternberg could only stare back.

The girl's eyes were brimming, but her face had not softened. "And one good storm could wash it away. We've had so many this year. I don't think it's wise to wait."

"Yes. I see that." The hollow widened in his stomach. All his life, just the idea of an exposed fossil had filled him with such curiosity that he could barely tend to the necessities of food, sleep, shelter. He wondered if that passion had left him forever. To be filled with what? He put his arm across his stomach.

"Soon, Lily. I promise."

Sternberg turned and limped slowly to his tent.

That night, he was haunted by one story, above all others, and he could not suppress it, either in or out of sleep.

# 1876

THERE WAS CONSTANT DANGER FROM INDIANS. THE MANY tribes of the Sioux—Pawnee, Cheyenne, Oglala, and others—were being pressed on all sides by white settlement. Sternberg, after receiving Professor Cope's draft, and as soon as the frost was out of the ground, had hired a team of ponies and a boy assistant and had left the ranch in eastern Kansas for Buffalo Park, the very edge of civilization. Following the railroad line, he had seen at every stop great heaps of buffalo bones glinting in the sun, and very few buffalo on the prairie. At the time, a buffalo hide was worth a dollar and a quarter, but even sport, passengers shooting from trains, would have greatly reduced the Indians' staple food. Though the carnage troubled his gentle nature, Sternberg had his mind on much older bones and the places he hoped to find them, in more dazzling masses of white—among several of the Creator's great cemeteries.

Sternberg was in his mid twenties, large-browed, already losing his hair but compensating with a thick mustache. He felt the glory of his unexpected chance every bumpy, tedious moment. The Kansas Chalk! Once the floor of the vast Cretaceous Ocean! He had waking visions of the creatures he had already found entombed there—huge fish and sea lizards, giant toothless flying reptiles. His excitement was such that he took no precautions against Indians. He did not even carry his rifle with him, but left it in the wagon when he limped out to explore the territory along the way, telling Jakob, the nervous boy, that he couldn't hunt fossils and Indians at the same time. It was the boy's experience and caution, not his own, that made sure the tent and wagon-sheet were of brown duck, which blended into the dry, brown buffalo grass and kept the two well-hidden as they travelled from canyon to canyon.

They had left civilization behind and made their own wagon trails, stopping to explore any exposures of chalk they found, from the mouth of Hackberry Creek in the east to the south fork of the Smoky Hill, a distance of a hundred miles. All along the dried, old watercourses, antelope, and wild horses with beautiful flowing manes and tails, roamed in great herds. Prairie-dog villages broke the ground in all directions. The sun beat down. They searched as much for drinking water as for fossils, though the water was alkali and barely drinkable. The silence was immense and cleared the mind of fear, directed everything to the task at hand.

Sternberg walked miles, his head down, the wagon following with its dry-mouthed driver and ponies. One late June afternoon, he inched along a ravine, both sides of which consisted of cream-coloured or yellowish chalk, with blueish chalk below. For hundreds of feet there was no vegetation except for the occasional scrawny shrub; mostly it was just bare rock, cut into ridges and mounds, sometimes beautifully sculpted into towers and obelisks. He crept like a ghost through a ruined city, his shadow spreading like a thin stain under halls of tottering masonry. The wagon creaked at his back, the horses' hooves echoing dully.

"Mr. Sternberg," Jakob rasped.

"Soon, soon," he promised vaguely, sweat evaporating off his brow. He sucked the pebble that rested on his swollen tongue, pushed it between his parched lips.

The day had been a failure, just like the previous two days. Acres and acres of blinding chalk without a single find. He knew he could find water at the river, but it was so far away from his work that he decided to push on in the hope of finding some nearer at hand. A howling wind blew out of the south, cloaking them in clouds of pure lime dust that stung the eyes. The heat had not abated. The sun was pebble-sized, fiercely white, almost the colour of the chalk he walked on, which reflected the sun's rays with a savage intensity. Sternberg, dazed, felt he was crawling across the very surface of the sun.

Finally, beyond a sprawl of rock, he discovered some small borings of crayfish in moist ground. Taking a line and sinker from his canvas pack, he measured the depth to water at a couple of feet.

"Here," he said to Jakob, waving him down from the wagon.

The boy, staggering, tried to push the shovel in, but his foot slipped and he almost fell.

"Give it to me," Sternberg said gently, sorry for the boy's condition; already pale, Jakob had become an albino, his bared skin frosted with dust, his lips cracked.

Sternberg dug the well as quickly as he could. Greedily, in huge gulps, they quenched their thirst with the little water they found, then immediately tended to the horses. Neither spoke, for there was nothing to say that hadn't been said before. Sternberg knew the boy would beg to set up camp and ease work for the day. But there were hours of sunlight left; the day might yet be redeemed. Another few steps in any direction might reveal a treasure unknown to science, unseen since Kansas had been the bottom of a tropical sea. This was the greater thirst. The boy could wait for dark to sleep.

But looking at him, his tiny Adam's apple beating out a sparrow's fear as he swallowed, his left shoulder hanging slightly from the pressure of holding the reins, Sternberg thought of his infant son, George, and took pity.

"We'll stop here, Jakob," he said, already deciding that he'd walk out on his own until dusk. Perhaps once the glare had dulled on the chalk beds, he would find something.

They set up camp, again in silence. Sternberg pitched the tent in the moist ground, in the shade of two tall pillars, while the boy retrieved some buffalo chips from the wagon to start a fire.

As he was pounding in the last stake, Sternberg heard the boy's mild voice, almost at his ear.

"Mr. Sternberg," he said apologetically, the wind bristling his fine, blond hair. The red that had returned to his lips made a livid scar in the surrounding white.

"Yes, what is it, Jakob?" Sternberg tried not to sound severe, but the boy's deferential manner often weighed on him. He didn't want to spare the time for it, no matter how much he appreciated that a child ought to show respect for his elders.

"I can't find any food. I think we're out."

"Out?" His brow darkened. He stood stiffly, brushing the dust off his trousers. Why hadn't the boy noticed before and said something, when they might have had a chance to shoot some game on the prairie?

The boy blushed, dimming the scar of his mouth. "I thought we had another bucket. But there's nothing. Just the ponies' corn." He hung his head.

These mundane details of survival—how they plagued a man when he wanted only to do his work! Drink, food, sleep: to be allowed one solid week without them. To think of how much he could accomplish!

He looked soberly at the sky. The sun, still blazing, had nevertheless begun its descent. They were forty miles from fresh supplies. He could take one of the horses. But then he'd have to leave behind the precious specimens he'd found during the earlier part of the trip, not to mention the boy. And the chalk beds—he might be the first hunter in this particular valley, in any of these valleys. If he left before thoroughly going over the ground, he might return to find that one of Professor Marsh's party from the college had arrived to lay claim to the finest specimens. Day after day, this fear drove him harder. He had something to prove to the professor who would not sign him on, but, more importantly, he felt a great responsibility to do well for Professor Cope, whose generous gamble on an unknown fossil hunter repeatedly gave Sternberg the energy to push on beyond his usual limits of endurance.

The fear of losing specimens decided him. "Parch some corn in the kettle," he told Jakob. "We'll try for an antelope tomorrow."

AN HOUR LATER, HE TOOK A FEW HANDFULS OF THE PARCHED corn with him and continued his head-down, laborious progress over the chalk. The wind kept up. It blew grit against his legs and into his face. The world condensed to a few square feet of dazzling white in all directions, occasionally punctuated by the shadow of one of the misshapen towers. He was looking for loose bones near the site of a wash, or any unusual protuberance in the chalk, his concentration so great that he heard nothing, not the howl of the wind, not the scrunch of his boots, not the throbbing of blood in his temples. He didn't even feel the chalk or the sun. He moved always forward, sweat evaporating almost immediately off his nose and lips, but thought of nothing.

Then suddenly he dropped to his knees and carefully brushed aside the thin layers of disintegrated chalk.

"Thank God! Thank God!" He looked heavenward, squinting into the sun. Something dark shimmered at the edge of the yellow haze. Sternberg shook his head. Heatstroke, he thought with dismay, and paused. Excitement prickled the back of his neck. He reached up with one hand, turning slightly as he did so. Something dark. But the shadow did not lap at his feet. It was still as the flesh that cast it. Instinctively, Sternberg moved his hand to his scalp. The Indian's black eyes narrowed. His lips parted slightly—with amusement or savage expectation, Sternberg couldn't tell.

The Indian was small, wiry and—Sternberg noticed this right away—very pale, almost white-skinned. He wore no paint. A single eagle feather stuck up from his narrow head, over which soft brown hair rippled with the wind. His breechcloth was the colour of the buffalo grass. He was so still, he didn't even appear to be breathing; but for his cloth, he might have been made of chalk.

A hatchet hung from his belt, but no scalps. Nonetheless, Sternberg mouthed a quick prayer, in preparation, knowing how high the passions were running between Indians and whites. People spoke of a big battle to come, of General George Armstrong Custer's battalion moving across the Plains from the east. But that would be north, in Nebraska and Montana, Sternberg comforted himself in vain. It really made no difference: the Indians roamed the whole of the Plains, considered the land

96

sacred, their traditional hunting grounds. A friendly Indian was less likely to be encountered than a hostile one. And yet, there was something odd about this Indian. His face was narrow, not broad like those of the Indians Sternberg had encountered near army forts and in reservations. And he had a high, sharp nose. But more than that, Sternberg felt drawn to the man's stillness. The chalk, the wind, the prairie grasses beyond, seemed to flow into and out of him. Sternberg stared at him now in much the same way that he stared at the chalk beds, for evidence of the Creator's power in the cold form of death. For death enveloped the Indian; it rose off his stillness like dust sweetly scented with blood. The blood, imaginary or not, assailed Sternberg's senses. For the first time, he regretted not carrying his rifle. Then he heard the screams.

"Jakob! Jakob!" His blood was in his mouth, but he didn't move. Darkness swirled out of the beating sun and splashed over the Indian's shadow, which slowly came forward.

"Jakob! Jakob!"

HE WOKE IN HIS TENT, HIS SONS ARRAYED AROUND HIS COT.

"The boy," he said desperately, trying to rise.

Charlie pushed him down gently. "It's all right, Papa. The boy is fine. Don't worry yourself."

"Boy?" Levi grunted. "What boy? He's been dreaming." Then, loud-voiced, "Papa. You're here. With us. In the Red Deer badlands. There is no boy."

Sternberg felt Charlie's cool touch on his sweating brow.

"No boy?" he said, then immediately thought of where he was and who assisted him. "Lily? She's not here."

"Asleep, Papa," Charlie said firmly, as if Sternberg had lost his sense as well as his hearing. "It's late."

"But you are all here."

George coughed uncomfortably. "Well, her sleep is probably deeper. The work is wearing, especially for a ..."

Sternberg sat straight up. "Yes, yes," he muttered, wondering how his sons could have so little awareness of the spirit of someone they worked with day after day.

Charlie put a mug to his lips. He tried to speak, spluttered through the liquid.

"A little Madeira, Father," Charlie said soothingly. "A restorative, that's all."

Madeira? Sternberg did not approve of drink, but perhaps madeira was allowable. But what did Levi mean, there was no boy? Did he not hear the screams?

Sternberg lay still, breathing heavily, letting the drink and the coolness on his brow spread through his limbs. The badlands? Lily was out in them, excavating. On her own. Tomorrow, he'd have to confront her about this.

"You've had a bad dream." Charlie again, the calm voice of his middle child. Middle, if you no longer counted ... Then he came fully to himself, wrenched back by the weight of absence.

He glared at Levi. "I know where I am. And the boy was not a dream. Do you think I have forgotten? Do you think he is gone from me? Do you think such a thing is possible?"

His son's unblinking features in the dim yellow shadows of the tent infuriated him further. "Are you so wise you can tell another when he is dreaming? Have you lived so fully in this world?"

Levi did not flinch at the words or react in any other way. Yet Sternberg immediately felt contrite. He didn't doubt the truth of what he'd said, that Levi had always lived within fixed limits, but he was sorry for the accuracy. Levi was a good man, and goodness did not require imagination. Or did it?

Sternberg fell back again and closed his eyes. The Great Plains flowed away from him, the oceanic grassland steppe waving and waving, shimmering, a close-up of the sun, spotted with the black of the buffalo herds, and the sky shimmering like an extension of the ground, great clouds thundering over in their own herds, and somewhere in the swirl and flow, still as his own skeleton in the chaos of his imaginings, the bones of extinct beasts, fixed like keys into doors that never really opened, beyond which lay Doomsday and Paradise and all the felt and unfelt mysteries of Creation, more than a man could apprehend without risking his mind and his soul. Little wonder that he'd dream, if dream was the word for memory in sleep.

And what of Lily? She was out there now, willing to risk so little a thing as one man's, his, displeasure, to gain ... what? Not a bone, not a specimen named after her. The trust of something greater than herself, the trust Sternberg had lived his whole life by.

Maud understood. More than the others, she had her Papa's soul. She loved to hear him tell of the great Cretaceous, she loved to hear him recite his most fanciful poems and stories. In her dark eyes, his boyhood. In her tender nature, his rest. In her life, his faith. And all torn away from him, as God tore His noble beasts from under the light and heat of His sun.

He opened his eyes. Charlie and George were all solicitude, and Levi stood still without the power of stillness. They were good boys; he had taken much solace from them at the time of Maud's death. Why could he not do so now? He wanted to tell them of his struggles and doubts, he wanted their help, even if it was not the tender help of a daughter. His lips parted, but he could not speak such words. They were grown men with their own pasts now, their own futures. Because he loved them, because he could still see in their eyes how much they counted on his strength, he would not burden them with something only he alone could face. It was a matter between him and the Lord, as it had been at the time of Maud's death, as it would be at the time of his own.

"I'm sorry," he whispered at last, turning his head away. "You are good sons, all of you. I have no accusations. I am tired, that is all. Some rest, and then, to work once more. That is medicine enough."

Soon after, his sons gone, he faced the strange memory to which his dream had fastened itself.

# 1876

WHEN HE CRIED OUT FOR THE BOY, STERNBERG WAS SUR-
prised that his own body did not immediately move. As soon
as Jakob's screams and his own shouts had subsided, when the
thought of running forward came to him in a jolt, the Indian
calmly lifted the hatchet off his belt. He did not wave it in the
air, or speak in an angry or commanding tone, or even change
expression. His penetrating black eyes weren't even making
contact, yet Sternberg somehow intuited that every flicker of
his body and features was being carefully observed. It was as if a
pillar consisted of nothing but eyes, layered deep beneath the
stone. Garbed simply in brown, his sinewy legs and chest bare,
almost the pallor of the surrounding chalk, the brave hardly fit
the popular image of a Plains Indian. And his face and hair were
so fair that, if not for his obvious composure in the landscape,
Sternberg might have believed him a white man. But he'd never
yet met a white man who could contain silence so naturally and
with such ease. There seemed no separation between the Indian
and the air.

Yet Sternberg did not regard the hatchet as anything but a
material fact. It kept him in place, his shadow half-covering the

exposed part of the beautiful mosasaur specimen, the Indian's shadow equally motionless a few feet away.

Sternberg did not know how to proceed. He had had almost no experience of "real" Indians, those who hadn't already been forced onto reservations. If he had, he might have accepted the necessity of carrying a rifle into the field. But then, with more experience, he might have been even more terrified. As it was, his concern split equally between the bones of the ancient beast behind him and the boy somewhere beyond the bluff for whom he felt responsible. He did not, at least initially, fear for himself. Because of this, he pointed violently in the direction of the faded scream and half-shouted, "He's a boy! Just a boy! What have you done to him?"

The Indian turned slowly, following the gesture. Sternberg noticed the small brown stone behind the right ear; it looked to be pierced into the flesh of his neck. Apart from the single eagle feather sticking up above the same ear, the stone was the Indian's only adornment. Was he, then, an outcast from his people? The thought made Sternberg painfully aware of his own likely fate. Whites had been massacred and mutilated all over the Plains, especially recently, ever since Custer had found gold in the Black Hills and prospectors had swarmed into Sioux territory: that much Sternberg knew from the papers. But if this man was a renegade or an outcast, who had attacked the boy?

Surprisingly, the Indian's look softened as he turned back. He raised the hatchet to his own scalp, then shook his head and made a quick sweeping gesture with one hand, as if clearing the chalk dust from the air.

The wind, which had lessened somewhat, now blew stronger again. Sternberg stared at the single feather, rippling fiercely above the sharp face. Dust whipped up between them; Sternberg could feel the mosasaur's bones emerging from its ancient grave. Relieved by the Indian's gesture, in which he interpreted that the boy's life had been spared, Sternberg could not resist a quick look down. Yes, the skull, and around it … praise God … could it be … yes … the four paddles! He almost dropped to his knees again, his fear overshadowed by the beauty of the specimen.

He felt rather than saw the Indian's shadow move forward. He flinched, expecting to be struck at any second. But no, for the sake of his wife and child, if not for the boy, Jakob, he had to at least make an effort to defend himself. He turned quickly, but the Indian, his hatchet at his side, was looking beyond him at the bones. Then, his dark eyes narrowing, almost vanishing in the sharp ridges of his cheekbones, he frowned at Sternberg and again raised the hatchet. This time he pointed at the bones, as if expecting something. But what? What did he want? Sternberg blinked dumbly at the mosasaur's beautiful snake-like tail, wondering what he was supposed to do, assuming that his life depended on it.

The Indian reached out with the hatchet and tapped the canvas sack. Then he pointed at the bones.

Sternberg couldn't believe it. But even if his own death lay at the end of this encounter, at least he'd have the satisfaction of seeing this wonderful specimen of the Cretaceous. That was something, perhaps more than he could have asked for. He crouched down and set to work.

Their shadows mingled so that it became unclear which body was moving. Yet the Indian stood so still that Sternberg, if not for his heightened sensitivity to other living bodies—antelope, deer or human—would have considered himself alone. Only the sheer enthusiasm for his work interrupted his unusual sensitivity, to the point where, now, it was fair to say that his work could be the cause of his death. If he hadn't been so intent on finding something, anything, of note in the chalk, he almost certainly would have been aware of the Indian's presence earlier, perhaps early enough to get back to camp, back to his rifle.

The sun burned into the back of his neck. He slid the butcher knife from his sack and began scraping, very carefully, around the bones. His initial enthusiasm was not disappointed. It was a rare find: the skull, intact, with the spinal column around it and the four paddles stretched out on either side. The skull was large, flat, and toothed like an alligator's, the jaws forming an anvil, the eye socket the size of a man's fist. It lay on its side, one of the front limbs gnarled below it, oddly resembling a hand with a hole where the palm should have been.

Gradually Sternberg chipped the chalk away. Then, with a brush, he swept the dust and flakes off the bones, which were pale yet darker than the surrounding chalk. He began to imagine the reptile returning to life as he worked, saw the eye socket fill in and turn to him, blinking away a million years of sunlessness, the jaws open. The image cooled him. He felt a tropical breeze across a marsh, smelled the sassafras and blooming magnolia, heard the great palm fronds beating overhead. He gripped harder on the handle of the knife, breaking the skin of the blister he'd formed on his last dig. The pain he recognized only briefly before it was forgotten. Lying on his stomach, leaning slightly to his left side, as if listening for the beat of distant horse-hooves, he continued to scrape with his right hand, blinking the sweat from his eyes, entranced by the rhythm of his breathing and the knife's scraping, the two sounds blending, becoming a meaningful voice speaking below the wind. Slowly, expertly, he brought the ancient bones into clearer focus.

104

TEN MINUTES PASSED. FIFTEEN. FINALLY, THE INDIAN UT-
tered one harsh word. Sternberg felt the hatchet blade on the
back of his neck. He murmured a quick prayer, his scalp prick-
ling with anticipated pain. In rapid succession, he saw his wife's
face, his son's, as clearly as if they stood with him. And then, to
his surprise, he saw a girl's face—it was his cousin, Esme. She
was smiling, waving at him—was it a beckoning forward? Was
she dead, then? The image dissolved into the white dazzle of the
chalk and the thick smell of dust.

The blade, flat to his skin, pushed down harder. Sternberg
tensed along his whole body. "My Father, My Lord, for the sake
of the glory of your making." He spoke aloud now, alone with
his God. "Blessed is the one who enters Your gates, blessed is the
one who has laboured in Your service."

The blade lifted off his skin. He was kicked in the side, hard
enough to turn him over. The sun swam in his eyes. Several
seconds passed before the Indian emerged from the dazzle.
Still, he wore no discernible expression. His eyes looked down
at Sternberg, and far beyond him at the same time. The Indian
gestured for him to rise. Standing, Sternberg felt light but not
weak; it was as if he had been released of some burden.

And then he was walking, back towards camp, the Indian
directly behind him. His sack and butcher knife and brush lay
beside the mosasaur's bones. He wondered if he would ever use
them again.

They moved into the sun, past the white pillars, those senti-
nels of God's long reach into the dim past. How strange it was,
Sternberg thought, to walk so quickly, with his head raised, over
this ancient cemetery. And how difficult too, despite the situation. He might have missed a specimen the first time by, or the
wind might have blown just enough to reveal the tip of a bone

that had been buried only moments before. But it was better not to look. He did not need the added suffering of having to overlook a new find. Besides, he had a more immediate responsibility: to save the boy if he could, and, somehow, to save himself. He did not hold out much hope, but he knew from previous experience, if not his faith alone, that no situation was hopeless. Believing so was a sacrilege, vanity of vanities. He would do all he could and put himself in his Creator's hands. That was enough, and the decision gave him comfort.

Three dozen horses shone black against the chalk. They stood peacefully together, nickering and blowing air. As Sternberg came closer, he saw that they weren't only black, but different colours: brown, grey, dappled. All were lean, strong, with something of the wild still in them. Perhaps, he thought, some had recently been among the wild horses he'd seen as he crossed the prairie—certainly the manes and tails flowed beautifully, cast rippling shadows.

Beyond these shadows, standing or squatting around the campfire, were the Indians. More colourfully ornamented than his pale captor, they seemed to flaunt the muted nature of their surroundings. Their faces, broad and dark, were flashed with red streaks, as were some of their chests. With a shudder, Sternberg noted several scalps hanging off belts, and some vests twined with what looked like human hair (he'd heard about that particular form of savagery). He could see no other Indian who even remotely resembled the one at his back. None were so pale or so simply dressed. And when they stared at him, Sternberg felt only that they took in what they saw, which they did mostly with indifference, though a few looks seemed hateful. These faces were recognizably human and almost put Sternberg at his ease, since his imagination could encompass their response to his presence. He could read in each face what they thought of him. But he could not read his captor's face at all.

They passed at the outer edge of the fire. Sternberg still couldn't see the boy. By the time the wagon came into sight, though, he heard him. A moaning and a rising, breaking series of sobs. Soon, Sternberg saw Jakob sitting on the ground by the front wheel, his arms behind his back. He appeared to be tied to the spokes. Sternberg was relieved to find him alive, though the boy's crying distressed him almost as greatly. Sternberg could not see Jakob's face, as his head hung down into his chest. But his cries washed against Sternberg's back as he was prodded sideways towards the gathered warriors.

For he saw they could be nothing else. Given the hostile climate on the plains, and the absence of women and children, as well as older men, Sternberg could deduce as much, even if there had been no war paint. Though he had paid scant attention to the Indian wars, and scant attention to anything but the beginning of his life's work, it was impossible to live in the West and not be aware of the rising tension. It was all some people spoke about, as if life consisted only of violence and the expectation of it. Yet there below, on the very ground that people travelled over, glorious evidence of life more mysterious and dramatic than any clash between Indians and soldiers. Ah, but how few ever looked! Or, if they happened to stumble upon a precious fossil, how quickly the vandal hand of man would destroy out of sheer ignorance.

But these Indians: Sternberg could not guess what form their ignorance would take in relation to fossils. They were heathens, yes, but they had their faith of a kind, which may or may not honour the ancient bones. Of course, they wouldn't know what the bones were, but perhaps their superstitions would keep them from being destructive. He looked at the wagon, three-quarters filled with sacks of specimens. Soon enough, he'd know the fate of all his hard work.

They had walked into the smell of scorched meat—antelope from the look of it. To his surprise, Sternberg realized that his hunger overwhelmed his fear. Where his mouth should have been dry, it produced a faint moistness. He breathed in the rich smoke, wanting to point to the fire and back to his mouth. If he was going to die, he reasoned he might as well do so on a full stomach.

But he did not have to gesture. The pale Indian pointed him to a bare space of chalk amongst the warriors ringed around the fire, then spoke rapidly and softly into the coming dusk. Seconds later, a chunk of meat, greasy and hot, was in Sternberg's left hand, and a gourd of spring water in the right. He ate and drank with relish, yet with control too. This hospitality worried him: what might it be preparing him for? Could there be anything, he wondered rapidly, looking around at the half-naked, paint-streaked bodies, anything worse than dying?

The pale Indian, who had vanished while Sternberg was eating, reappeared. He squatted to prod Sternberg in the ribs with the end of the hatchet, not roughly but with insistence, commanding him to rise.

As they walked away from the fire, two dozen pairs of eyes turning to watch, a dozen others never shifting from the flames, another Indian stepped out of the dusk and fell in with their strides. In the rapidly fading light, Sternberg saw that his face was large and crooked, almost broken in appearance, as if it had been repaired once but inexpertly, the pieces not quite fitting together smoothly. He wore several feathers in his hair, which hung in two long braids. The pale Indian was not tall, but the braided one was even shorter, and walked with a slight roll, as if he was not used to being on the ground.

The two Indians exchanged a few words, then fell into silence, a silence that was quickly broken by the rising moans of the boy tied to the spokes of the wagon wheel. Sternberg could not bear the sound; it was piteous, heart-rending, and grew worse as they came within a few feet of his slumped form.

"Jakob, have courage," he said quietly. "Never despair. We are in His hands."

The braided Indian spat twice on the ground, then spoke quickly to the other, who did not reply. Then, to Sternberg's astonishment, he found himself addressed in English.

"You are in the hands of men. But it is good to have courage. Pah!" He held his hand to his nose and, with a wave, dismissed the figure on the ground. "That is white's courage, children or men."

Sternberg breathed in. The boy had fouled himself. But who could blame him? He was a boy, and he had good reason to be afraid. More than anything now, Sternberg wanted to protect him. Having recovered from the shock of hearing English out of the Indian's mouth, he made his bargain.

"You say you are men. Men do not harm children. Let the boy go, then do as you will. My fate is in greater hands than yours."

The dusk had become grey chalk grains. Nearby, a horse neighed, the sound rippling away like water as the braided Indian responded to Sternberg's words.

"The boy helps you work. So he stays."

Sternberg looked at the pale Indian. His eyes, firmly set on watching the last of the sun die, nonetheless reflected everything, even Sternberg's wonder. He didn't seem to be there at all. Sternberg could think of no way to approach him; it was exactly as if the chalk, the last of the light, the first stars, the blood in the veins of those around him, were housed in his stillness. Without understanding why, Sternberg felt hope in the Indian's apparent unearthliness. He waited for him to tell the braided Indian to speak.

In a moment, the pale Indian did just that.

"Bring the boy. Quickly," the interpreter said.

Sternberg bent to Jakob and spoke as gently as possible to him as he undid the ropes. The boy's pupils seemed to throb. His jaw opened and closed silently.

"Have faith, Jakob. He has not forsaken us."

The interpreter snorted, then spoke in his own language to the pale Indian, who only raised his hand, as if he wanted to blot out all speech. Then he murmured something so quietly that Sternberg thought a breeze had fallen from his lips.

"Bring a lamp," the interpreter said.

Sternberg looked at the pale Indian as he responded. "We don't use lamps. Only fire."

The interpreter relayed the message. Again, the pale Indian showed no expression. He spoke rapidly in his own tongue, ending with what sounded like a command.

The interpreter hesitated, his eyes blinking, his face in shards.

The pale Indian spoke harshly, and the interpreter turned away. In a moment, he had blended into the dusk.

Sternberg, who had been stroking Jakob's forehead, stopped. The boy had fouled himself again. Sternberg plugged his nose, then pointed down, and made a cleaning motion with his hands.

The pale Indian nodded. But he did not turn away as Sternberg helped Jakob out of his trousers. The boy was almost completely limp, the life already draining out of him. Sternberg removed his own shirt. With difficulty, he mopped up the boy and his underwear as best he could, then helped him back into his pants. It made little difference to the air, but Sternberg was happy to be doing something.

The interpreter returned with a blazing torch and what looked like a sack of buffalo chips. The pale Indian took the sack and spoke his tongue again.

The interpreter nodded, but looked confused. He seemed to be questioning everything he was told now. He looked at Sternberg coldly.

"He wants you and the boy to dig up the bones. To give him the hand. He will tend the fire. He wants the work done quickly. Do not worry that you will be harmed. Do your work. That is all."

Sternberg gaped at the interpreter. "The hand? What hand?"

When the interpreter had relayed Sternberg's question, the pale Indian showed emotion for the first time. He narrowed his black eyes and snapped out something in his own language.

"Your life is at stake," the interpreter explained indifferently. "Do your work."

Sternberg decided that he'd find out what the hand was when they reached their destination.

It was dark by the time they arrived at the mosasaur. The few stars, small as chaff, emitted almost no light. And the wind, which had earlier died down, began to gust again. It swirled the torch into an unravelling crimson scarf. The faint crackle of the wood inside it was all that broke the silence, now that the boy's whimpering had ceased. He seemed, finally, to have accepted the comfort of his employer's faith, or else he was just exhausted. Sternberg had to support him at times, reach out and put an arm around his waist. Terrified of being scalped, the boy seemed already dead now that no sounds came from his mouth. Sternberg felt oddly that he was escorting a corpse to its grave. The fire shadows on the chalk only gratified and excited such fancies; they were walking in a crypt, except the bones they sought had not been entombed by men, but by water, wind, earth, and time.

The Indian walked beside them, even slightly ahead. Sternberg could tell he was in a hurry, but he did not know why. His own curiosity, as much as fear, made him keep the pace.

Even in the dim glow of the torch, the specimen was beautiful, the one side of its anvil-shaped skull distinct in the chalk, its rows of sharp teeth preserved in the jaw, its vertebrae curving away beneath the breastbone. It was rare to find so much of a skeleton in one place; usually the bones were scattered over a wider area, with the main cache often the last to be found. But this was more than a weathered fragment, and Sternberg immediately went to his knees for a closer look. He grabbed his butcher knife, pressed his body full-length on the chalk and said to Jakob, "Here. Here. Shine the light here."

When the light did not come, he turned and looked up with irritation. One glance at the boy's limp posture and drained face quickly reminded him of the situation. He was about to gesture to the Indian when the light was lowered to a position just behind his head, so close that he felt his skin was burning. Then the Indian lay on his chest beside him, touching the beautifully preserved front limb of the mosasaur, stroking it, and speaking his tongue in a kind of chanting whisper.

Sternberg watched the man's jaw move in the flickering

shadows, his hand caress the ancient bone. The single feather he wore dangled down the side of his face, twisted there like a loosened flame. His words sounded like worship.

Sternberg took a closer look at the limb. It was broad-palmed, with a hole in the centre, the finger bones pointed straight in the one direction, as if at something. With a start, Sternberg realized what the Indian thought it was—a hand, a human hand! He looked again. Yes, to the untrained eye, it looked human enough, though far too large. But perhaps the Indian's superstition allowed for giants? Certainly he spoke to the bone and touched it as if it could understand.

The torch was burning down, the light flickering more and more.

"Jakob," Sternberg said calmly, without turning. "Take the sack and build a fire."

But there was no response. The Indian, finally, came out of his trance and pulled himself upright in one quick motion. Sternberg followed.

They looked back together on emptiness. The boy had run off. For a moment, Sternberg thought this would change everything. But the Indian's only reaction was to dump the chips out of the sack and put the last of the torch to them. Soon, a sizeable fire threw greater light over the specimen. The Indian grabbed Sternberg by the wrist that held the butcher knife, then pointed at the limb.

It was clear now what he wanted. Sternberg, because there was no other choice, set to work.

The night deepened. Occasionally a bird screamed, something killing or being killed, it was impossible to say which. The wind wrapped the flames over Sternberg's shoulders; he seemed in the grip of the very limb he was so carefully digging out. The

Indian squatted beside him and hardly moved. Hours passed. It grew colder. The fire weakened. But by then, Sternberg had scraped away most of the chalk that held the limb in the ground. Soon, he could lift it out and present it to the Indian. And then what? His usefulness past, would he then be killed? Absurdly, all he could think was what a shame it would be to die and leave this wonderful skull behind. If Marsh or one of his party didn't happen this way, a precious gift from the Creator's glorious past would be eaten away by the elements, lost forever. And the limb—what would happen to it? Would it ever return to those who could appreciate it as a sign of the Creator's genius, power and even wrath? Would the learned men of the scientific community be able to protect and preserve it for future generations? The questions were useless. He flaked away the remaining chalk and, carefully placing his hands beneath the bones, prepared to lift them out.

The Indian shouted. One harsh word. Heart pounding, Sternberg turned. The Indian's eyes were shining, trained on the mosasaur limb. He dropped the torch to the chalk. It burned there, casting a long, flickering shadow. On his knees, the Indian gently placed his hands under the bone. Then he waited, as if listening to some voice on the faint wind only he could hear. Sternberg was mesmerized; he did not even consider taking the opportunity to flee. The Indian raised the bone to a point just below his face. He stared at it, rapt. The firelight dimmed. The Indian lifted the bone slightly towards the dim stars. He was almost kissing it. Then he looked on the torch glow reddening the skull and other bones beside the cavity where the limb had been. The wind blew his single feather against his cheek and he winced at the touch. But still he did not move from his knees. Sternberg waited, holding his breath.

The torch flickered out and only the fire a few feet away cast light on the chalk. Finally, the Indian looked at him. Their eyes locked briefly and Sternberg felt he was being pierced through, though his skin was not broken.

The Indian looked away and murmured to himself. Then he stood, the bone balanced lovingly in his two hands a few seconds before he placed it carefully in the deerskin pouch at his waist. He gestured for Sternberg to get up and relight the torch, which he did. Then the Indian pointed back the way they had come. Bewildered, but feeling oddly as though he'd risen in a state of grace, Sternberg obeyed.

They walked back to camp, the Indian slightly behind. Sternberg, coming to himself with each second, began to pray repeatedly for the boy's escape. He had given up the mosasaur, even his own life, when the Indian had fallen into some sort of trance and then come out of it, looking drained, yet somehow steeled at the same time. Whatever his resolution was, whatever ritual he had performed with the limb of the mosasaur, the Indian's demeanour suggested to Sternberg that he would not survive. Perhaps, if he had acted quickly, if he had struck out while the Indian was in his swoon? No, it was foolishness—he had no such physical skills. His fate was with the Creator, let it be. But the boy might escape; that was a worldly consolation.

They reached the wagon, its tarp of brown duck flapping in the wind. Soon they would reach the campfire. Despite himself, Sternberg began to tremble: it would not be pleasant to die. He had heard many horrible stories of torture since he had come to Kansas as a boy. And these warriors were not likely to be gentle killers.

Sternberg felt a firm hand on his shoulder. He turned to see the Indian staring at the covered back of the wagon, one hand pulling the mosasaur limb from his pouch. The Indian gestured violently at the back of the wagon. Sternberg's heart emptied: not all of his specimens too, not all his months and months of hard labour! Take my life, he prayed, but if you do, please Lord, preserve these examples of your glory for the world. Then he moved towards the wagon and pulled back the tarp, as directed. The Indian held the torch closer. The heaps of burlap sacks, slightly bulging from the protective buffalo grass around each fossil, seemed to catch fire. Sternberg almost leaped forward to pull them to safety.

But then the Indian was at his side. He had put the mosasaur limb back into his pouch. With his free hand, he reached into one of the sacks. He pulled out some grass, fingered it briefly, let it drop. Then he removed part of the spine of a tylosaur, revolving his hand clockwise to study it. Sternberg swallowed hard. How much he'd toiled to find each of the specimens in those sacks! The Indian placed the spine fragment down, then opened a few more sacks and looked at the contents.

Sternberg was suddenly very tired. He slumped against the wagon, turning his face from the Indian's handling of the precious bones of the great reptiles and fish of the Cretaceous Sea. Why didn't he just smash them? Or was he going to pray to every single bone? Then what? He couldn't carry them all in his pouch.

Suddenly the Indian shouted into the darkness. After a few moments, Sternberg heard the clop of hooves on the chalk, and soon all the horses appeared at the edge of the dying torch-light.

A long-faced, toothless Indian in a massive war bonnet grinned down from his mount. He said something lightly to the pale Indian.

116

But the pale Indian pointed and spoke decisively. Several Indians dismounted and began to hitch Sternberg's ponies to the wagon.

The pale Indian spoke in almost a whisper to a young brave who then disappeared around the front of the wagon. More words. Sternberg was directed to get up behind the toothless Indian on his horse. The smell of scorched meat was heavy on the man's lean body. With a shudder, Sternberg felt his bare chest scrape against what might have been the scalps of other white men.

Finally the pale Indian swung lightly up onto his own horse, and led the party out of the chalk bluffs, down onto the prairie. Sternberg heard the wagon clattering behind. He wondered briefly if Jakob had been caught and made to drive the ponies. But, looking back, he caught a glimpse of the young brave at the reins. Ahead, the torch suddenly shot down like a comet and blazed a few seconds before becoming black as the star-spaces. The horses galloped faster, the pale Indian rushing ahead. Sternberg could not see him, but somehow knew he preferred to ride alone.

The minutes stretched out. Now the grass skirled the hooves, blew half over in the unblocked wind. Sternberg continued to pray, but the smell of the Indian was like a wall against which words smashed to pieces. He concentrated instead on the rhythmic pounding of the hooves.

Abruptly it stopped. The horses pulled up, scattering dust and tufts of grass.

The Indians were completely silent. Sternberg saw the pale one off to one side on his own, looking back. The horses snorted and shook their heads; their manes rippled like the grass at their forelegs.

When the wagon appeared, the pale Indian approached it. Then, to Sternberg's astonishment, he replaced the young brave at the reins. Even more astonishing, Sternberg was ordered down off the horse, blindfolded and helped up into the wagon beside the pale Indian. Then he heard the reins snap. The wagon bucked forward.

Sternberg did not know how much time had passed. At least an hour, perhaps two. The wagon seemed to spin like a ship in a torrent. Fast, then slow, then faster, around and around, then straight forward. He felt he was falling and recalled those few seconds in his uncle's barn as his body dropped through space until the hard ground broke him back into the world. Or, at least, partway back, into the shadows of the unconscious. But then, he had not been guided by any human form; no one steered his descent, or the Creator did. And now? It was hard to believe that the Creator steered through the body of a savage, and such an unusual savage as well. But he had to believe it. The Lord works in mysterious ways, His wonders to perform. He mouthed the phrase with some hope. The blackness whirled on.

Finally they stopped for good. The sound of wind soughing the open spaces, the smell of the heated earth, the dryness in his throat and mouth: they might have arrived anywhere on the plains. Or maybe the plains had gone. Sternberg felt, as he had once or twice before in his fossil-hunting life, that time did not exist in a straightforward way. This sound—could it even be the waters of the Cretaceous Sea falling on their marshy shore? It was easy to believe that the wagon had left the known world behind. He closed his eyes, and the second darkness washed into the first. When he opened them, would the great bones have found their home in the flesh again?

The Indian's hands touched his head gently, undid the blindfold. Sternberg blinked into immensity, stars like a throw of dust, darkness close as a buffalo's hide to its flesh. Apart from heavenward, he could see only a few feet in any direction.

The Indian ordered him down to the back of the wagon. Then he pulled back the tarp, removed two sacks and dropped them on the flattened grass. Sternberg stifled a cry. The Indian turned and touched his hand to the hatchet at his belt. Yet when he returned to the sacks, he dropped them with greater care and directed Sternberg to do the same, which he did. No other choice seemed possible. He gathered up the back-breaking labour of months and, as gently as possible, added to the pile of sacks faintly visible in the dim light of the heavens, sacks full of ancient life—the shells of great turtles, the spines of giant fish, skulls of mosasaurs and pleiosaurs and other swimming reptiles, bone after bone after bone, each the rung to a ladder that was pointed towards the stars but had hardly gone beyond the height of a man. Sternberg almost wept, feeling his mind descend the rungs. Yet there was something—he couldn't understand the sensation—almost logical in what they were doing. Let the dead lie, he thought. Except the Creator Himself had chosen to bring them before the eyes of man, for his learning and deeper humility. No, these bones were meant to teach the world of His glory, past and to come. It made no sense to lose what they brought to civilization. So why did the wind sound so much like the humming of a choir? And why did the savage beside him move his flesh like a brother spirit, born to the same sacraments of solitude?

When the sacks had all been dropped on the grass, Sternberg and the Indian stood silently over the pile. The wind touched them lightly, twirled the Indian's feather. Only the sudden snort of one of the ponies seemed to break him from his trance.

He made Sternberg dig, held the shovel out in his hand stiffly. Sternberg was surprised—he had thought they were done, he had even thought that, with the Creator's guidance and his own uncanny sense of direction, he could find this spot again, were he alive to do so. But it was not to be. For whatever purpose, he was meant to undo everything he had done over the past months, right down to the returning of the bones to the earth. Again, as he worked, he could not feel the outrage he was entitled to feel. Perhaps it was simply the silence and isolation (the Indian merely taking the place of the boy) that made this task a replaying of the original reverence. Or perhaps it was the lung-drowning beauty of the Creator's night, the rich musk of His earth—how could a man, even digging a grave for knowledge, not stagger in his senses at the majesty of his tiny role in such drama?

Sternberg dug hard, until the sweat ran and he tasted his own salt. He swayed at the edge of the deepening dark. If he fell now, if the edge of those stars cut into his neck like a hatchet blade and he collapsed into the sudden grave, he could not be better prepared to die. On the wind, he heard a lost hymn, one of his mother's favourites, and hummed to himself as the hole deepened.

AFTER A WHILE, WHEN THE HOLE HAD BECOME A FEW FEET deep and wide, the Indian gestured for Sternberg to get down into it. He prayed rapidly, but resolved not to show fear, not to give the Indian that satisfaction. If he was to die, he would die in praise of the Lord, not in terror. Yet he was trembling violently as he dropped into the hole. The ground level came to his thighs. He waited for the Indian to shoot him, or perhaps order him to kneel. Would he bury him alive? Any kind of savagery was possible.

A sack was handed down to him, then a second, a third. Ten sacks, twenty sacks. Finally, all forty-four lay piled around Sternberg. He stood in them up to his knees, and tensed for the crack of a rifle.

Instead, the Indian's body loomed over the hole in the dim starlight. Then he reached his hand down. Sternberg took it and was pulled up.

The Indian handed him the shovel again. Completely bewildered, but relieved, Sternberg began to fill in the hole. The earth returned to its darkness, the bones to their sleep. He worked quickly and efficiently. The wind was like a balm on his brow. He didn't even feel sickened by the loss of his specimens. The earth closed in great black waves over the bones of its giants; they were becoming small as the stars. The Indian stood motionless. Sternberg felt he might have been taking the earth out of that body and shovelling it back in.

But as soon as the hole was filled, the Indian wasted no time. He motioned Sternberg back into the wagon where he blindfolded him again, then snapped the wagon into a jerking, bouncing motion across the prairie.

The whirling darkness rushed back. Sternberg closed his eyes, tried to keep the position of the stars he'd scanned from the hole fixed in his memory. And if he failed, he'd only have to work harder; the chalk of Kansas contained riches enough for whole worlds of men to uncover. The thought that the Indian might kill him even yet seemed somehow a weakness, a failure of spirit. It was possible, but what wasn't possible in this life? The stars blurred, their edges frayed by the wind. The smell of the horses' flesh wafted up from the warm grass and earth. He breathed it in as his sense of time faded. The same ship, the same sea, the same wild passage.

The wagon stopped again. Low voices. Horses neighing, then pounding the earth. Sternberg noted for the first time that his hands weren't bound. He waited. Only the wind now, the same long, devout worship of its song over the earth. He undid his blindfold and sat staring at the stars. What position had they held? Already he couldn't recall.

More alone than he'd ever been, he got down off the wagon, walked around to the back and rummaged behind the tarp. Only a few empty sacks had been left and some clumps of buffalo grass. He prayed in gratitude to the Creator for his life, standing like a shorn cross in the prairie, his blood pounding. Then, breathing slowly, calming himself, he thought of the boy he'd have to search for, praying too for his safety. But even this thought of another did not alleviate his solitude, which yet was strangely pregnant with witness. Sternberg felt the bones and the eyes and the skin of the hidden beasts all around him. He felt naked, stripped of all sensation. Worlds within worlds. Space, earth, grass, wind.

He could not remain so; he forced himself back. With resolve, he mounted the wagon, chose his direction and returned to his labours on the floor of the ancient sea.

# 1916

HIS VOICE WAS WEARY, WITHOUT THE USUAL DELIGHT IT contained when he told the stories of his past. Lily stared at him, half concerned, half angered. What did yesterday matter? His words barely registered.

"Magnolia, sassafras, all the remarkable beauties of the late Cretaceous. But you have seen these, you know their beauty. I don't have to explain."

He turned to Charlie and Levi, then to George on the other side. Lily saw their heads bob, like worn-out nags at a trough. Even in profile, Mr. Sternberg's face looked all wrong. She wondered if he might be dying. When he looked straight ahead again, she met his eyes through the thin smoke. His face was reddened by the firelight and his whole body suddenly trembled. Was he cold? Or was he reading her mind and finding the disobedience there, the betrayal? He looked to the sky, as if he couldn't bear the sight of her.

I've hurt him, Lily thought. He's sick and I've hurt him. But as soon as she considered stopping the excavation of the skull, she could feel the bone pulling at her, she could see its exact position in the stone, as if Scott already held it in his hand. The image was so powerful and so comforting that it washed away her guilt and she had to force herself to remember all Mr. Sternberg had done for her. The faithfulness of his bedside vigil, his tenderness once she had recovered, his generous practical assistance: were these to be forgotten now that a greater human bond had entered her life?

The wind blew the smoke her way. She coughed, and the sound made her aware of the silence that followed it. Looking up, she saw that Mr. Sternberg's jaw was hanging open. His face was all fire and shadow. The sight of a burning moon would hardly have been more shocking.

"Mr. Sternberg," Lily said softly.

He stirred and spoke again, without looking at her.

"And so … I went to work. And I've been working ever since, for the greater glory."

And then he turned such a desperate gaze on her that Lily felt certain he was about to die. She vowed to make one last effort to show him the skull.

"Goodnight," he said weakly, rising and heading for his tent.

Lily quickly caught up to him.

"Mr. Sternberg. Wait! Please!"

He stared at her and seemed to recoil. To her surprise, his reaction irritated her rather than moved her to compassion. All this because she wanted one fossil? No. There had to be more to his weakened condition. But Lily all at once found herself desperately thinking of strength, of Scott and the future, as if Mr. Sternberg was deliberately keeping her back.

"Have you decided when to come with me?" she said almost coldly.

He shook his head. "Lily, the bone has been in the rock a long time. A few more days will not …"

124

It was as if he had struck her. "Days might not matter to the bone, but to Scott …" Lily felt the tears rise, but fought to keep from crying them. "And one good storm could wash it away. We've had so many this year. I don't think it's wise to wait."

"Yes. I see that."

But he seemed to see nothing. He stood like someone stricken blind who was trying to remember the sighted world. He suddenly put his arm across his stomach, as if to keep from being ill. His voice was almost a whisper.

"Soon, Lily. I promise."

She watched him limp away and felt almost no pity. She had tried, after all. She had done what she could to include him in her future. Now he had forced her to go on by herself. Already, her ears picked up the curious ringing promise in the dark-smothered stone.

# 1916

"YOU WHAT?" THE CAPTAIN STOPPED WRITING AND LOOKED up at Wheeler. A shaft of sunlight fell onto the trodden, slick grass outside the officers' quarters. Amber-coloured, it looked sticky as blood. For a few seconds, Scott, his eyes shut, tried to think of honeybees, tried to turn the distant guns into swarm hum. But the usual shouts and barks and engine-gunnings of reserve didn't allow for such easy escapes. He opened his eyes. The captain's jaw hung open, but he hadn't spoken again after Wheeler had repeated his request. He must be a decent sort, Scott guessed, with at least some sense of justice. Probably the mandatory service just an hour ago, which the men mostly endured in sullen silence, held him back from turning Wheeler down immediately. Or maybe he was what Wheeler would call a fellow traveller. Whatever the case, the captain paused long enough for Scott now to believe that Wheeler might just get the permission he so desperately wanted.

The captain coughed. He was thirtyish, narrow-shouldered, with a deeply cleft chin, one of those men who, immediately after shaving, looked unshaven. Scott assumed he'd be unsympathetic to any request out of the ordinary. But then, what was ordinary in a war?

"All right, Private. If it matters so much to you, I won't stand in your way. Fact is, things are pretty quiet as it goes." He looked off over the rubble of buildings, the black road running between like a charred snake's tongue. "You might as well take your buddy along. Two sets of eyes are better than one."

Just then, another officer, two decades older, appeared. After the salutes and a quick explanation from the captain, Wheeler found himself the object of effusive admiration.

"Now that's fine, that's the spirit!" The older officer pumped Wheeler's hand. "I think we can even spare another man from their unit, Captain. I can't think of a more important detail. It's what we're here for, after all." Then he muttered something lowly about the godless Hun, and fell into a staring silence, eventually broken with, "Good luck, men. I'm sure you'll find it. He'll be guiding you."

After more salutes, when Scott and Wheeler had walked away, Scott suggested they invite Macpherson along. He knew how exhausted the older man was, in body and spirit, and a chance to escape the army for a few hours was likely to be enthusiastically embraced. Wheeler agreed. But he was so excited and relieved to have his request granted that he would have agreed to a walk into no man's land in broad daylight. Just don't get preachy, Scott begged in silence, but was grateful enough for the break in routine that he'd have put up with some sermonizing. At least with Wheeler, it came from someone who knew what it meant to put his life on the line.

Macpherson was overjoyed at the prospect of a long march and a search, especially one away from the army. He didn't blink at the reason.

"It's your comfort," he said gently to Wheeler. "I have my letters from Emily. Why, even Scott here has his bone book.

And I'd walk the whole front to get my packet of letters back. Couldn't go on without them, I don't think." The thought shadowed his thin face, which seemed little more than a flicker of skin between charcoal bars. His forehead shone dully, brittle as eggshell. Scott often wondered how the older man managed to keep going. Maybe it was the same way he did, with his mind always on something to get back to, and, more immediately, on the possibility of surprise that wasn't deadly. Such as walking casually and freely down a black road, free of the pack's regulation weight, with a glorious late-summer sun breaking the cloud cover, and every mile becoming less rubbled and cratered, quieter. Scott marvelled at the clarity of the birdsong—truly a sound from another life—and at the sight of farmers and their hands at work in the fields, harvesting potatoes, turnips and various grasses, hay, straw. The usual stench of decay and urine and gasoline faded, replaced by the drugging musk of windfall fruit in unshelled orchards.

For a while, the three men listened to the birds, their boot steps, their even breathing, amazed by this change in routine. Good old Wheeler, Scott grinned, you had to hand it to him; he really did have the courage of his convictions, and army life had only revealed more clearly to Scott the scarcity of that virtue.

The road became packed earth and grass as it ran beside a clear river. The banks were flush with the sun-spangled water, and knee-high grass shimmered between it and the road. To the other side were more fields, and distant figures following behind horse-pulled wagons. Every mile or so appeared a stone farmhouse and low, companion barn. It was so quiet the three soldiers could hear the trickle of current coming along with them, like a horse wearing a Christmas harness. Even the big guns had fallen silent.

The air changed from fruit musk to rich grass, then back again. Scott hardly noticed the heat, or that he was drenched with sweat. He glanced back a few times at their three shadows, as if to be sure that they still walked in their bodies and hadn't left them behind in some smashed trench or snag of uncut wire; it was easy enough to believe that only their spirits had been released from a painful bondage.

They rounded a bend, passed a low stone wall blackly shadowed with squat apple trees, and came to a narrow, arcing footbridge over the river.

"It's this way," Wheeler said, and his voice dropped.

Scott knew why. The direction looped northward back towards the war. As if in mockery of their brief escape, the guns started up again, thudding out the familiar map of shell craters, ashen, stunted trees and ruined buildings.

Before the bridge, the three men had been content to enjoy the change in their day. They spoke at odd intervals, mostly to point out some other beauty in the landscape or to express again their disbelief at being free of the endless work details.

"Look! No shovel!" Macpherson had laughed, swinging his arms from side to side. Somehow, it would have been an invitation to violence if they had done more than enjoy what the day was giving them. Each walked as if carrying his life in a brimful bowl. Not once did Wheeler mention God.

As soon as they crossed the bridge, however, their mood changed. The day remained bright, the birds still flitted, singing all around them, men and horses still walked the fields. But the road became pitted; they had to negotiate shell holes. The fruit musk evaporated and the grass smell weakened. Now, with every mile, they walked back into what they'd left, except the army was no longer there with its tents and machines and shouts.

The three crept carefully along the road's edge, close to a brackish ditch. Orchards like burned-out fires appeared, one tree standing untouched in the ashes, its apples grotesquely red. A truck, with a smashed windshield and only two wheels, pointed nose-down in the ditch. Three old women with empty baskets walked by them and did not look up. A faint chemical smell strengthened and eventually blended evenly with the grass. The guns smote the sky without pause.

Wheeler led them with increasing confidence down a branching lane towards one of the common stone farmhouses and accompanying thatched barn. Much farther north and there wouldn't have been any buildings left to find. But the one they moved towards was untouched, and the lane smooth and still shadowed by its windbreak of trees. A smell of manure and cut hay thickened the air. The three soldiers dragged their shadows slowly through it. Where had the river gone, Scott wondered, suddenly aware of its absence. Now the birds were ominous as burst shrapnel. He looked at Wheeler's flushed, sweating face, round and full as a harvest moon, and it depressed him. The solace it depended on turned his stomach. How could he keep his faith with the proof of its irrelevance, even foolishness, all around him? Sometimes, despite everything, Scott felt he hated Wheeler, hated his unwavering enthusiasm. It wasn't just courage or innocence, it was stupidity. Sometimes, cruelly, he wanted to ask Wheeler to baa like a sheep if he felt so much like accepting the war as part of God's plan. These feelings swept over him at low points like a bone-chill reeking of blood and oil and smoke, and he could quell them only by thinking of Wheeler's decency, his genuine good-heartedness. In the end that counted so much more than his religion, especially up the line.

But now, even Mac appeared sullen.

"Are you sure this is it?" he grumbled. "I don't remember this."

The farmer striding towards them confirmed the rightness of Wheeler's sense of direction. There could be no mistaking him. He was in his mid-sixties, yet gave an overwhelming impression of great strength. Short but thickly built, he had one slightly dipped shoulder that made him appear to be continually pushing and bearing up a massive weight. His moustache was long and drooping, he had awful black teeth and skin the colour of sand.

"Artois, wasn't it?" Mac whispered. "Something like that?"

The farmer stopped and waited for them to come across the yard, swarming cats at their puttees. Scott shook the creatures away, sickened at the touch of them, the ceaseless hunger; they could have been rats. A fine dust, a chaff, filmed the air, smelling fresh but irritating the eyes and skin.

Wheeler rubbed at his eyes before he spoke. The farmer watched without expression. His shirt was open to the waist. Thick tufts of grey hair thrust out from his chest.

"Bonjour," Wheeler said. He pointed at the barn. Its opening was half-blocked by a large wagon of loose straw. "We were here before. We slept in your barn."

The farmer chewed his moustache as if it was a stalk of grass, but said nothing. He showed no signs of remembering anything. His body held up the heavy gold sunlight and he did not strain to waste any energy on speech.

"We're Canadians," Wheeler added hopefully.

Again the farmer just blinked back.

Macpherson leaned forward. He possessed a naturally deferential manner which, combined with his age, tended to win

132

the confidence of locals. The farmer was no different. His face relaxed slightly as Mac spoke.

"Excusez-moi, Monsieur. This lad here, he has lost something very special. His Bible. He thinks it might be in your barn. Unless you have found it already …"

The farmer turned slowly towards the barn until he was bearing it on his shoulder as well. He turned back with a grin as black as pitch. "No. I have not found it." He began to laugh, and the sound came from a great depth, as if out of the earth. The sunlight shook off him like chaff.

The three soldiers looked at one another. Macpherson shrugged.

"Monsieur, s'il vous plait," Wheeler pleaded. "It is a special Bible. My mother, ma mere, you understand, she signed it for me when I left home for the war."

The laugh broke off like a gunshot. The black mouth closed. "I will show you," he said respectfully, and led them to the barn.

The farmer's son had been killed in the first year of the war, Scott recalled, and two grandsons the following year. Yes, that would explain the lack of expression. But the laughter? Scott didn't see anything particularly amusing in Wheeler's mission. It was a bit earnest, certainly. He didn't think he'd make the effort to recover Mr. Sternberg's book, no matter how important Mac believed it was to him. Besides, he wouldn't need to bother, since he had so much of it memorized. But Wheeler was in a panic, had been ever since losing the Bible. He was convinced that he was going to die without its protection, and confessed to being afraid of dying if he couldn't have God's word and his mother's inscription on his body at the time. Scott had had to persuade him not to run back for it without official permission, had explained that they'd likely pass close to the area again, and that it would either be in the barn or in the farmer's possession (a long shot, he knew, but Wheeler had to be pacified somehow).

But here they were, amazingly. And since the farmer claimed not to have the Bible, they'd just have to spread out and cover the floor of the barn. It wasn't a large building, so it wouldn't take long to search.

They followed the farmer around the wagon and into the dark opening of the barn.

"Arretez," he said to the boy forking straw out of the wagon and into the darkness. Chaff consumed the air. They pushed through it, then straightened up in the thick dark. The farmer burst out laughing again. It seemed the ground beneath them was trembling.

Shafts of chaff-laden light angled in through chinks in the roof and walls.

"It isn't funny!" Wheeler reddened. Then, more angry than Scott had ever known him to be, he pointed at the farmer and spluttered, "You ought to be ashamed. It's not funny. Ashamed ... you ought ... I thought ... I thought you French were godly people." He seemed to be struggling for air.

Despite their friend's dismay, Scott and Macpherson exchanged subtle grins. The barn was stuffed with straw, the whole floor covered to almost head height. The boy had been tossing more in, like dumping water into the ocean.

Scott felt bad for Wheeler. It was a terrible loss for him, and Scott knew that he'd have to find some way to convince the younger man that it was for the best, perhaps even part of God's plan. Maybe the old farmer would have a Bible to spare. It would be in French, most likely, but the words were still the same. As

134

Scott turned to Wheeler to make the suggestion, he was shocked to see that his friend had rolled up his sleeves and had grabbed the pitchfork away from the boy.

The farmer blinked at Scott, and his black laughter died again.

"Come on, you two!" Wheeler said, thrusting the fork into the straw. "There must be other forks around."

The farmer began to grumble in French. Then he reached out and firmly held Wheeler's elbow. "Non, non!"

Wheeler whirled around and put the fork tines right up to the man's face. His voice was a low snarl. "You don't understand. I have lost my Bible here. And I am going to find it."

Instinctively, Scott and Macpherson stepped closer to Wheeler. Seeing this, the farmer reconsidered his opposition, and even seemed impressed by Wheeler's resolve. He addressed Macpherson when he spoke.

"You will put it back?"

Macpherson looked stunned. He turned to Scott for his opinion.

Scott had no desire to dig through a whole barnful of straw for a Bible that likely wasn't there, no matter how much it meant to Wheeler. He'd had more than enough of digging. Sure, this wasn't mud, and there weren't any shells or snipers about, but the damned repeated motion would be the same.

"Come on, Vic," he said quietly. "You can't be serious."

"What do you know about it?" Wheeler snapped, stabbing the fork back into the straw and pulling a heap down. "You think it's a game, like finding dinosaur bones. You think it's just words. You don't know anything about it!" He gasped as he worked. Blood quickly flushed his round cheeks. "Go and lie in the sun. I don't need any help."

Macpherson widened his eyes at Scott. Neither had ever heard Wheeler speak so aggressively, not even about the Germans. But the mention of dinosaur bones gave Scott a pang of guilt, not only because Wheeler had brought the fossils to him, but because he was reminded of Mr. Sternberg's equal devoutness. *My Life in the Bone Yards of the West* was filled with praise of the Lord. Why, he even described the badlands as "cemeteries of Creation," and spoke of enduring hardships for the sake of revealing the Lord's ancient treasures to man. But then, his hardships, trying as they were, were nothing like the horrors of this war. Scott couldn't believe that even a man as devout as Charles Sternberg could describe the Western Front as a cemetery of creation. Of course, he'd blame the carnage on the vandal hand of man, as if God took no part in it, no part in the doings of that hand. But did He not create it? And if so, should He be absolved of the responsibility?

The thought of the Sternbergs softened his opposition to Wheeler's plans. Despite all the destruction and suffering he'd seen, Scott could not dismiss religious faith when such a man as Charles Sternberg depended so heavily on it. To hear him speak of the glory of the Lord was like hearing Macpherson speak of his daughter's love. It was a comfort, and you no more had to love Macpherson's daughter to appreciate the warmth she brought to life than you had to pray to God to benefit from the strength others took from doing so. Mr. Sternberg never preached for conversion, only out of a joyous expression of what sustained him. Scott felt he could honour that much of God at least. He turned to the farmer.

"Bring us a couple more forks. We'll put all the straw back when we're done."

Wheeler paused, a grin cracking his red face. "Thanks, Scott. I didn't mean to blow up at …"

"It's all right. Besides, I figure the longer we're here, the longer we're away from there. Eh, Mac?"

"That's the truth. I think the rest of the boys were being detailed to run some trench stores up to the front. I'm glad to miss that." He reached down and flung a piece of straw into the air. "And this is a darned sight lighter than mud."

The farmer returned with three pitchforks and said that the boy would help. Then, holding Wheeler by both shoulders, he said seriously, "I am sorry, mon ami. I too am a man of God. I wish you luck." Solemnly, he lowered his shoulder into the sunlight.

"Well," Scott said. "Where should we dig to?"

Sheepishly, Wheeler gestured with his pitchfork to a back corner of the barn. "That's where we slept, remember?"

Scott didn't, but he knew that Wheeler had a sharp memory for such details. In fact, it was his friend's attention to detail that made his loss of the Bible such a surprise in the first place. Wheeler's explanation was simply that he didn't think it was possible he could lose it. The war made that sort of logic commonplace.

Macpherson suggested that they fan out and make a trench towards that corner, working four abreast and throwing the straw behind. He tripped self-consciously over the word "trench," but no one commented. The French boy, dark as a creosoted stake, hurriedly bent to the task. The others joined in.

As he worked, chaff swirling in the sunbeams, the half-dark and almost-silence obscuring even further the linear sense of time, Scott realized that this was the first time he'd done any digging in France that was anything like what he'd done in the badlands. Prior to this, he'd dug to fill sandbags or graves or new trenches, but the silence was always accompanied by the threat of sudden death. A shell could come over any time, a flare could go up, or, less dramatically, he might be ordered to do something more dangerous. Then, too, he'd mostly been digging in mud or in broken, smoking earth, within range of the stink of rotting flesh and acrid chemicals, constantly aware that he might dig up the remains of a recent or older carnage. There had been no cause to think of the badlands, not even when he'd set to work right after reading from Mr. Sternberg's book, not even after the English engineers had brought him the bones (which he carried secretly, carefully wrapped in a sweater, in his haversack). The perils of soldiering eliminated both past and future; the task at hand was all one could handle. Though, at rest, the past and future were never far away.

But now, for the first time, the rhythm of Scott's digging proceeded without anxiety. It was a warm day, he'd been for a long and pleasant walk through a countryside still able to renew itself, and no one was about to order him to stop and join a detail to the front. Even the big guns throbbing in the distance, noticeable when he paused, seemed connected to that larger, resonant silence of the earth, the silence out of which a mosquito's buzz was the wick burning down to fire the falling star, out of which the faint, dizzying ringing in the baked stones became the same ringing in your body and in the bones you sought to uncover. That eerie silence, which governed the whole of the western half of North America, contained within it your own death and the destruction of the dinosaurs. God's heartbeat, Mr. Sternberg called it. And he would add that any noise man could make, any violence especially, wouldn't alter the flow of a single cell in the blood that fuelled that heartbeat.

Scott was comforted. It seemed designed that he should have such thoughts while searching for the book of God's word. Despite all he'd suffered, he was not an unbeliever. He'd been raised a Christian, and while he did not actively practise religion, he had not dismissed it either. Like many soldiers, he was irritated by the army's insistence on mandatory attendance of church services and by the chaplains' unearned exhortations to fight because "God was on our side." But he'd never yet encountered a man who, in the terror of a barrage or in the grey minutes before going over the top, didn't appear to be praying.

The smell of straw, and of men sweating to throw it, knew no national boundaries. Scott could have been home. And the earth was the same, layered and seamed with minerals and trapped life. And there were men, learned men from great museums, young men like himself with dreams of working for science, who were suffering on the opposite side of the trenches. Hadn't Mr. Sternberg mentioned many times, in person and in his writings, all the dealings he'd had with the museums at Munich and in Bavaria? Weren't specimens dug out of the great West, even now, on display in Germany, with tiny labels attached, explaining they'd been found by Mr. Sternberg or Barnum Brown or Professors Cope or Marsh? And didn't ordinary Germans stop before them, stricken with humility and awe?

Scott let the easy rhythm of the work and the delights of the country air recharge his thoughts with excitement and hope. The time would come, he knew, when his real life would begin again.

"Whew," Macpherson exclaimed, wiping his brow with the back of his forearm. "It might not be as heavy as mud, but there's plenty of it."

Scott felt suddenly abashed; there was no reason why Mac should have to do any work at all. The man needed a break. You could see it in his eyes; they were heavy-looking as stones. And his cheeks were so hollow when he inhaled that he seemed permanently on the verge of a coughing fit.

"Why don't you go on out and find a shady spot, Mac? The three of us can do this."

Wheeler chimed in. "Yeah, why don't you, Mac?"

The older man shrugged as he took his canteen of water off his belt. "Never look a gift horse in the mouth, as they say. Let me know if you want a rest." With obvious relief, he retreated back along the widening trench and disappeared.

The boy had paused mechanically, but once Macpherson was gone, he resumed his work. Scott and Wheeler did the same.

An hour passed. They had made a golden trough into the corner and were spreading out over a wider area. Intermittently, Scott and Wheeler spoke, but only to say, "Sure is warm," or "It's bound to be here somewhere." Somehow the search demanded as much silence as possible. Scott was grateful that Wheeler, for whatever reasons of his own, saw no need to talk. As for the French boy, Scott wondered if he was in fact mute. They worked on.

Scott uncovered a grey mass in the straw. At first he could not tell what it was, but, wiping the sweat from his eyes and bending closer, he saw that the mass was alive, a squirming nest of baby mice. Ash-grey, blind, still curled foetally, their tiny limbs lifting up against the sudden light, they struck Scott as too vulnerable to be alive. He shuddered at their small writhings and coilings.

Hesitating, frozen by the soundless motion, he felt the tomcat brush his leg. With a terrible speed, the scrawny, jaundice-yellow cat began to devour the mice. The crunching of bone, the gorging swallows (as if the cat was about to heave out what it had just taken in), stirred Scott to a sudden rage. He swung at the cat with his pitchfork, but it only moved off briefly, mewling in piteous outrage, before it crept back to its feast. Scott shouted "Get away, you!" and swung again. This time the cat only looked up, grey dangling from its mouth, and quickly returned to its chewing and swallowing.

"What is it?" Wheeler said, appearing alongside. "Oh," he chuckled. "Tom's lucky day."

Scott's grip tightened on the handle as he recoiled at Wheeler's amusement. He cast a look of such disgusted anger that Wheeler shrugged, mumbled something about cats eating mice being common enough on farms, then stood silently by.

Helplessly, Scott hoisted the cat away with one strong swing of his boot, then forked the remaining mice as far as he could into the deeper straw to one side.

"Let him search himself if he's so hungry," he gasped, almost immediately feeling ashamed of his behaviour. After all, what was a cat eating a nest of mice compared with … "I'm sorry, Vic," he said after a few seconds. "It just shocked me, coming on it like that."

Wheeler nodded. "Cats are useful, but I don't like them much." He slapped Scott on the shoulder and beamed. "I have a feeling this will change our luck." He bounded away, back to his part of the golden trench.

Sure enough, a few moments later, he cried out, "Aha!"

Scott hurried over.

Wheeler had dropped to his knees and was quickly brushing

141

away loose straw. In a few seconds, he lifted the small black Bible into the air.

The French boy grinned, but only briefly. Then he looked back down the trench, with the straw sliding off both sides. Scott followed his look, and thought, "Let it cave in, let us spend the rest of the war trapped in a barn full of straw." But already his stomach muscles had clenched. The found Bible meant one thing: a return to the fighting. Now the guns sounded like guns again, and seemed to be closing in from the north. Scott realized he had no idea what the day was like, how late it was. They had a long walk back, and it would be more pleasant in sunlight. With mounting gloom, he recalled the dark clouds massing over the guns as they arrived at the farm and the stone farmer's unending burden.

"Blessed is the man that walketh not in the counsel of the ungodly," Wheeler whispered, his head bowed. "Nor standeth in the way of sinners, nor sitteth in the seat of the scornful. But his delight is in the Law of the Lord, and in his Law doth he meditate day and night." He lifted his head and, blushing, sweat gleaming on his skin, finished rapturously: "And he shall be like a tree planted by the rivers of water, that bringeth forth his fruit in his season, his leaf also shall not wither, and whatsoever he doeth shall prosper."

The golden chaff swirled around them. Scott blinked and looked down the darkening trench to find the sun.

"Amen," Wheeler said alone.

Then they helped the French boy fork back the straw.

# 1916

STERNBERG WOKE AND LAY STILL FOR SEVERAL MINUTES, gradually recalling that he was not a young man in the Kansas chalk, that he had not just buried forty-four flour sacks of fossils on the prairie, that he did not need to rise and search for the boy, Jakob, nor find him, witless, wandering in a circle, his hands fixed to his intact scalp. No, he was an old man in a tent alongside the Red Deer River in Alberta, Canada, and the child he sought would not be found this side of Heaven. The pain took him again. She seemed now to be his youth too, his strength, everything he felt the ebbing of. Her face ... Ach, the nights were always hardest. Fancies of every kind plagued him. Yet—and here was the frightening part—he preferred the fancies with all their heartache to his daily existence. Maud was alive across that border, alive with everything that the Creator had ever breathed the breath of life into. But here, she was dead. He would walk out into the denuded, toppling badlands and labour in the blazing sun in the nattering clouds of mosquitoes. For what? So he could nightly close his eyes and live his real life again.

Sternberg had had this idea for years, but never so vividly as now. The idea that the world of sleep was the true world, where all artifice dissolved, and that the waking life was a falsehood, a brilliant shadow. More and more, he had to force himself to believe in the stone and sunlight that he could feel, he had to force himself to believe that he felt anything. What were the bones of any life compared to the flesh on them, the eyes that moved in the flesh?

Crazy Horse, for instance. The world said he was stabbed and killed at Fort Robinson, not long after the massacre at the Little Bighorn. But if that were true, how could Sternberg know more about him, night after night, than what he'd known at the time? Why could he hear a dead Indian speaking to him in English, an Indian who almost never spoke, even in his own tongue? Because he was alive, as Maud was alive, as the Creator's vanished beasts were alive. Only a foolish man would deny the truth because it happened behind his eyelids while his body lay still.

His heavy body, this sack of bones the Lord hadn't delivered unto the earth. Sternberg groaned and pulled himself up. He dressed and stepped outside. He couldn't sleep twenty-four hours a day, unless death were sleep. But it was not in his hands to live or die. As long as there was daylight, he'd labour in it.

The camp was still, though darkness had begun to lift off the river. A faint smear of pink crested the valley to the east, but no light unshrouded the million years of erosion. Sternberg saw the sun as a great brush, clarifying the bones at the bottom of this ancient sea. After all, what wasn't a bone hunter? The sun, the wind, the rain: everything was searching, all the time. And an ordinary man, too. A rancher on the prairie above, a merchant in one of the great cities: their days were nothing but one continuous search for the final truth hidden in their own flesh.

All at once the thought of work struck him as sacrilege, an absurd flaunting of lies in the face of what was most truthful, most important. Soon the boys would be stirring, Lily and Kim as well, and the plan for the day's work would be discussed. George would need help blasting the rock above his promising chasmosaur, and Charlie would continue the careful excavating of stephanosaurus, one of the many crested duckbills that swarmed Alberta a million years ago. Levi and Lily would provide assistance where needed.

Lily. The thought of confronting her about the skull wearied him so greatly that he reached a sudden decision. He was up before the others. He had a perfect opportunity to go off on his own without raising suspicion. New specimens had to be found, as the field season could not last more than another two months. The boys could not possibly know if he spent the day walking or resting instead of searching for bones. Once he was out of sight around a bluff, he was free to do as he liked, free of having to answer to his children, free of having to face Lily's intense hope.

He prepared his collecting kit, then walked quietly past the cold ashes of the fire to Kim-Lu's wagon and tent. The old man was snoring lightly in the darkness, and Sternberg was careful not to wake him as he found some buns and dried bacon in the stores. He returned to the open area between the tents and looked up. The billion stars were fading, dimmed back to impressions of stars. The light in the east slowly broadened, became a wide slit through which the sun would eventually emerge. It would be glory and praise enough for a man to watch this in wonder. Yet Sternberg had almost never stood still to appreciate daybreak; his glory and praise kept his neck bent to the hard stone. But not today.

He returned to his tent and scrawled a quick note to Charlie:

*Left early to scout new sites. Levi to help George with blasting. Lily to help you with dig. Back by nightfall.*

*Father*

Then he took the note to the campfire and weighted it with a stone on one of the chairs. A cough came from Levi's tent. Sternberg didn't want to talk with anyone, at least not on this side of the border between worlds. He shifted his kit comfortably over his shoulder and walked out of camp, up to the rise and into the pink light.

By ten o'clock, it was already warm enough to force him to take regular drinks of water from his canteen. He stood several hundred feet above the floor of the valley, on a cliff he had reached by making handholds with his pick, and then, at a crucial point, clutching onto some scrub juniper forced up through the cracks in the stone. A small cloud of mosquitoes followed him everywhere, hanging off his mesh veil like flies to honey, droning their incessant hunger into his good ear. He let the water flow down his throat when he knew that sips were more sensible. But sense was a burden now. For hours he had walked the badlands, forcing himself not to look for specimens, wandering by an instinct that was other than a hunter's. At first this had proven a considerable strain, almost painful, but gradually he had found a new rhythm. Once he accepted that there could be a greater purpose, even if a man couldn't name it, he felt calmer. It was only for a day; the difference might just teach him more than years of study or worship over the Scriptures. Ach, if only it wasn't so hot.

It's age, he reasoned, all of this, the fatigue, the doubt, the guilt. But where is it written that age is infirmity? He looked down on the valley. The river shone like a frosted snakeskin

146

twisting away to the east through a prairie Egypt of mysterious stone shapes. At this time of year, the colours were vivid in the formations, the ochre of the iron and the black of the coal clear in the sunlight, the lighter sandstone sandwiched between. Instinctively, Sternberg stared at the layer which he knew from the Judith River beds in Montana as the Belly River Formation. Here lay the richest deposits of fossils. His sons would be working it now. Earlier, he had heard one of George's dynamite blasts—the chasmosaur lay under thirty-five feet of sandstone. Now they'd be removing the rock to build a road.

Roads. In such a place. Roads that went nowhere except to death. Roads that would never be used again once the bone hunting was done. The absurdity of it turned his face away from the Belly River Formation and back to the sky, which was a light blue and getting lighter with the heat. An ominous sky, he noted, observing far off a few puffs of white cloud. The heat mingled with the musk of the sage at his feet. Wherever he stepped, he fuelled the embers. Often he had believed the heat of this ground would make the whole valley such a furnace that men and horses could not travel on it. He had known greater thirst in his work, but never a more intense heat. It was a wonder that the flesh didn't just burn off and leave bones among the footsteps, or that a hawk didn't blaze into a comet as it struck its kill.

Sternberg limped on, away from the view, climbing higher. The mosquitoes hovered like the palm of a black hand.

By noon, his canteen was nearly empty and his lips were parched. The sun, pearl-sized and white-yellow, hung directly overhead. He sat on the edge of the prairie, in a circle of burnt grass dotted with small stones. The badlands below, bronze and crimson, looked gentler, rounded into sibling shapes that stretched to the east as if it truly were the East of scripture. A heat-haze blurred the hard edges of the bluffs and buttes and hoodoos. Sternberg sat with his bad leg stretched before him, the other knee lifted, his head resting on it. Five hundred feet below, the river of cold, pure water might have been a hollow bone. He knew he'd have to get back there, but the heat was so intense he could not even contemplate rising. At least the mosquitoes had given him a brief respite. He gazed through the mesh at three million years of Creation, according to the learned men of science. Nothing was there but bones. It didn't matter how high he climbed. From the stars, he'd look down on the same decaying story. Men and horses here were only bones caught on a slower tide, drifting for a few years until covered over with the same silt and mud. The valley dropped away at his feet. Sweat burned off his skin. From a long way off, a rumble and a fading to silence. George at his work.

Something was collapsing inside him and he couldn't stop it. He couldn't stand. Dear Lord, he prayed, you have taken yourself away forever. There was no wind, but he heard a murmuring behind him. He thought of turning. He thought of dying. His throat was baked stone. An image wavered before his eyes.

IT SUDDENLY GREW VERY COLD. SNOW DRIFTED HEAVILY all around him, yet he remained hot, burning. The Indians, perhaps fifty or sixty of them, appeared darkly out of the swirling flakes. A handful of old women and small children rode on horses that stumbled heavily, as though about to fall. An old man had already fallen, and a young woman had bent to help him up. The party paused, breath pouring from their mouths. A child cried, another whimpered. A second young woman clutched a baby to her chest and looked wildly around with scorching eyes. A young man walked back from the front of the party. He wore leggings but only a thin shirt. The rest of the Indians, Sternberg noticed with surprise, were equally underdressed for the cold. Strangely, he could feel the ice of it, and yet he sweated, his whole body a live coal. Why were they shivering? Why did the child cry so? Let me hold her.

But he couldn't move. He watched the young man in leggings as he stood over the fallen old man. The same soft murmuring. Then the young man closed his eyes, tilted his head until he was facing the snow. He stood this way for half a minute. Finally, as the child's crying rose to a steady wail, the young man turned. A horse had collapsed onto its front legs. The old woman on its back tried to get it to rise, but she had no strength in her own body. She moved her legs once, then stopped, her head hanging.

The young man spoke firmly into the darkness. Another young man, as poorly dressed, appeared out of the flakes. He held a rifle, which the first young man took from him. He lifted the old woman off the horse and carried her away to a place off to one side. Then he returned and put the gun to the horse's head. There was a loud crack, as of an axe hitting wood. The horse slumped sideways. Blood spattered the snow.

The young man worked quickly. He pulled a large knife from his belt and dropped to his knees beside the horse. He pushed it over slightly, stuck the knife into its belly and split it open. Guts hissed out. The young man stuck his hands into the steam and pulled more guts out. Then he spoke softly to the young woman standing nearby, and rose. The young woman with the scorching eyes clutched her baby even more fiercely to her chest, then relented as the other woman gently explained. She gave her baby to the young man. Two other children, including the one, a girl of about three, still wailing, were brought forward. He took the baby in his arms first, whispered to it, then stuck it into the steaming belly of the horse. He did the same with the wailing girl. Her cries were muffled by the horse flesh, which the young man pulled together. Then he and the man who had given him the rifle pulled the dead horse onto a wooden travois hitched to one of the standing horses. Slowly the party staggered off into the storm.

Sternberg watched with his mouth open. The stench of the gutted horse flowed into his burnt throat, but he couldn't force his jaw together. Blood sparkled on the snow. The stones that ringed him began to shine, blinding him.

Then the scorched prairie reappeared, only the grass was higher. Someone was dragging something on a wooden sled. Or was it a stoneboat? Who were the figures doing the pulling? George and Levi? Sternberg knew there were bones on the sled. He had often used stoneboats in the badlands to drag out the huge, plastered blocks of fossils. But that required horses, not men. The figures doing the pulling were human. And they wept, Sternberg realized, not quietly, but without restraint, raising their lamentations to the sky. In the distance, Sternberg could see a fort. Over it a flag fluttered with stars and stripes. A group of soldiers in blue uniforms stood outside the gate. Surprisingly, Sternberg could see the fear in their eyes, as if he stood with them. But he didn't. He walked behind the sled. A canvas sheet lay over the bones, only they weren't just bones. The weeping, wailing, came from the mouths of an old man and old woman. Sternberg stared at the old man's face, a sharp profile, almost familiar to him. He stared until the face slipped off the skull.

A gust of wind blew the top of the canvas sheet back. A single feather dragged in the tall grass. The slipped face, drained completely of blood and even sharper in profile, settled on the corpse. Sternberg could see where the bayonet had gone through, low in the abdomen, piercing the vital organs. As he watched, the face opened its eyes; they were black, far-seeing, a hawk's eyes with human thought behind them. The corpse threw off the canvas sheet with a bloodless hand to reveal its gaping wound. The other hand reached in. Sternberg began to stumble, but he kept his eyes on the wound. It widened, blood flowed from it, a child's face, the girl from inside the horse, years older ... no! ... another girl, a young woman more familiar ...

He was falling and the Indian's voice came to him. "It is easy to die. Any day is a good day for it."

"Where is she?" Sternberg cried. "Is she warm? Tell me if she's warm."

The Indian took the brown stone from behind his ear and carefully placed it in the ring of small stones on the burnt grass. "I lived to watch my people die."

"Is she in Heaven?" Sternberg demanded. "Is she with God?"

The Indian considered. His eyes had the distance of dead stars, but his mouth was kind. "We can't mourn for a whole people as we can for one child." He leaned forward. He was so pale that Sternberg believed he could look through him. For the first time, the Indian met and held Sternberg's gaze. The wind gusted, bringing heat. Single brown feathers, one after another, fell out of the sky and drifted down all five hundred feet into the valley.

The Indian did not smile, but his voice was softer than it had been. "You will see her again," he said.

The mosquitoes had returned, droning in Sternberg's good ear. The badlands shimmered below. Where was the sun? He raised his head and almost fell over with dizziness. The sun was past its apex. He couldn't swallow. One last drink from the canteen and then back into the valley. It was a long way down, but he felt strangely refreshed, hopeful. Soft words played around his hearing, raised him and led him back the way he had come.

# 1916

MIDDAY, A HEAVY RAIN. SCOTT'S UNIT, FILLED WITH NEW drafts, was hunkered down in deep V-shaped pits they'd just managed to dig under continuous enemy shelling and rifle fire. There was nothing to do except keep up the same crouched tension that had been kept up for hours already, since before daybreak. The pits, some of them at least, were loosely connected, and Scott did his best to help the new men. Every ten minutes he would rouse himself from an almost torpid state and go to the others. Wheeler, as always, stroked his Bible and mouthed its words (Scott guessed that he was actually yelling, but he didn't move close enough to tell), while Macpherson sat with his back to the pit wall and hid his head in his greatcoat. Other experienced soldiers stared into their hands clasped white on their knees; one or two wept uncontrollably; a few whistled as if walking down a country lane. The noise, never ceasing, yet intensified and fell away, so that shouted conversation was possible, making the worst of the new men's fears desperately audible.

Scott had smoked what might have been his thirtieth cigarette since the morning, but they had little effect. Each explosion hit like a punch to the stomach; his nerves seemed to swing openly in the air. It was all he could do to force himself to check on the new men. White-faced and shaking, he stepped into a connecting pit where a new draft, a young, clean-shaven boy, was pressing himself against the wet wall and crying in a thin voice "Mom! Mom! Oh please. Make it stop! Mom! Mom!"

"Shut up for Chrissakes!" another member of the pit yelled. "Can't you just shut up?"

Another thunderous crash descended. In the aftermath, the boy began to wail, shrieking for his mother in a voice that hardly seemed human. Others from nearby pits began to curse him.

"If you don't shut up, I'll kill you! I mean it! I'll kill you!"

Scott looked at the other soldier and saw that his fury was just another form of the boy's shrieking. But he well knew that men were capable of anything when the pressure was intense enough. Briefly, he thought, maybe the boy would be better off strangled quickly, put out of his misery. Then he shook the thought aside and grabbed the soaked, mud-splattered body by the shoulders.

"It's all right! It's all right! I'm here, I'm here!" And he held the weeping soldier to his chest until the screaming stopped, replaced by a white, shuddering blankness. Then Scott had to move on. He was willing to do what he could for others, but he would not give up his own long-protected instinct of self-pres-ervation. Pity for the new drafts was itself a dangerous weakness and could not help them, he knew that. There was no help, not really. And so the first responsibility was to survive.

He crawled back to his pit. Wheeler did not even acknowl-edge him, but simply kept moving his lips, his eyes raised into the downpour, oddly glazed. Scott leaned against the muddy wall. Smoke drifted overhead—or was it broken cloud? A shell screamed over, very close. It sounded as if a row of houses was being sped through the sky.

"Oh please," he moaned. "Please stop."

The air reeked of blood, piss and chemicals, as if these things all came out of the rain, dumped out of the heavens.

Two hours later, nothing had changed. Scott, down to his last cigarette, could not keep from shaking. The rain didn't help; it was almost sleet and drove down like hammered nails. There was no way to help anyone else now. He leaned one shoulder against the wall of the pit, fumbled to light the cigarette.

Suddenly a small avalanche of mud slid down directly beside him, and Scott, his hands numb as his senses, did not even reach for his rifle. He thought, quickly and against all his usual defenses, "It doesn't matter. I don't care."

And by the time he'd recovered and thought to defend himself, it really didn't matter. For he was looking into the moon-wide eyes of a young Englishman who was so slight and short he could have been ten years old. His uniform was torn on one shoulder and his face was a shocking mix of mud, pale skin, and lips like a blood print.

Looking at him, Scott thought of a grotesque checkerboard, as though he was looking at a tiny chunk of the scarred battlefield. It was all there, the mud and the wasted dead and the blood of the dead with eyes wide and roaming as the sea looking out from the carnage.

Disgusted with himself, Scott fought to regain the impossible reality of the situation. Here was a young Tommy escaping the shells, or trying to.

"Where did you come from?" Scott shouted.

"Just yonder!" he shouted back, pointing in the direction over the parapet. "Me sergeant were killed. Then six more. I coom."

His uniform was so mud-plastered that Scott could not identify his unit, for all that it mattered. And he shook violently down the whole length of his body, a body thin as some men's legs. He couldn't have been more than fifteen or sixteen.

Sweet Jesus, Scott thought. He's not short, he just hasn't grown.

The boy blinked out of his terrible shaking and was too dazed to answer any more of Scott's questions. The shelling swelled again with a series of splitting crashes, and soon the boy had snuggled tight against Scott, as if trying to burrow inside his flesh.

Oddly sickened by his touch, Scott moved away, but the boy followed, cringing with each shell-burst that sounded closer. The whole time, he kept crying out in a high-pitched voice.

"Yan! Tean! Tether! Mether! Pip! Cesar! Azar! Castra!"

Horrified, Scott pushed him away, but gently, afraid he might shatter.

But the boy snuggled back, still crying out. "Horna! Dick! Yan-a-dick! Tean-a-dick! Tether-a-dick!"

Scott grabbed him and shook him. He put his face as close as he could stand to the red-lipped, mud-caked, trembling face and shouted, "What the hell are you saying? Dammit! What are you saying?"

"Mether-a-dick! Bumfit! Yan-a-bum!"

"Are you crazy?" Scott shook him harder.

Finally, the boy looked him straight in the face. "Oh sir," he said pleadingly, "I'm from Hawes." He gasped and his jaw worked silently, as if swallowing the mud off his cheeks. "That's how we count the sheep at home. I can't stop!"

Scott saw that there was no use in trying to do anything with him. He let the boy snuggle tight against him and tried not to

156

shrink from his absurd voice shouting out the count of the shells exploding nearby. One shell burst just over the parapet of the neighbouring pit and sheared off the arm of one of the occupants. Scott watched the man crumple to the mud.

"Tean-a-bum! Tether-a-bum! Jigget!"

The other occupant of the pit crawled past his dead comrade, slithered over a heap of mud and pressed close to Scott on the other side. Scott felt the man's arms and legs twitching convulsively.

A shell burst on the left, scattering mud over the pit. A steel helmet pinged off Scott's rifle, then a haversack came hurtling through the air and fell apart at his feet. He gazed stupefied at the contents: a pair of socks, a towel, a toothbrush, a razor and a tin of bully beef.

The shepherd boy never stopped his count.

A new man sprawled into the pit, clutching the air like a swimmer from the water. His helmet was gone and he made wild animal noises, shaking as if in an ague fit. He crawled on hands and knees past the one-armed corpse in the neighbouring pit, and passed Sergeant Menzies coming from the other direction. Menzies tripped over the corpse but got up immediately and huddled alongside Scott and the others. Scott shouted a question at him, but Menzies didn't answer, though he appeared to hear.

Then the earth erupted and mud rained down for several minutes. The mud in the neighbouring pit slid over, carrying the dead man with it. His remaining arm ended up stretched out at Scott's boot. The wrist was hairy and there was a watch on it.

Amazed, Scott saw that it was going. Four o'clock, it read.

"Four o'clock," Scott said aloud, watching the digits as if they were flies swarming on the face of the dead.

"Yan! Tean!" The shepherd boy shouted, and kept it up, almost without pause, until the barrage finally stopped eight hours later, as the dead man's watch ticked into midnight.

# 1916

STERNBERG WALKED FOR HOURS, PAUSING WHEN HE COULD find shade. Moment by moment, he had to force himself *not* to look for bones, to unlearn the expertise he'd accrued over the decades, even to deny his mind's uncanny gift for locating fossils. He tried to recapture the snowy scene with the Indians and the crying children, but it was already fading, along with the harsh image of the corpse on the sled and the gentler one of hopeful words: "You will see her again."

For the moment, the heat seemed to dissolve everything, including his own past. The sun raged, silently, without motion. The air was transparent stone. Sternberg felt he had to shift huge blocks as he cautiously descended to the valley floor, finding footholds where he could, straining to see through the mosquitoes. The stone rang beneath his feet, a sort of insect hum without insects. His boots seemed to crunch bone whenever he placed them down. The river didn't appear to get any closer. Perhaps he wasn't walking down? Perhaps he was circling, the way a hawk or eagle circles, downward but slowly.

But he felt neither such lightness nor such power. His bad leg ached, his good leg felt heavy and the mosquito-drone in his ear gave him the disturbing impression that he was always slightly off to one side of where he should be.

He skidded slightly on a small decline and fell hard. Then he tried and failed to stop his brief slide with a pick. At the bottom, he put his other hand out and touched something sharp and firm. For a few seconds he didn't look, just breathed evenly and told himself to be more careful—the next slip might occur in a more dangerous place. He decided to find some shade, take a longer rest, let his body recover enough to get him safely back to the river. Then he looked down at his hand.

It was resting, plain as a butterfly, on a human rib cage. Sternberg did not recoil at the sight—no bones had the capacity to shock him. Those of the ancient beasts filled him with awe, but never fear. Yet he was disturbed when he followed the rib cage up to the skull. It lay, facing up, as if grinning at the God who had taken its flesh away. Sternberg felt his own skin draw tighter over his cheekbones. Between the dead and the living, how much difference did the body make? He knew his spirit wore the same futile grin, no matter what expression his flesh manufactured.

The skeleton was partially clothed. Or, rather, a few shreds of black clung to its ribs. Some visitor to the badlands who'd wandered off, Sternberg guessed. Occasionally, city folk with an interest in the unusual landscape—often a relative of a nearby rancher—made the trip out for a few hours of sightseeing. Had there been any reports of missing people? Try as he may, Sternberg could not generate any interest in this find. He tried to will himself into feeling, into responsibility: he should mark the exact location, notify the proper authorities on his return.

Sighing, he started to rise. But as he did so, he caught a rippling motion out of the corner of his eye. He let his weight settle to the earth again, then turned with astonishment to the skeleton.

Flesh was growing on it. Sternberg blinked rapidly, wiped at his eyes. The bone was vanishing as the skeleton reclaimed its living form. Ribs, pelvis, skull: all were quickly covered over. And, as the flesh returned, the black shreds multiplied as well, stitching together to form dark pants and suit jacket. Sternberg froze, mesmerized by the returning face, waiting for the eyes to emerge, terrified that he was about to meet his own gaze.

But when it came, it wasn't his. It was familiar somehow, yet he couldn't be sure.

As Sternberg leaned slightly forward, swaying from just the waist, his bad leg stiff in front of him, the skeleton—more rightly a corpse now—vanished. Sternberg dropped his head into his hands. If this were a trial, if he was intended to witness scenes as unsettling as the gutting of horses and the fleshing of skeletons, he'd have to find the strength to face them as a man of belief. Weakness would serve no purpose. God demanded courage of the living. Sternberg knew that either he'd stand and keep moving or he'd stretch out and die right where he was. Perhaps, he realized with a sudden insight, his skeleton was meant to replace the other.

WHEN HE RAISED HIS HEAD FROM HIS HANDS AND LOOKED around, he found himself standing on the floodplain near the camp, Bible open in his hands. A few feet in front of him stood his small congregation. But he turned away from it, closing the book gently as he looked westward.

Strands of mist rose off the earth. The shadows of the cottonwood branches lay in thin trenches before him. It was very still. He did not know whether he had the ability to speak. Had he just spoken? The Bible had been open in his hands. Why couldn't he hear the echo of the verses as he always did?

Sternberg recognized the young man immediately. He stood only ten feet away, his hands clasped together and hanging in front of him. In one hand he held a dark hat; in the other a book. But all of creation shone in his eyes—they were as dark as a badlands night with its promise of an always startling and rewarding dawn. It was a look Sternberg recognized but had seen rarely in others, never in his sons. The young man stepped closer.

"Amen," he said softly.

"Scott," Sternberg started to say. "You're back. You're safe." But only "Fine morning" came to his lips.

The young man nodded as his eyes, slowly scanning the denuded horizon, crashed with wonder.

His eyes, Sternberg noticed with a shock. His dark suit. Sternberg stared, searching for exposed bone.

"Yes, very fine," the young man agreed. Then, as if he could no longer hold back his speech, he began what sounded like a long-prepared and rehearsed address.

"Mr. Sternberg, it's a great honour to meet you, Sir. I have read your book with great admiration." He held it out, tapped it firmly with the finger of one hand. The hat dropped to the ground, but he ignored it, his words following fast upon the slight pause. "And I have seen the wonderful results of your work mounted in museums. I must tell you, sir, I stand here in homage to what you have given the world."

The warmth Sternberg had felt the first time he'd heard those words, just over a year before, flowed into him again. And the excitement of meeting someone that he knew, right from the first sight of his figure in the launch on the river, possessed

162

the gift for fossil hunting—a bone sharp—also returned. Standing there again, he could hardly contain his joy. Yet, to his chagrin, he found he could speak only the words he'd spoken at the time. And so, slightly guarded, always on the lookout for spies from competing bone diggers (a lesson he'd learned well from the great Cope), he responded to the young man's enthusiasm with probing questions.

Where had he seen his work mounted?

In Ottawa.

How did he know to find him in the Red Deer?

From speaking with the curator in Ottawa.

Why did he not simply write a letter? It was a long journey from the East.

The young man explained that he'd been working as a ranch hand in the West, that he'd been saving his money so he could make an offer.

Sternberg blushed at his old suspicions, but again, to his consternation, he could not quell them; everything had to be played out exactly as the first time. So, probing further, he learned that the young man, Scott Cameron by name, had visited these badlands as a boy a dozen years before, that he'd been fascinated by the valley and its fossils, that he wanted more than anything to learn the trade of fossil hunting. Slowly, as had happened the first time, Sternberg's defenses began to melt. He possessed a keen instinct for the genuine, and this young man was genuine, even to the point of producing a billfold and offering to pay to be allowed to work as an assistant.

For the second time, Sternberg smiled at the offer. He had only one question remaining, but it was the most important one. He stretched an arm out towards the hoodoos and in a hushed voice asked, "What do you feel when you look at this valley?"

The young man did not smile. His eyes once more scanned the horizon. Then, returning, they met Sternberg's own intense gaze.

"Humility," he said.

That same rush of joy, as if the Lord had made him a precious gift! Sternberg revelled in it again as he had on that morning, felt it carry him buoyantly to the handshake, and then towards his waiting, no doubt very curious, congregation. Perhaps now his trial was over? Perhaps God had carried him back to give him a fresh chance to stave off the demons of doubt and weakness that assailed him? Excitedly, he introduced Scott to his three sons in turn. Then, with the joy so intense he felt his heart must burst, with the sun rising behind him and the remainder of his mortal life straining towards the light, he said:

"And this is my daughter, Maud."

And there she stood, sallow-skinned, her thin arms extended from the pale nightdress, her mouth trembling, sweat beaded on her forehead. "Papa? Papa?"

This was not the same. This was fresh horror.

COME AT ONCE STOP DAUGHTER ILL STOP COPE STOP

Sternberg put his hands over his face and sobbed her name again and again.

Finally he dropped his hands and was silent. He saw that he was sitting just where he'd fallen, at the bottom of the steep slope. And the skeleton that had vanished was right there beside him. Sternberg half turned at a rumble of explosives. George getting down closer to his chasmosaur.

The sky darkened. A metallic taste filled the air, as if the iron concretions of the valley had been swirled into motion by an invisible wind. Sternberg began to pray.

After a few moments, he stopped, the words hollow. To what purpose was this trial leading, he wondered, and fought off the desire to lie down and cease making any effort at all. He had struggled long enough and hard enough. Besides, Maud rested with the Lord. How could he ever doubt her eternal peace? Yet the cold words of the telegram echoed around him; he could not shut them out.

Off to the west came another deep rumble. The horizon blackened.

Sternberg stood with difficulty, swatted half-heartedly at the mosquitoes and limped off in search of shade.

# 1975

LILY LET THE PILE OF LETTERS SETTLE TO HER LAP. SHE
dropped her reading glasses onto their chain. She had dozed
off and on through the night, but the seat was uncomfortable
and she was unaccustomed to being away from home. The
sleeplessness did not disturb her, however; she felt it as a kind
of bridge back to the young man who had written the letters.
After all, from everything she knew about the conditions of the
Great War, he had lived for years with broken sleep. If anything,
Lily would have wanted to be even less comfortable—what right
did she have to an easy existence? It was enough that she had
survived him.

She shifted her weight towards the window. Daybreak was approaching. The world was a mixture of blue and black shadows
falling off rocks and pines. Or fallen, because everything was
so still, fixed as the mountains that seemed to close around the
bus.

Lily watched the darkness lift, listened to the occasional
coughing somewhere behind her, and stroked the old letters as
if they were fur. There was little point in speculation, she realized. The Good Lord in His time would reveal the purpose of
her journey. Yet she could not simply give herself up to passive

waiting; the imminence of a resolution made her more alive than she'd been in years. And though her thoughts, as the miles passed, were mostly melancholy, she still felt an overwhelming gratitude.

By the time the bus pulled into the mountain town and the driver announced that they would have a one-hour breakfast stop, Lily knew what she wanted to do. In the first light, which seemed as delicate and frail as the skin of a newborn, she walked along the small, empty main street. The scent of pine filled the air. The mountains were black, inlaid with blue-green, and surrounded the town like the sides of a teacup. Lily went into the only café, bought a scone, and asked the young woman behind the counter to direct her to the town's cenotaph.

"The cenotaph? Oh, I don't know. I just moved here for the summer." She pushed back her long blonde bangs and turned deferentially to an older woman sitting at a nearby table. "Maggie. This lady wants to know where the cenotaph is."

The woman, older than Lily herself, looked up as if every second person wanted directions to the place of the honoured dead. She had long grey hair and a face like crumpled parchment. But her eyes were a deep, animated blue.

"Yes. She does. And there's many would do well to follow her."

Lily shivered with sudden cold. The woman spoke as if out of expectation. And when she kept her shining eyes on Lily's purse the whole time, Lily instinctively clutched it to her side. Absurdly, she felt like exclaiming, "They're mine. You can't have them."

"You're not far from it, my dear. Just out the door to the right, two blocks down till you come to the statue of the bear— you can't miss it—turn right again, up the mountainside an-

168

other block. Then you'll be at the park. The soldiers are in the middle, where they always are, under." She didn't grin at the last word, or scowl, just stared harder at the purse.

"Thank you," Lily answered weakly, pulling the purse around to her front and backing away. Just as she turned to go, the iron-haired woman said, almost as though to herself, "They're all dead, you know. You won't find one with a warm mouth."

Poor soul, Lily thought, departing quickly. But she was afraid for the first time, and ashamed of her fear. Nothing has changed, she scolded herself, all is still in the Lord's hands. She shook the fear off and walked with a firm purpose to the little park.

The cenotaph was just like the one at home, a pyramid of granite, perhaps twenty-feet high, ten around, inscribed with the names of the dead in two wars. Lily approached it curiously, half expecting to read Scott's name there. But he had been born and raised in Ontario. His name would be etched on another stone.

Quickly, because she did not want to be late for the bus, Lily bowed her head and said a small prayer for all the dead soldiers. Then, lifting her head and opening her eyes, she stepped forward and put on her reading glasses to better read the names.

"Cartwright," she said softly. "Innis. Meggert. Lemington. Macdonald. De Vries. Besher." Then Besher again. And a third time. She paused, thinking forlornly of the family, perhaps even the one mother, of those young men. For they were all young now, had become younger with the decades, even the survivors. Lily continued on, her voice tangled in the notes of the bird-song.

"Anderson. Watkin. Riley. Jenner ..."

# 1916

AFTER THEY HAD RETURNED FROM THE MISSION TO RECOVER the Bible, and as twilight approached over the noisy area of billets, Scott wrote his letter of request to Mr. Sternberg.

It was not an easy letter to write, but he took courage from the example in the older man's own book, *My Life in the Bone Yards of the West*. As a young man, Sternberg, in desperation, had written to the great Cope to ask for help in beginning his scientific career. Scott didn't feel he was asking for so much, though in the world of science he knew that reputation was a greater asset than money. Perhaps, then, he was asking for the one thing that would be hardest for his former employer to give? If he had had time, he would have sought Lily's advice, or maybe even Charlie's, but somehow he felt a great urgency about this letter. He needed to write it, now, before he went up the line again. Just knowing that it was bound for the badlands, as he soon hoped to be, would give him the necessary strength to face the terrors of the trenches again.

*Dear Mr. Sternberg,*

*I hope you will not mind receiving a letter from me. If I have not written before, it is because I did not have any reason for*

*troubling you. I know you are a busy man, especially now that*
*the field season is coming to a close. But you'll perhaps excuse me*
*for writing when I tell you that, against all sorts of odds, I have*
*come into the possession of several bones belonging, I believe, to a*
*small carnivorous of the late Cretaceous period ...*

Scott held the pen still. Was it wise to mention the bones
at all? Perhaps the censor would consider such information
unusual and suspicious enough to bring to the attention of his
superiors—what, then, would they do? He couldn't be sure, but
since he dreaded having the bones taken away from him, he
decided he'd better keep their existence a secret. But how to
proceed with the letter?

Scott sat against the wheel of a farm wagon, his knee up,
notepad perched on his thigh. Around him, the machinery
of the war was beginning to move again—a variety of trucks,
limbers and horse-pulled guns filled the torn, black road of the
village as the afternoon darkened. Men marched by, songless,
tight-faced, their expressions taking on the deeper colour of the
sky. Scott's unit could be ordered out at any moment. He realized he didn't have time for niceties. He'd just have to hope that
Mr. Sternberg thought well enough of him based on their time
together in the badlands. He began again, scribbling hastily:

*Dear Mr. Sternberg,*
*I am writing to you from France. But at some time in the*
*next few months I expect to go on leave to England and plan to*
*visit again the great British Museum in London where so much*
*of your valuable work is displayed. If it is not asking too much,*
*might you write me a brief letter of introduction to the chief pale-*
*ontologist there? I realize this is a large request, and I do not make*

*it lightly. Some information regarding carnivorous dinosaurs of the late Cretaceous period has come into my possession, and I am eager to seek the advice of the most learned man of that wonderful museum. I will explain further at some future date. But please understand that this letter of introduction would mean a great deal to me, as much as your own first letter from Professor Cope once meant to you (thank you again for the copy of your book, which I have been returning to often with much pleasure).*

*If you are willing and able to grant me this request, Lily or Charlie can direct you where to send the letter.*

*Respectfully,*
*Scott Cameron*

That would have to do. If the mention of Cope was perhaps too personal, it was too late to change it now. Scott quickly sealed the envelope, addressed it to Steveville, Alberta, and took it to the field post-office, which was just another canvas-covered wagon, though it might as well have been made of gold as far as the soldiers were concerned.

Coming back, he met Wheeler. For once, his friend's exuberance was muted; his eyes were heavy as they met and held Scott's.

"I hear we're in for another trip to ..."

Scott put up his hand to cut him off. "You'd better say an extra prayer." He thought of his own future, the skull perhaps on its way across the Atlantic, the bones in his haversack, the shocked expression on the face of the chief paleontologist at the British Museum when a soldier emptied a sack of Cretaceous fossils on his desk. Nonetheless, he added quietly, "For all of us," before turning back to get his kit.

# 1916

THE AIR WAS BLISTERING, BUT NO MARKS SHOWED IN IT.
The stone hummed. Everywhere Sternberg looked was a shimmer, a trembling, more dreamlike than dreams. He thought for
a moment that he was already asleep, or that he'd walked away
from his body and left it beside the skeleton. But surely the spirit
wouldn't feel such heat, it wouldn't sweat and ache. He pushed
on, around a smoothed bluff, to its north side. The cherty fragments underfoot threatened to bring him down at every step. In
the slight shade, which seemed only a dullness and not a dimin-
ishment in temperature, the trailing juniper among the sponge
moss and purple crocus seemed fragile as any weathered bone;
the sudden colour did not comfort him, but gave a suggestion
of coolness that only heightened his thirst. He could not rest
here.

He wandered eastward, trying to aim down but feeling again
that circular drifting of a bird of prey. Towards what kill, he wondered grimly, then considered it was his own death he was hunting. You will see her again. He could only just hear the words
falling from the Indian's lips. The prophecy couldn't have been
realized in that last pathetic image of Maud in her nightdress,
ill and trembling. No, the Indian meant something else, some-

thing deeper, Sternberg was sure of that. But would he have to die to prove that prophecy? He was prepared to do so, if only in body; he knew a man should face death as he should face life, with praise of the Creator. But a man could not trick his god, no more than he could trick his own soul. His great fatigue after a life of hard struggle and suffering—surely that would count for something on the Day of Judgment. The Lord was merciful. What pain He allowed on the earth, what suffering, would be forgiven. And forgiveness, surely, would include his reunion with Maud. Mysterious ways! To put truth in the mouth of a dead savage. A wonder. As wonderful as revealing a million years of the earth in the middle of the prairie, as wonderful as a splash of colour in the barren depths. Yes, a wonder, but Sternberg could only think of it. All his feeling was spent on his own sorrows; there was nothing left for Creation.

He did not even consider the abandoned coal shaft as a gift, where once he would have prayed in gratitude. Now he only clambered up the slope, into the thin gap in the Edmonton Formation.

Darkness. Coolness. A fine black dust on the walls, covering the ground to a depth of fur. He walked in, deeper and deeper, going in no direction he could tell, then sat reclining against the stone wall. In a matter of minutes he was asleep.

"PAPA?" HE HEARD HER VOICE BEFORE HE SAW HER. IT WAS rainwater, dew, pond of lost years. His aching body grew boyish in it. He turned.

She was sitting on a chunk of cottonwood, her knees together, her body slightly forward, her delicate features clear in the firelight. She wore a white gown, simply embroidered. The sleeves belled slightly from her thin arms. The neck frill almost

176

reached her chin. He immediately recalled her mother on their wedding day. The child had always taken after her.

Sage flowed from her presence. Rich, heavy, the promise of plenty in barrenness. Yet her skin was scarred and waxen, sickly. He had not seen her in illness. A day late, that was all. It might as well have been eternity. He reached out his hand.

"Don't cry, Papa. Please. Please, Papa."

He could not hear her for the resurgence of his grief. "Could you not be as you were in the full of life? What cruelty is this, to have you marred for all time?" He felt the fever of her hand scorch his bones. It was too much. He raised his face to the heavens and was about to shout the questions to the darkness when her voice stopped him.

"Papa, can't you see? This is for us. It is His mercy. This is my living hand. Can you not feel it?"

He felt the slight pressure in his palm and realized, with a shock of pity, that she could press no harder. Was this eternity for her, her final illness never reaching the peaceful release of death?

She answered calmly, as if he'd spoken aloud. "No, Papa. I am at peace. This is God's mercy, to give us what we did not have on earth." Her voice dropped, became almost inaudible. "A final parting."

"Final? Maud, don't speak so. I have you with me always. Nights … you must know this, you must sense it. After years, we are closer now, we talk as of old. I have told you so much I had forgotten." Sternberg paused, almost as if the hand he held had gone cold while the flesh still burned. "And yet, it is never like this when we speak. I cannot hold you. There is no sage, the fire gives no heat, you are as you were that spring, beautiful, before the dread disease …" He broke off, bowed his head. The fire crackle drowned her breathing. He looked up, afraid she had gone.

But she remained, staring at him with such pity in her wide eyes that he might have been the one dead. Then he remembered. "Maud," he chose his words carefully, so as not to startle her; her presence seemed fragile, like a deer watching a man approach across the prairie. "Have I joined you? Are we to be together now?" The thought consoled him, removed the awfulness of her reference to finality. An immense peace flowed into his body. He was tired of the long struggle.

But she shook her head gently. Her hair shone brighter and softer than he remembered; it still seemed a cruelty that her skin was sallow, her cheeks slightly sunken, their bones prominent. He wanted to reach out and stroke her hair, but he was afraid. He wanted only for her to remain, even if they did not speak. What did questions matter? Explanations! He'd spent his life working for men driven to find the truth in Creation, even to the point of denying it. But the answers they sought, that he and his sons helped to find, were nothing compared to the loss of a child. Can it be true, Lord, he lamented. Will I never be with her again?

She smiled, slowly closed, then opened, her eyes. "Papa, be kind to yourself, to Mama, to my brothers. What you seek to know, you have known; what you would question, you have lived. There is nothing I can tell you." She coughed hollowly and her hand pressed his again. "I am still your child," she ended, a fierce appeal in her gaze.

He was ashamed, so ashamed that for several moments he could not speak. It had never occurred to him that the dead might yet require the strength and guidance of the living. Could he still reach her, then? If so, that promised a future. Surely there could be no purpose to her spirit's need if what he gave on earth did not improve her rest. He returned the pressure of her hand.

"Child, what can I do? I am here. I have not stopped loving you. I love you more. I …"

She reached forward and lightly stroked his rough cheek. He felt his tears break on her fingers.

"Maud," he continued in a whisper. "What can I do? Tell me, child. What do you need?"

"One time, Papa," she said weakly through her own tears, "as you used to do. Your stories … I have missed them so."

"Of course, of course," he rallied quickly, assured that his speaking now could hold her there. "I would like that too, more than anything. Here, daughter, take my other hand. What shall I tell you? Your favourites were always about …"

"Professor Cope," she finished for him. "And yours too, Papa."

"Yes, yes, you're right, Maud, they are my favourites. Such a man, the world has never seen the like …" The warmth and snap of the fire triggered his memories. He recalled their first expedition together, just after the Custer Massacre, along the Judith River in Montana. Oh yes, an exciting time. She was looking at him so expectantly, yet with such calm. He thought back forty years, and as he did so, the shadows gathered and drew in.

# 1876

STERNBERG STOOD AT THE TRAIN DEPOT IN OMAHA, WATCH-ing the east for a pillar of smoke. It was early August, very hot. He mopped his brow repeatedly until his handkerchief was sopping. On any other occasion, he would have been dressed casually, in a loose shirt and trousers under his weathered, much beaten slouch hat. But today he had to wear clothes more suited to, and usually reserved for, Sunday worship: a dark suit and tie, and his felt hat held mostly in his hands. The severity of his dress caused the other few people waiting at the depot to take him for a preacher. He smiled to think how surprised they'd be to know he was a fossil hunter waiting to meet, at last, the man who had made his work in the great cemeteries of Creation possible.

Sternberg pulled anxiously at his collar. The man waiting with him, Hank Isaac, who had also been hired for the upcoming expedition, gibed good naturedly, "Relax, Son, it ain't the Second Coming."

"No, it's not that," he smiled in response, not the least embarrassed. "In fact, it's the first."

"Aw hell, Charles. He ain't but a man same as us. And he's a good fellow too. Mostly. It don't pay to get on the wrong side of his temper, though." Isaac laughed so that his Adam's apple bobbed wildly in his thin, reddened throat. "For a man that don't cuss, he's good at getting his point across when he's riled."

The conversation wasn't helping Sternberg relax. He'd have preferred to hear that Edward Drinker Cope was a quiet and gentle sort of man, but Isaac never mentioned these qualities. He'd been with Cope four years earlier on an expedition to New Mexico, and had taken away from that experience the simple notion that Cope was just like anyone else, only moodier and prone to "wild talking" about animals and scripture and the like when in one of his good moods. "A religious sort," Isaac explained, "but not so you'd notice most of the time. He was too busy working."

Try as he might, Sternberg could get few other helpful details. All Isaac would add of a personal nature about Cope was that he had an independent income from his wealthy father.

"I 'spect that's how he dodged the war," he added with mild bitterness. "But I'd have sooner trucked around Europe than go to Bull Run too, come to that."

Isaac wasn't a man to take an interest in learning, in science, and referred to conversations in these areas as "wild talk." Generally, he wasn't much impressed with their employer's standing in the world. "If he wants to pay good money for help getting these old bones out of the ground," went Isaac's thinking, "then he's got a loyal helper in me."

The air thrummed with unseen insects, as if the heat of the sun had spawned an audible light. Sternberg held his hand against the glint, but could see nothing but waving grass stretching to the horizon.

"Come on back to the depot," Isaac suggested, tugging Sternberg's elbow. "Get out of the sun. He'll get here when he gets here. Your watching's not going to speed the train up any."

"I'd prefer to wait outside, Hank, thank you. But you go on back. I don't mind waiting on my own."

"If you say so, Charles," the older man drawled, turning away.

Sternberg watched him go. He was a good man, a hard worker, and strong despite his small stature. Not much over five feet and thin as campfire smoke, Isaac was nonetheless unmatched for hauling equipment and handling horses and wagons. Or so Professor Cope had written in his most recent letter, which Sternberg kept folded in his breast pocket. Certainly Isaac had a wiry, muscular frame; it was plain to see he had strength of body. Spirit, however, was another matter. Sternberg had never met anyone so terrified of Indians. Isaac shrunk into himself at the sight of them, like a spider thrown into fire.

No, that wasn't exactly true. Sternberg knew of someone even more terrified. For a moment, he let the memory haunt him, as it had periodically for months. The non-stop trembling, the eyes fixed wide, the jumping at every sound: it was awful, more awful than the boy's eventual self-killing. He shut the memory out, forced himself to focus on the present. Mr. Isaac's fear, at least, wasn't debilitating in that way, though he had seen five of his companions shot and scalped the summer before, only barely escaping himself. It was a story he told Sternberg only once, shuddering the whole time. He preferred not to dwell on it, he said. But not talking about something, Sternberg recognized, wasn't the same as not dwelling on it.

He squinted back into the sun, his eyes stinging. It seemed

time hadn't moved. The sun, so pale yellow that it was almost white, suggested that it had no intention of ever setting or rising again. Only a few hawks, like old train tickets, disturbed the air. Squinting, Sternberg couldn't even be sure the distant hawks weren't his own eyelashes. Time was haze and hum.

But gradually another sound came out of the earth, another darkness flickered on the horizon. A low rumbling, a slight vibration, the dirty white smoke. Sternberg swallowed hard. His mouth was dry.

Isaac's shadow lay like a rake on the beaten ground.

"Well," he said, grinning and clapping Sternberg on the shoulder, "it ain't likely the Saviour, but someone's coming. Hope you got a dictionary of Latin words to hand." He chuckled. His Adam's apple looked like a small animal trying to burrow free.

As the train pulled into the station, Isaac said, "Come on, he'll be 'specting us."

Nervously, Sternberg followed into the smoke, clatter, cinders and hissings of the train's arrival.

They waited on the platform amidst the unloading of trunks and disembarking of passengers, most of whom Sternberg didn't even notice. He didn't know what Cope looked like, but he was sure he'd recognize him simply by his bearing; such a man had to stick out in any group of people. Sternberg leaned forward, his heels almost lifting from the planks.

"He's a Friend, you know," Isaac blurted out. "Even writes them tracts for them. I 'spect that's why he don't favour guns any, though he ain't dadblamed fool enough not to carry one. With all these savages ..."

"What?" Sternberg reeled with the new information. "A Friend? You didn't tell me that. Why didn't you say so before?"

But it was too late. The haunted look had returned to the older man's lean face. His eyes seemed to follow some invisible spill of blood. He wasn't listening to anything except memory.

Sternberg racked his brain for what he knew about Quakers. They were peaceful men. Strict, severe, honest as the longest day. He'd known a Friend in Kansas. An abolitionist, but he wouldn't fight for the Union. Both sides of the conflict harassed and tormented him for his pacifism, but he'd never wavered. People of conscience. Plain of speech and dress. Somehow only part of that description appeared to fit what he knew of Edward Drinker Cope. Wild talk and plain speech certainly didn't fit together. And what about the man's already legendary reputation for competitiveness with other bone hunters? Some said he hired spies to keep track of Professor Marsh's field crews. That didn't sound like a Friend, at least not one who authored tracts.

A tall, handsome young woman stopped a few feet in front of him. Dressed completely in black, she seemed to be propping up her companion, a man some years older than herself. For a moment, Sternberg found his view obstructed. With a slight bow, he moved a little to one side.

"How do, Professor?" Isaac said suddenly.

Sternberg whirled around so quickly that he almost wrenched his neck.

The shadow at the side of the young woman detached itself slowly and extended a hand.

"It's good to see thee, Mr. Isaac." The voice was a high, tremulous extension of the body which wavered like a blade of prairie grass. "Thou has kept well, I pray, since our previous travails?"

Collecting himself, Sternberg closed his jaw. Unbelievably, this frail figure appeared to be the man he'd come to meet.

"Tolerably well, Professor," Isaac answered, bending to take up one of the large bags the Negro porter had put down. "A few close scrapes, but I come through all right."

Sternberg felt again the familiar shudder of Isaac's recent past, and then something else: he was being stared at.

He met the gaze, and it froze him. The face was remarkably attractive: high cheekbones, the nose strong but finely proportioned, the slightly cleft chin jutting out with authority, the brow high and clear. It was a large skull, but then, Sternberg reasoned, how could it be otherwise to house such a brain? His moustache was full and curled up at the ends, making a perfect symmetry with the shape of his thick eyebrows and the waves of his full blond hair, neatly parted down the middle. The whole effect of the face was one of balance, of classical lines. But the effect was at once enhanced and undermined by the restlessness of the man's large eyes, a blue not quite light enough to be of the cornflower, nor dark enough to be of the midday sky. At times, the eyes rested neatly in the configurations of the face, in the sculpted lines of the bones and hair. But then, suddenly, as if some other intelligence invested them, they trembled, riding the registers of the voice, rendering the whole notion of order ridiculous. It was as if a dragonfly had sunk the blue of its wings into fire. And yet, there were dark rings below the dazzle of the stare, almost deep enough to form pouches. And the frame kept threatening to collapse.

Sternberg could not look away. He clenched his teeth to make sure he'd kept his jaw shut.

"And this must be Mr. Sternberg."

The handshake was firm but remarkably cold. Had he been resting his hand in ice? Despite himself, Sternberg shrank inwardly from the touch.

"It is a pleasure to meet thee at last. I said to my wife, as we came along the platform: yonder man, doth he not possess the look of a bone sharp? By the light of He who guides us, I said, that must be Mr. Sternberg."

"This is a very great honour, sir," Sternberg managed to utter through dry lips.

"Nay, man, never call me sir. Professor is how the world knows me, so let the world call me by its knowledge, as we call the great fossils we find by what our learning dictates. But gentlemen, my manners." He turned slightly to the woman, who'd been watching him with obvious admiration and solicitude. "Behold my wife, Annie." He grinned. It was no surprise to Sternberg to see that the Professor's teeth were perfectly even and white.

"Good afternoon," she replied politely to their greetings before quickly turning her attention back to her husband. "Edward, dear, you need to rest. Has your headache eased any? Let me rub your temples again."

The Professor turned his head obediently towards her. With long-fingered hands, she firmly pressed the sides of his skull.

"Yea, that is the very balm," he sighed, closing his eyes.

Isaac coughed with embarrassment. "I'll just take these along to the wagon." He staggered off, as though carrying two buffalo calves under his arms.

Sternberg didn't know what to do. The professor continued to sigh, his head resting on his wife's ample bosom. She was a comely woman, Sternberg couldn't help but notice. Observing her tender ministrations reminded him of his own recently wedded wife and their baby. How long had it been now since he'd seen them? The Lord only knew when he'd see them again.

"As the rain falleth on the petals of the flower," the musical voice whispered, "so the touch of a woman …"

"Edward!" Mrs. Cope suddenly raised her husband's head, as if it had burned her. "Remember where you are," she whispered, blushing.

He grinned at Sternberg like a boy who had just stolen some candy. He stretched and lifted his eyes to the sun.

"Where I am? Oh, I am in the West, I am in the field. And soon I will be plucking the very flowers of the field!" He lowered his eyes and stared at Sternberg. The blue motion of his gaze was almost dizzying. "Dost thou feel it too, man? The pull?" He rapped his chin, then one elbow, then his chest over his heart. "A magnet. That is all thy frame is. A magnet to His glory and His mystery. Yea, why dost thee tarry? Where are the horses? Oh how I have missed the smell of horse flesh. And the manure too. Wife, do not frown so. Is not the horse a natural beast? Is any product, then, of the horse, not natural unto the Light?"

She blushed, shook her head. Sternberg had the distinct impression that she was well used to such talk. For himself, he found the man's enthusiasm for work contagious, but oddly incongruous to his fragile appearance.

Isaac returned, and Cope immediately corralled him, ushering him to the side with one arm, as a hen might shield one of her chicks. Even so, Sternberg had no trouble hearing the conversation. Strangely enough, Cope hardly bothered to lower his voice. Since he and Isaac stood to Sternberg's left, the side of his good ear, their words floated clearly to him.

"I saw thee and Mr. Sternberg from the train," Cope said.

"Why, the man can hardly walk. With such a limp, surely he is of little use in the field. Can he even ride a horse?"

Sternberg's affection for Isaac swelled at the man's reply.

"I've heard it said he can mount a pony bareback and cut one of his mares from a herd of wild horses."

The professor nodded, then turned back with a sly grin. Did he expect me to hear that, Sternberg wondered, and the question brought to mind the man's icy touch. One thing was definite: if Cope was not a queer man, he was certainly queer for a Quaker.

"Mrs. Cope will accompany us as far as Ogden," he said, the grin dissolving. "Let's get started. I wish to send a telegram first. Those accursed printers! If you leave them to their own devices, nothing would ever get printed. Gentlemen!"

"He was up all night," Mrs. Cope explained to Sternberg as they proceeded to the station in her husband's wake, "working on a monograph. I could not convince him to sleep."

Sternberg watched the professor at the telegraph window. He gesticulated wildly, then returned to them as if he'd not moved his limbs in hours. Sternberg thought he was a chameleon, though of mood and motion, not colour.

"Never mind about the wagon. Mr. Isaac, retrieve the bags. Now that I'm here, I've decided that there's no reason to tarry. We'll reboard this train. It will be leaving shortly. I've arranged for the wagon and horses to be returned and for your bill of fare to be settled. Here are thy tickets!"

"But Professor," Isaac said apologetically, "all our clothes and tools are at the hotel. We reckoned you'd be spending the night, since you've been travelling ..."

"Blast ye, man! Do you think I have time to waste?" His eyes seemed to rage against their sockets.

"Edward," his wife said soothingly.

"Haste ye, then! Take one of the horses and be back before the steam rises. I'll not be staying here when others are bound for the bone fields!"

Sternberg accompanied the hurrying Isaac to the wagon and helped him unhitch a horse.

"Moody, didn't I say?" Isaac chuckled between gasps.

Sternberg watched him go. He wasn't sure if he wanted to return to the storm inside the station, but his own excitement decided him. It would be strange if such a man as Professor Cope *wasn't* anxious to be at work. Sternberg, his own eyes hungering for the sight of bones, hurried back to the station.

The sun creaked a little over him, like a wagon wheel turning over in a rut.

A few hours later they were speeding along over the treeless plains of Nebraska, steadily gaining altitude. Sternberg, Isaac and Mrs. Cope tried to make themselves comfortable in the spartan, plank-benched coach, while the professor found a more isolated spot to continue writing; he had a monograph for the United States Geological Survey to complete before the fieldwork started.

Sternberg, out walking to stretch his legs, happened upon the great man in an otherwise empty coach not far back of the engine. He was on his knees, his tiny journal held down firmly with one hand onto the plank, his other hand pushing the hair up from his forehead. The coach rattled terribly; the light was dim. Cope muttered long scientific phrases to the sooty air, pushed his hair higher until it formed a miniature shock of wheat.

Sternberg watched in silence from the doorway, entranced

by the frantically uttered phrases: *Genus Tinoceras.* Order *Dinocerata. Ornithosauria.*

He had planned to speak to the professor, to learn something more of what he hoped to achieve on the expedition, but the man's intensity silenced him. The passion was naked and wild. It was easy, at that moment, for Sternberg to imagine the boy that Cope had been. Dishevelled and muttering over his research, he might have been eight years old, dissecting a frog. And yet there was no mistaking the mature energy either—a boy can play seriously, but not with such a direct purpose. Cope's ambition, of which Sternberg had heard rumours, was so apparent that it seemed unlikely even the capacious wastelands of the West could contain it. No wonder he was so frail and exhausted, if that was how he routinely drove himself.

Sternberg was about to step back out of the rattling, soot-dusked coach when the professor suddenly snapped his head around in his direction. The wildness flared higher in the eyes, which, despite being bloodshot, were dancing. A smear of soot blackened his large brow. He looked like a man torn from a dream, though his voice bespoke no terror, only a strangely muted enthusiasm.

"There's so much," he said simply, his hands still flat on the planks so that he resembled a caged tiger. "Too many lifetimes. I'd need an army. And then every soldier's skill would have to match my own."

Sternberg strained to hear the words over the roar of the engine, but the confident tone carried their message regardless. And somehow the confidence was inoffensive, as if he had said "certain trees drop their leaves in the fall." The matter-of-fact acceptance of his own gifts was strictly scientific. Even so, Sternberg could think of no reasonable response. He knew what the "so much" was; he'd experienced the same joyous hunger at the prospect of delving further into the mysteries of Creation. But Cope's reference to this miraculous plenitude contained a darkness, as if he also dreaded it or somehow resented its greatness.

"And I'm on my knees!" He straightened up, throwing his hands in the air in the same motion. "On my knees for the blasted government! Should a man ever be on his knees for anything but prayer, Mr. Sternberg?" He grinned boyishly. "Unless it's for a woman."

Sternberg noted the return of the public man, felt the defenses spring up around the nakedness. He thought he detected a gleam in the bloodshot stare. Whatever the case, Cope's reference to prayer was disquieting, especially when followed up by the mention of women. Sternberg, while registering his unease, chose to pass over it quickly. Yes, he thought, feeling the vibration of their journey in his marrow, there was much to be done. Above all else, he was deeply in the professor's debt for the opportunity to participate in such a glorious labour. That was enough.

Cope returned to his monograph. He snarled the strange words out in the swirling space between his face and the paper. Sternberg could almost feel his body sinking from the great man's consciousness, as if he were just another specimen to be noted before moving on to the next.

But this dismissal seemed natural, the way an antelope or coyote or rabbit took note of a human being, seeing them but without especial regard for their individuality. Here is a bone hunter that can be of some use to me—that was the apparent extent of Cope's engagement with his young worker.

Not the least bit offended, Sternberg backed out of the

coach, bearing the image of Cope's intensity like a burning branch into his sleep.

THE JOURNEY PROVED TORTUOUS, THOUGH NOT THE EARLY stages of it, not the train ride into the highlands of the Great Divide and on into the majestic cliffs and ranges of Weber and Echo canyons, where the forests were dwarfed into miniatures by the immensity of the Rocky Mountains around them. Sternberg mostly stared out the window, awestruck by the scenery as the train was devoured by it. Only the Almighty architect, he enthused silently, could imagine and then carve such beauty.

At Ogden, in Utah territory, two things changed. Mrs. Cope left the party to return east, as conditions were soon to become uncomfortable for a lady. Again, Sternberg and Isaac were exposed to a scene of unusual affection, in which the professor, his head nestled on his wife's bosom, simpered like a child while she stroked his temples and entreated him, with much weeping, to be careful and to look after himself and to be sure to rest. Cope promised to send many telegrams. Then, grinning widely, staring up at her with his blue eyes full and his voice deep, he added, "Good wife, my dear Annie, how I will miss thine ministrations!" To which expression, strangely, Mrs. Cope noticeably stiffened. Red flushed her cheeks. "Edward," she said lowly, "you promised." But Cope merely blinked up at her, obviously delighting in the reaction he'd elicited. Sternberg and Isaac merely exchanged puzzled glances.

The other change was the mode of transport. From Ogden the three men rode on a narrow-gauge railway to Franklin in Idaho territory. Much to Sternberg and Isaac's surprise, Cope did not mention his wife again, though he did send a telegram at Franklin, presumably to her. His conversation, little though it was as he struggled to complete his monograph, growing visibly weaker by the hour as he did so, focused increasingly on the badlands of the Judith River Basin in Montana.

"I'm expecting much treasure, gentlemen," he said, running his tongue over his lips. "Old life, which we shall make new." Then he chortled, leaned forward and added darkly, "A new field. Untouched. None of Marsh's lumber-fisted crews have been anywhere near it. At least not according to my latest information."

Sternberg understood the competitiveness, though it was only a low flame in his own character, and decided to ignore it. If the work was done well, that was reward enough. And besides, he believed that the Lord's cemeteries of Creation held glory enough for a million bone hunters. He found it surprising that a man of Cope's intellect should waste energy on competing with someone for whom he obviously held little respect (he referred to Marsh as a charlatan and crook). But as the professor did not speak often, Sternberg did not yet know the extent of his employer's obsession in this regard, if obsession it were. He chose instead to dream of the treasure that awaited them in Montana.

At Franklin, the relative comfort of rail travel ended. The three bone hunters, along with a dropsical-looking man who claimed to be a doctor, and a broad-shouldered youth striking out as a ranch hand along the Missouri, boarded a Concord coach for the six-hundred-mile journey through the dry, barren plains of Idaho. It was a nightmare ride: they travelled ten miles an hour, day and night, stopping only for meals of hot soda biscuits, black coffee, bacon and mustard, for which they were charged the exorbitant sum of a dollar each. But much worse than the rapid, bumpy progress and poor sustenance was the dust—thick clouds of it, kicked up by the team of six horses, coated their clothing and filled their eyes and ears. And since the weather was so warm, and the coach further heated by the closeness of the bodies inside, the dust stuck to the sweat on the passengers' exposed skin and gave them the appearance of having jaundice.

It was almost impossible to sleep. If, worn out from prolonged wakefulness, one of the men dozed for a moment, a sudden lurch of the coach into a chuckhole would smash his head against a post or his neighbour. Only when buttoned into the leathern apron in the seat beside the driver could a passenger remain still enough to sleep.

Professor Cope, alone of the men, fared better. On just the briefest acquaintance, others seemed aware of his uniqueness and went out of their way to lighten his burden. The would-be ranch hand, for instance, took Cope's head in his arms and held it there for several hours, allowing the exhausted man (he was still toiling over various documents) some much-needed sleep. Seeing this, Sternberg couldn't help but recall Mrs. Cope, by then many miles on her journey home, and of her tender ministrations to the great skull. While the youth did not cradle the head so gently, nor stroke the brow, he nonetheless conveyed a sense that it was a privilege to be so close to such a distinguished gentleman.

The rollicking journey continued. Outside the coach grew a darkness so heavy it pulled the stars closer to the earth. Sternberg found it hard to believe they could be going anywhere except into complete isolation from the rest of the civilized world. He hung from the coach strap as if he was being lowered, generation by generation, into prehistory.

The horses jolted to a stop.

Before anyone else could react, Professor Cope had sprung awake and reached into one of his boots. To Sternberg's amazement, he pulled out a derringer and hurried to the front of the coach. Might there be an ambush? The country was alive with hostile savages and various kinds of thieves. Sternberg couldn't adjust to the absence of motion. Dizzy, frightened, he stared into the black space where Cope had vanished.

"Snap out of it, man!" came a quick curse from the darkness. Then a sound as of a hard slap, followed by incoherent mumbling. The professor thrust his head through the black space.

"Gentlemen," he said with controlled rage, "the fool at the horses is a damnable drunkard. He hasn't the wits to hold the reins. If there are no objections, I'll guide the team to the next station. It can't be far now."

Without waiting for a reply, he withdrew. Sternberg heard him speak to the man buckled into the seat beside the driver. Seconds later, the man himself appeared with the intention of exchanging places with Sternberg. Simply, as if no reason were needed or given, the man said, "He wants you up there."

Sternberg made the move quickly and without comment. Cope waited impatiently, clenching and unclenching the reins. The driver slumped lifeless between them.

"I should leave the fool on the trail," Cope snarled. "That would sober him up fast." He paused. "I wouldn't put it past Marsh to hire …" he began, then cut the thought short. "No matter now." With a violent lunge, he snapped the team into motion.

Like the other passengers, Sternberg had no time to react to Cope's new role. But, given time, what would they have said? It was folly not to continue. And, Sternberg comforted himself, men skilled enough to find the barest tip of bone in rock should have no difficulty finding a horse-changing station on the plains. In any case, Cope's decisiveness created its own confidence.

The coach plunged forward into the thick clouds of dust. Sternberg coughed, rubbed at his eyes, happy to be moving again, happy that the dust and the smell of horse flesh dissipated the odour of whiskey rising off the driver's unconscious form, but disturbed, also, that the form seemed lifeless. Thinking of the dead, Sternberg gave over his will to the professor's urgency.

They found the station without trouble, changed horses, acquired a new and sober driver, and continued northward.

The journey improved once the coach reached the Rocky Mountains. For one thing, the scenery was transformed from the bare and monotonous to the spectacular, all breathtaking peaks and declivities, bluish shadows and snowcaps. For another, the dust disappeared and the air grew cooler and sweeter. Yet there were new trials: the passengers had to get out of the coach and walk up all the steep ascents.

Still, despite the difficulties, Sternberg's enthusiasm grew. He was, in fact, so eager to begin what he increasingly saw as his unique celebration of the Creator, that he had made no attempt to hide his profession. Once, while Cope was asleep, the youth asked the pertinent question: what are you fellows heading for? And Sternberg, not many years older than the questioner and therefore willing to meet his warm optimism, told him briefly about the fossils. The youth's eyes widened and he shook his head.

"I've never heard of work like that. You must be really smart fellers."

Sternberg nodded in Cope's direction, then whispered, "No. The professor is a brilliant man, but Hank and I are just workers." He smiled. "We're not much different than ranch hands, I suppose, except we're trying to herd beasts that have been dead a long, long time."

At some point, while Sternberg was explaining the barest rudiments of fossil science to his companion, Cope blinked awake. Almost immediately, before he had time to straighten up in his seat, he cut Sternberg off in mid-sentence.

"Dost thee know this man?" he snapped. "Take care! Our work is best done amongst ourselves."

Later, more calmly, he explained to both Sternberg and Isaac that the West was literally "crawling with Marsh's spies," and that they had better be "tight-lipped" if they hoped to remain in his employ.

Sternberg, abashed and repentant, vowed to do as Cope said, if only because he didn't want to cause trouble. Personally, he did not like looking upon every stranger as a threat, nor did he believe it necessary. But the Professor knew his business better than anyone else, so there was some sense in acting as he wished. In any case, Sternberg was content to be alone with his thoughts, for they brought him closer to the work he knew he had been put on the earth to do.

Finally they reached Helena, where they were forced to rest for a few days as the coach underwent some repairs and a change of driver and horses. On arrival, the passengers felt the excitement in the streets before they understood it. People were speaking animatedly in small groups along the boardwalks, and there was a general thrum of activity—two or three horses went galloping past, their riders bent low, some shopkeepers were assessing their front windows, a small boy ran into a saloon and did not reappear. Sternberg could see that something unusual had occurred, and his body tensed. Something had darkened the air, even though it was a sunlit noon.

When the coach stopped at a stable behind the saloon, an employee burst out with the news. The Indians had defeated Custer and the Seventh Cavalry at Little Bighorn. It was a massacre! No survivors.

Sternberg looked at his companions. Isaac had gone pale, motionless; the vague look clouded his eyes again. Cope, on the other hand, merely asked when the fight had occurred and who the Indians were. But he cut the stable hand's excited chatter about revenge with a blunt declaration of intent.

"This won't stop us."

Then he asked when they might expect to be on their way again. The stable hand, a wheat-haired, freckled youth, blinked stupidly, but did not answer. Instead, he began to recount what he'd heard of the butchery, emphasizing the indignities that had been done to the corpses.

Cope turned away and gestured indifferently with one arm. "I expect we can arrange for rooms and a meal at the inn just there. And perhaps someone at that establishment has a better understanding of how we are to proceed on the next stage of our journey." He walked briskly off, leaving Sternberg and Isaac to gather quickly and follow.

When they caught up with him, in the lobby of the hotel, they found a crowd of guests huddled around the proprietor. A large-bellied man with a sagging moustache and high Eastern accent, the hotel owner quivered with excitement as he waved a piece of paper in the air.

"This is a copy," he cried grandiosely, "of the last letter General Custer wrote before he entered the valley of death. Let me read it to you, citizens, if I can do so without my voice breaking."

Sternberg noted Cope's response. He crossed his arms over his chest and sighed, seeming to have accepted that, for a few minutes at least, his own plans would have to wait.

"There are only two lines," the orator thundered. "We have found the Indians and are going in after them." Then, lowering his voice, he ended with, "We may not come out alive."

A graveside silence fell over the listeners. A strong wind knocked at the wooden shutters. Someone's watch ticked loudly.

What did this mean, Sternberg wondered. Was this the start of a general uprising? Would the Indians throughout the West go on a killing spree?

A few muttered curses broke the silence, at which point Professor Cope moved away from the banister he'd been resting against and calmly addressed the proprietor.

"Sir, my two companions and I have need of your hospitality until we can make arrangements to leave for Fort Benton."

"Fort Benton?" the man replied, clearly annoyed that the effects of his reading had been so quickly undermined. "What, man, haven't you been listening? The Indians are on the warpath. You don't want to be going anywhere."

Cope smiled. "Oh yes, we certainly do."

Sternberg was amazed: did the great man think the massacre was another ploy by his enemies to keep him from the rich fields of the Judith Basin?

But Cope's answer to the current difficulties put Sternberg's mind to rest on that score. Cope believed the tragedy had occurred, but he knew it wasn't tragic for his purposes.

"Nay, the Indians will not trouble us. They will be no threat for a while."

"How can you …" the man began to argue.

Cope leaned slightly forward and spoke in a lecturing voice. "Every able-bodied brave will be with Sitting Bull and he won't come north until the army forces him to do so. And the squaws and children will be hidden away in some fastness of the mountains. Judging by previous encounters of this type, I calculate that we'll have at least three months in which to make our collections in peace. We'll leave the field as soon as we hear that Sitting Bull has been pressed so closely that he'll be forced to seek safety on British soil, across the Sweet Grass Mountains into Assiniboia."

"Collections? What sort of collections?"

Sternberg sensed that the other guests did not take kindly to Cope's manner.

Shocked by his admission of purpose, the professor responded deferentially, "Oh, rock samples. We're employed by a mining company to scout new territory." With that, he turned and walked to the desk and began making arrangements for rooms with the clerk.

AT FORT BENTON, A COMMON ENOUGH FRONTIER TOWN AS far as Sternberg could tell—playing cards blowing like leaves through the dusty streets, whiskey for sale in open saloons, wooden buildings that appeared so flimsy they might have been simply hardened dust—Cope had to restrain Isaac from returning to Helena.

"I tell thee, man," he growled, his nostrils flaring, "the Sioux are nowhere near. You're safer with us than a babe is at his mother's teat."

Isaac quailed as if the wind were a sharpened blade. At Helena, prey to every wild and uninformed tale of Indian savagery (a rumour had arisen that the Sioux had carved Custer's heart out of his chest and eaten it), he had announced his decision to quit the expedition. At first, Cope raged. Then, finding this reaction ineffective, he plied his impressionable hired man with a winning combination of logic and whiskey until finally his methods won the day.

But now, in the naked forlornness of the frontier, about to leave even that tiny vestige of civilization behind for the desolate badlands, Isaac's courage weakened again.

Cope, with a sigh and a look at Sternberg that said, "Ah, what burdens I must carry," softened his tone, put an arm around the dubious man and spoke cooingly straight into his ear.

"Would I lead thee to thy death? Nay, and I have too much work to do to meet my own death at the hands of savages."

And so it went—the Indians would be more likely to attack a settlement anyway, not to wander through the badlands—as he skillfully steered the nodding, beginning-to-be-convinced Isaac towards the saloon and another few shots of courage.

Suddenly alone, Sternberg decided to take a walk up the windblown street of grit and dust. For some reason he couldn't pin down, a gloom had come over his spirits. It had been growing since Helena and the professor's response to the news of the Little Bighorn massacre. How could a man who so valued creation be so indifferent to the destruction of it? And it wasn't even as if Cope disliked the army. On the contrary, he praised it glowingly, claimed he could not do his research in the West without the reassuring presence of the bluecoats. How often, he acknowledged, he had ridden with cavalrymen and relied on their military maps when no others existed, how many good friends he'd made among the officers of the various scattered forts (and their good wives too, he'd added with the usual boyish grin).

So why the cold reaction to the massacre? Perhaps it was Cope's wisdom not to mourn what could not be changed. He could not be an uncaring man, given all of his other winning qualities, especially his enthusiasm for the work of fossil hunting and his fascination with all forms of life. Already, Sternberg had been held spellbound by vivid descriptions of the coyote's and rattlesnake's physiognomy and behaviour, descriptions Cope poured out offhandedly, as though he were chatting amiably about his close friends and relatives. And truly, Sternberg saw, the man's genius and greatness lay in his love and respect for all the marvellous workings of the Creator.

The snarling references to Professor Marsh, the grinning references to womanhood—these were trivial matters, understandable even, considering the great pressures that Cope worked under. That he functioned so well was a miracle in itself—to live with the rigours and demands of such intelligence was a feat few could manage without slipping into madness.

Sternberg walked on. Soon he saw a bulk of dark through the swirling dust. He moved towards it. The wind blew the day's heat full into his face and the grit stung his cheeks. The dark shape grew into several smaller shapes heaped together. Sternberg stopped and gaped at them, feeling as if a black wave had crashed over the silence, leaving a new, more resonant absence of sound.

The shapes were buffalo heads, forty or fifty of them. Most were placed without any apparent order in front of the stagecoach offices. A few were nailed high to the beams across the large window, a few others positioned in a recess in the front wall. But most just lay in the dust. The heads were huge, the horns like grappling hooks ready to swing them into a fire, the fur ash-black but dust-caked. Sternberg shivered. The eyes of the buffalo were open; several fixed directly on his own. A few, dribbling with wounds, resembled rotting blackberries. It was hard to tell if they were eyes or crawling bluebottles. He half-expected a huffing and snorting to break the silence of their still gazes. The other heads, those heaped in the dust and not look-ing at him, seemed deliberately pointed towards some meaning. But Sternberg could see no meaning in the various directions and no purpose in the display. Likely it was an advertising gim-mick—he'd seen carcasses and bones of animals used similarly in larger towns, usually by railroad companies.

But not so many, not so recently killed and not in such a remote outpost. The animals themselves looked more lost in death than usual. Some of the heads, turned upward, propped against others, suggested the bodies below were fording some stream; their eyes, though motionless, appeared to whirl.

Sternberg felt the wind swirl the loose strands of his hair, the same wind that rippled the dust-caked fur, bent the prairie grasses, pushed clouds across the great sky and howled in the star gaps. There was no other sound. He sniffed at the dusty heat. Without forethought, he prayed for the success of the ex-pedition, though he knew that the prayer wasn't personal but had something to do with knowledge, civilization, the end to senseless slaughter. He was not sentimental; he'd lived too long in the West to expect much tenderness towards God's creatures. But his life's work forced his hands onto the bones of extinct creation, and he could not pretend the touch did not carry with it a sorrow for the splendour that had passed forever from the earth.

He raised his head, stared for a moment into the myriad looks of death, then turned and walked back quickly the way he had come. All the way down the street, he felt the eyes on his back, as if, finding some last surge of life, the heads had slowly twisted around to the east to watch him disappear.

THE PROFESSOR HAD BEEN BUSY IN STERNBERG'S ABSENCE. He had hired a half-breed scout and a cook, a fat, cowlicked, grumbling man named Austin Merrill.

"Doth thee note his great girth, Mr. Sternberg?" Cope enthused. "I believe the man knows well how to eat."

Once he'd completed arrangements for the human part of the expedition, Cope, with difficulty, and after paying an exorbitant price, secured an outfit—two worn-out mustangs, a fine, if moody, three-year-old colt, and a stalwart-looking older horse. Along with several saddle ponies, and the wagon supplied with food and equipment, the outfit was complete and the journey to the badlands began.

For several days, they followed a series of wagon trails through a territory of vast, waving grassland and spectacular mountain scenery. Awed, Sternberg took in the ocean-like ripples extending in all directions, a lulling vista broken only by occasional sightings of buffalo, antelope, deer and wolves. When he found himself dangerously hypnotized by the high grass, he raised his eyes to the snow-covered peaks of the Bear Paw Mountains to the north, or else looked at his unusual employer. Periodically, Cope burst into shouts at the intransigence of the moody colt, who proved not to be a good leader of the team. But mostly he sat silent and straight-backed on the wagon, a diary sometimes taken from his shirt pocket and fiercely scribbled in, then just as fiercely put away.

At night, in camp, while they feasted on the rich dishes Merrill had fashioned from the game the scout had brought in—generally ducks, antelope or deer—Cope said little; his hand, however, almost never stopped moving across the page.

"Letters and notes," Isaac explained in an awed but uncomprehending way. "He's always writing up some kind of paper for one of them smart Eastern journals. I heard tell he's written thousands of 'em. Does it mostly to get the better of that Marsh feller, far as I can gather. Hardly sleeps."

Sternberg soon realized that there was no end to the surprises where Cope was concerned.

One muggy, ominous afternoon, the colt was proving particularly uncooperative, balking at every low thunder roll, rearing up on its hind legs, swinging its head savagely from side to side.

"Blast the creature!" Cope cried, jumping down. He ordered Isaac to unhitch the horse and tie it to one of the hind wagon wheels, then told Sternberg to climb up on top of the wagon with a club to prevent the colt from trying to climb in.

With a whip in one hand, butt end down, Cope approached the horse with his other hand outstretched, speaking gently to calm him. The horse, however, reared and struck out with its front hooves. Narrowly escaping the blow, Cope stepped back, raised the whip, and with the butt end hit the horse behind the ear. The animal collapsed with a piercing cry and lay stunned for several seconds. But when he struggled up, and the professor again approached with outstretched hand and tender words, the colt struck again. Once more Cope knocked him to the ground. For the second time, the horse, wild-eyed, struggled up and made another attempt, though much feebler, to strike. One last blow from Cope, however, did the trick. After that, the colt welcomed the professor's advances, accepting with little snickers of pleasure the caresses bestowed on him, and, when untied, almost dragging Cope after him in his anxiety to get to the traces. Even as the lightning flashed and thunder rumbled across the heavens, the horse did not act up again.

The party ventured on. Sternberg caught edgy, flashing glimpses of Cope, straight-backed, his blond hair loosely flowing to the storm, and had a sudden, disturbing vision of another blond-haired, iron-willed hunter crossing the Great Plains to his fate. But Sternberg shook the vision off as nonsense, the sort of thing newspaper writers would dream up for a gullible readership. Cope was a scientist, not a soldier. And he wasn't on the hunt for Indians. His game was not human or alive and it travelled at a speed only God could fathom. Even so, the lightning's jagged halo around Cope was disquieting. He seemed to advance in staccato bursts towards his goal, as if he came closer than any other man to the travelling speed of the bones he pursued, which was the speed of eons. Despite his growing unease, Sternberg could not help but admire Cope's single-minded passion, nor could he deny his own rising excitement at their quest. What unknown treasures awaited them? And what glorious proofs of the creative riches of the Creator? Looking to the dark horizon between the lightning flashes, he saw the summits of what resembled a low range of mountains, and knew, without being told, they were within sight of the Judith River badlands.

TWO DAYS LATER, THEY SET UP CAMP AT THE MOUTH OF THE muddy Judith River, near where an Indian trader had a store in a stockade. Across the river was a sight that immediately panicked Isaac and the cook. Isaac began wildly to pack his things until Cope, in a weary, exasperated tone, explained.

"Crows, Mr. Isaac, not Sioux. Note the shape of the lodges.

See how the poles stick so high above the point of intersection? Does thee not see how it forms the shape of an hourglass? Only the Crows build such lodges. Striking, are they not?"

Sternberg stared across to the other shore. Thirty or forty Indian tipis were set up in a grassy meadow near the bank, smoke pouring out of several of them. What appeared to be hundreds of dogs skulked around the tipis. But few Indians were visible.

"A buffalo-hunting party," Cope continued, "not a white-man hunting party. If I know my tribes at all, and I humbly submit few know them as well as I, for I have made a particular study of those I am liable to be in contact with, these Indians will become friends. Once we set up camp, I shall pay them a social call." He sighed. "Despair not, Mr. Isaac. Thou shalt not be forced to accompany me. But perhaps Mr. Sternberg has more of an anthropological interest."

And so, a few hours later, Sternberg followed Cope across the shallow river and into the Crow camp. Dismounting, they were surrounded by dogs of every imaginable colour, some snarling but keeping their distance. Cope growled, baring his teeth, then leaped forward. Some dogs turned tail and ran, others backed away slowly, still snarling and barking, but a few approached tentatively to sniff at the chuckling professor's outstretched hand.

Cope, however, quickly lost interest in them when he spotted an odd structure just to his right. It was a wooden scaffold raised on four thick, forked sticks. On top of the platform of the scaffold lay a long bundle of yellowish hide, the same material from which the tipis were made. Underneath the scaffold, on the ground between the four sticks, lay a dozen long lodgepoles. One pole, however, leaned against the scaffold and pointed almost vertically skyward. From its top point dangled a scalp.

Cope's blue eyes twinkled.

"Mr. Sternberg," he said lowly, "this is a rare treat indeed." He moved closer to the scaffold, and stood motionless, staring at the bundle.

Sternberg followed. Seconds later, he was almost knocked down by the stench of decay. His hand flew up to plug his nose.

"Yes, it is not a recent death." Cope knelt to run his fingers along one of the poles. "The death lodge has been taken down." He stood again, looking towards the tipis. "Just as well. I would not want to intrude upon a fresh grief." He turned to Sternberg with widened eyes. "It is well it is you and not Mr. Isaac with me. The scalp would have him halfway to Fort Benton by now. Ah, but Mr. Sternberg, what fascinations his timidity keeps him from encountering. The Crows and death, for instance. Their word for soul, *iraxe*, is connected to their word for shadow, *iraxaxe*, and also with ghost, *apara'axe*. So, you see, it is no wonder they believe the dead are not always dead, that they come back. The owl has cried for this warrior, though. If my senses don't deceive me."

Yet Cope did not even wrinkle his nose. Overwhelmed, Sternberg barely heard what the professor said.

"I once heard of a Crow warrior, Mr. Sternberg, who was believed to be dead, but got up again the next morning." Cope chuckled. "He told everyone that the dead were camped together and were better off than the Crow. Doth that not make it easier to face the foe, Mr. Sternberg? Yea, a most sensible view for a race that lives on the keen edge of survival."

But Sternberg had wandered several feet away, his attention drawn by an even more disturbing sight—several dozen bone-white buffalo skulls lined in the dust, all pointing in one direction, towards the camp. It was an eerie enough image in its own right, but when he recalled the jumbled mass of buffalo heads in Fort Benton, their eyes rotting and gazing blindly in all directions, a chill passed right through him. He could make no connection between the two sights, yet they were too similar not to be linked. Gaping, Sternberg almost convinced himself that the Crows had somehow recovered the buffalo heads from Benton and set the skulls up in a logical pattern for some deeper purpose.

Cope's voice directly in his sound ear shattered his imagining.

"For the buffalo hunt, Mr. Sternberg. See how they all point towards camp? When the hunt is over, the skulls will point out again."

This explanation, however, was little comfort. Sternberg could not shake the disturbing link between the sloppy, rotting deaths in Benton and the scoured, orderly deaths at his feet. He felt as if he'd travelled in one great leap closer to a darkness he did not want to enter.

"Ah," Cope started in delight, "here come our hosts."

A brave and squaw approached slowly. The brave could not have been more different than the last Indian with whom Sternberg had come into close contact, the young, pale warrior in the Kansas chalk. This Indian was middle-aged and over six-feet tall, so swarthy as to be almost black, with a large and perfectly straight nose. While his dress was not extravagant—it consisted of tan breechcloth, leggings, shirt and moccasins—he did wear several chains of buffalo bone discs around his neck and over his chest. What really shocked Sternberg about the Crow's appearance, however, was his long black hair. It flowed freely around his face and down below his waist. But not quite freely, Sternberg noticed as the Indian turned slightly—down the centre of his back to just above the ground hung a braid along which were fastened, at every four inches or so, rawhide switches decorated with elk teeth. The hair below each switch appeared slightly different in colour and texture, though Sternberg wondered if his senses were being faithful.

The squaw, also tall and dark, wore a long deerskin dress completely studded with elk teeth. Her long hair was parted evenly at the forehead and hung in two braids. The parting was reddened, as if blood had been rubbed into it.

Sternberg looked around nervously to the high-hung scalp over the scaffold just as the Indians stopped. He quickly looked back. Up close, the Indians were even more remarkable. Their hair was greasy yet glossy, and a sweet, herb-like smell flowed from it. The man had little balls of pitch in the hair above his forehead, perhaps to keep it from falling into his eyes. The woman's dress was like a field of stars.

With an effort, Sternberg forced his jaw shut. Yet he could not keep himself from gawping at the man. For a savage, he had a surprisingly noble bearing. Sternberg supposed he was a chief, and struggled to think of how he should show respect.

Cope, however, took the initiative. After speaking for several minutes to the pair in their own language (Sternberg was not surprised at this point by his employer's linguistic knowledge), and after much mutual nodding and pointing, Cope suddenly reached into his mouth and pulled out his false teeth.

The Indians stepped back, wide-eyed.

Cope popped his teeth back in, then turned and winked at Sternberg.

"Do it again! Do it again!" the brave shouted in English.

The professor obliged. While the Indians spoke rapidly between themselves and pulled gently at their own teeth, he whispered to Sternberg, "I've found it a useful practice in the past. In

211

my experience, Indians admire magic and link it with power. To explain to them that I am a professor of Natural History at the esteemed institution of Harvard means nothing. To show them my most prestigious government monographs means nothing. Ah, but to remove my teeth ... when I did this before a party of Sioux in the Dakota territory two summers ago, it prevented an outbreak of hostilities." He grinned again. "And the Sioux even gave me a name: Magic Tooth." Cope pointed towards a few Indians in the swelling crowd.

Following his directions, Sternberg saw two braves and a squaw off to one side, their hair raggedly shorn and their faces heavily and freshly scarred.

"Relatives of the deceased," Cope said soberly, nodding towards the scaffold. "The Crows cut their hair when they grieve. Did thee note the attachments on our friend's hair? I'm certain he's lengthened his own with the cuttings off the mourners'. An unusual practise, but then, Mr. Sternberg, grief and the unusual are well-mated. If I should ever lose my Annie ..." A shudder seemed to pass through him. His eyes watered.

A second later, he had whirled back to the Indians and was repeating his performance with the teeth. After he had done so a dozen times to the immense mystification and pleasure of the assembled crowd, he spoke to the tall man in Crow for several minutes.

Sternberg waited, his gaze drifting back to the row of buffalo skulls. Everywhere in this landscape death and bones were prominent. It was a veritable treasure house of death. These Indians used bones for decoration and ritual. Perhaps the warrior in the Kansas chalk had wanted the mosasaur limb for the same reason. Yet there'd been something about the intensity of his interest that seemed purposeful in a way that transcended earthly matters such as clothing and food. It occurred to Sternberg that the pale Indian would not be amused by Cope's false teeth.

Ten minutes later, returning to camp, the professor declared that they'd have no trouble with the Crows. His eyes blazing all of a sudden, he added, "It seems that great buffoon, Marsh, and his coterie of crooks and potato gatherers have yet to appear in the Judith beds. We are as Adam in Eden, Mr. Sternberg. The Indians assure me there are many bones where we are headed. We'll break camp at dawn. Get up!" And he exploded his horse through the shallow water.

True to his word, Cope led them away from the mouth of the Judith at first light. To Sternberg's astonishment, the Crow camp, scaffold and skulls included, had vanished. Isaac and Merrill took their departure as an ominous sign.

"Sitting Bull must be near," Isaac said, his knuckles white on the Winchester across his lap.

"I tell thee, man," Cope railed, "there is no threat! The Sioux are hundreds of miles from here."

"But why have they gone, then?" the cook interjected.

"Am I to read the minds of savages now?" Cope groused. "Mr. Deer is scouting. If there's trouble, we'll know in good time. But I tell thee, we are as safe as in the cradle bower. And once in the badlands, we will be as alone as Job with his conscience. It is as gospel, I tell thee!"

Cope's certainty had a calming effect, and when the expedition crossed the sparkling Missouri and the muddy Judith once more, it did so in sedate, if not exactly good, spirits.

Finally, one evening just past dusk, they stopped to camp in the valley of the Dog Creek. All around them, pressing like a form of low, heavy cloud dragged down by the weight of innumerable skulls and spines, stretched the vast labyrinth of the badlands.

"Gentlemen," Cope announced, leaping lightly off his mount. "Welcome to the Happy Hunting Grounds." His chuckle of delight was so infectious that even Isaac did not blanch at the sideways tribute to the Indians' religion.

Sternberg looked around. Above their camp rose twelve hundred feet of denuded rock in great beds of black shale. Beyond the sheer ebony steepness, the first stars glimmered, as if in promise of the specimens to be found. Sternberg breathed in the cooling evening air, still rich with heat, dust and the heady metallic taste of baking stone. At last, after such a long and wearying journey, the real work was about to begin. Happily throwing off the gloom he'd carried since Helena, Sternberg helped set up camp.

A short while later, as had been his custom since leaving Fort Benton, the professor stood over them at the fireside and preached, by memory, from Scripture. Eyes flickering in the light, his great head raised as if in defiance to the thick black walls, Cope thundered out the text, his hair unruly as he smote the air with an open palm, his words, endowed with the calm of his faith, forming a bizarre contrast.

"And God said, 'Let the waters bring forth abundantly the moving creature that hath life, and fowl that may fly above the earth in the open firmament of heaven'. And God created great whales, and every living creature that moveth, which the waters brought forth abundantly, after their kind, and every winged fowl after his kind, and God saw that it was good."

Cope went on, without pause, striking the air, emphasizing the words "God," "life" and "good." He appeared to be directing his mounting wrath at some hidden listener. Sternberg sat enthralled, though oddly unnerved by the familiar text.

The professor concluded, resoundingly, with "And God blessed the seventh day, and sanctified it, because that in it he had rested from all his work which God created and made. These are the generations of the heavens and of the earth when they were created, in the day that the Lord God made the earth and the heavens!"

Cope paused to let the words echo off the smoky blackness. His hair gusted like flame, his eyes drew in the night; they were hooded like a reptile's, but with a hawk's gaze.

Sternberg, as was becoming almost customary, was startled by the professor's next words.

"There are those amongst us, gentlemen," he growled, "—madmen, though they wear the very devil's cloak of cleverness—who would not see God's hand in His own creation, who would strip us of that glory. But have we not stood in these vast spaces, in these bone yards littered with the tangible proof of His power to create and destroy and recreate in our living eyes, and known, yea, felt through our sinews to the spirit, this silence as not an absence of sound but as the closest approximation to the Holy Spirit as we are to experience this side of the grave? Gentlemen, what use is any rhetoric before that which the naked soul receives direct from the source of its making? We are not greater than we know, we are smaller. This silence, this Western silence that surrounds and awes, is but the faintest echo of God's heartbeat. We lean towards it, almost hear words in a tongue we recognize. Gentlemen, it is not the crow's caw at birth I speak of, it is not the crow's caw at death—though these are verily the handclaps of the Holy, nature's supreme joy at our great privilege to know the pulse of creation. Nay, I speak of the meadowlark's song between, piping up from these ancient bones around us—it is this joy, this power to discover, this science, that presses us for a few precious seconds to the bosom of our Father, and we hear the truth, the only truth; it beats so loudly that starlight pours in our eyes and the blood knows other worlds. Are we so clever, are we so deadened, that the life in us does not hunger ceaselessly for more life? Are we soulless men bent over desks, waiting until the crow calls us out? Nay, nay! Joy is the knowledge of God's greatness!"

All at once, his rapt look gave way to one of intense scorn. His voice rumbled with disgust.

"Mr. Darwin, chief among the soulless, would have us believe otherwise, gentlemen. He would make of the earth a smallness, a matter of mere natural laws, governed by blind chance. Consider the arrogance of such a mind!" He reached into his coat pocket and pulled out a large railroad watch, which he then dangled off its chain over the fire. With his other hand, he gestured towards the stars, the surrounding country. "And is this to be creation, the earth and all its wondrous life a mechanism set going and left to run down without an ordering intelligence? Doth even man construct a timepiece and not adhere to time? Is this logic?"

Cope dashed the watch into the flames.

"I can choose thus," he roared. "And can God not claim a greater power? Who cast these scattered bones into the rock?"

Sternberg glanced over his shoulder, half expecting to see the bones rise and come forward, like whistled dogs to their master. But only the dark looked back at him. Isaac coughed uncomfortably, stretched his arms in a gesture of fatigue, which Cope ignored.

He lowered his eyes and voice. "Gentlemen, I will say this to you. Tomorrow we take up the chisel to break into stone. That is a natural law. And thus the Lord employs His laws. Natural law is but God's chisel breaking into matter to create new life. Do not be fooled. Doth God not temper the wind to the shorn lamb? He is in everything. Yea, tomorrow we will find evidence of His paradise in the barren rock!"

The words flowed away into silence. Cope smiled at the dying fire. "What do hours matter to us here in the land of all ages?" Softly, he concluded: "It is a great pleasure for me, gentlemen, to have devout workers in my camp. Why, at Como Bluff in Wyoming, when I preached, the damnable heathen of a cook would brush his teeth or go on chopping wood!"

He laughed pleasantly, then announced that they should retire to their sleep.

With a renewed sense of faith and camaraderie, and an inflamed kinship with his employer's ambition, Sternberg found his bedroll and, after several minutes of rapid, fire-flickering images, oblivion.

AS SOON AS THE FIRST STREAKS OF DAYLIGHT APPEARED, the party breakfasted. Afterwards, Deer left to scout the area, the cook returned to his kitchen, and Isaac set off to search for a better water source. Meanwhile, Cope and Sternberg headed to the field, picks tied to saddles, collecting-bags dangling from the pommels, and a lunch of cold bacon and hardtack in the saddlebags.

Whenever possible, Sternberg rode on the professor's right side, since he was totally deaf in his own right ear. His mount, a treacherous black mustang, continually tried to regain his freedom and had to be restrained by means of a curb bit that tore his mouth to pieces.

The professor, oblivious to these difficulties, grew animated, absorbed in his thoughts on man and science. In fact, he seemed to be speaking to himself, as he looked straight ahead and rarely turned towards his riding companion. Sternberg once again had the unnerving sense that the voice that came to him was as knowledgeable and remote as God's.

"A man should not be all intellect. That is the danger in science. Darwin, Wallace, Huxley, that damnable Marsh—such men believe they can reason their way through life. But how, how, faced with the glories of the Creator, can they reason away the cosmos, bird flight, a woman's heart? Doth experience teach them nothing? And mystery is no enemy to man—it is his greatest friend. Without it, we are as the extinct beasts whose bones we seek. Imagination and feeling. God has given us these faculties to praise and honour, not to deaden.

"When I was a young man, I tell you in all honesty, I was prone to plunging into the very depths. I lost the Way. I believed too much in the power of man's knowledge, his science. But I could not, try as I might, believe away my feelings, I could only ignore them. Ah, the madness of it! Mr. Sternberg, would you believe, once, travelling in Europe, I sketched the fossils in museums as if I had made them myself? It's true. I believed, the world of science gave me to believe, that I was the Creator and not the seeker of truth. Oh the very depths! Yet it was only intellect. In my heart, I felt the misery of my separation from the Way. But I could not see salvation. I was intoxicated with knowledge. Mr. Darwin could not rival me. So much life to discover, so much power to reveal. But it was not mine! I was a child playing with fire. And it was myself I burned.

"Only will, Mr. Sternberg, the power to choose, that greatest gift of the Lord, saved me. Dost thou know what I did? I gave the

218

fire back to the Creator. I burned everything. Before leaving the continent, I made a bonfire of all my notes and sketches, two years' worth of research. Ashes, ashes! Ah, but happily so. That knowledge is smoke in the stars now.

"And yet, I knew God's design is in all. He would not give science to man if we were not meant to pursue it. But as seekers not creators, humbly in service, not arrogantly drunk on power.

"And doth it not occur to thee, Mr. Sternberg, that the mysteries exist to keep us sane? I have thought long on this. In the very conflagration of my research, I saw it was thus. The Lord provides mystery to save us from ourselves, from over-thought. Distraction is a mercy. If I do not have it, I soon am lost to fancies, soul and heart sicknesses that plunge me …

"But look at this country! Even its graveyards teem with life! A seashell where there is no sea, a fossilized turtle shell on a mountaintop, redwoods and cypresses, their very seeds in the cracked clay, bayous where now is only alkali and …"

Sternberg listened, entranced. How little he knew of science! He swore to himself that in the coming winter he would apprentice himself to the discipline, read as much as he could, seek advice from Cope as to what books would be most valuable. If only, he went on in regretful speculation, he'd had the opportunity to study his passion at college—perhaps then he would have been worthy of the company of a man like the professor.

At that instant, Sternberg's mustang reared up, front hooves in the air, until he was almost standing at full length on his hind legs. Sternberg yanked on the reins until the bit dug in. The horse neighed in pain then burst forward, taking up a position on the opposite side of the professor.

Cope did not look up. Though he couldn't quite catch the words, Sternberg saw that the professor's mouth kept moving.

What wisdom was being lost on account of this cursed mount? It did not even occur to Sternberg to regard the great man's obliviousness as unusual—how could anyone hold so much information in the mind and be expected, simultaneously, to concentrate fully on his surroundings?

Finally, happening to look up, Cope saw that Sternberg had vanished. Then, turning, he exclaimed in surprise, "Why, I thought thee were on my right, and here you are on my left!"

Repeatedly, as they climbed up the narrow, stony trail, Sternberg would bring his mustang around to the right. But, when he again became so entranced by the professor's monologue that he loosened his hold on the reins, the same rearing up and bursting forward would result. In frustration, Sternberg vowed to exact every ounce of the professor's mass of knowledge when they weren't at the mercy of their four-legged transports.

AT THE VERY TOP OF THE BADLANDS, NEARLY A THOUSAND feet above the river, they reached the Judith beds. Tablelands and level prairie stretched away to the north, offering plenty of grass for grazing. So the two bone hunters picketed the horses and prepared for the perilous descent into the gorges in search of fossils.

"Fort Pierre Group, Upper Cretaceous," Cope murmured as he slung his kit on his back and strode off towards the edge of a ridge.

Sternberg could feel the kinetic energy burning off the man. He seemed all exposed nerves as his eyes widened and his large head turned in each direction, taking in the remarkable vista. Sternberg followed and looked out over the vast expanse of stone.

Long ridges, terminating in perpendicular cliffs whose bases touched the river a thousand feet below, extended back into the country for miles. The ridges were often cut by lateral ravines into an astonishing array of peaks and pinnacles, obelisks and towers, and other shapes so unusual that no single word could describe them. Even to look into these stone sculptures was to travel with the eye a narrow and winding path, with sides dropping away at forty-five-degree angles.

Sternberg trembled at the sight. The sunlight itself seemed afraid to walk on that stone covered over with broken shale like jagged bits of black glass. The badlands were mostly in shadows. A few isolated scrub spruce and juniper looked puny and forlorn on the sides of the ridges; what reason did they have to exist, Sternberg wondered, if not to give the crows, black as the shale, somewhere to light?

Cope turned, his eyes like planets, and formed his hands into a prayer beneath his jutting chin.

"Valley of death, valley of life," he said simply. Then he raised his eyes to the heavens and thundered, "Lord, how can we not be thankful for Thy beneficence?" Turning to Sternberg, he grinned and said, "Sharpen thine eyes, Mr. Sternberg. And pray for calluses." He leapt over the top of the ridge.

Blinking in astonishment, Sternberg followed and soon took up the concentrated posture of his employer. Together, inching forward on their bellies, they scoured the sandstone ledges jutting out like titanic windowsills from the dust-covered slopes of the ridge. Before long, they found what they had travelled so many miles and at such effort to find—the teeth and bone fragments of the great lizards of the Cretaceous.

Sternberg's excitement was great. He had never seen fossils of the massive carnivores, not even in dissociated fragments. Suddenly the sun burned hotter, felt older, the stone echoed with thunderous approaches. He had to turn onto his back to calm his breathing. Could the world be so miraculous, he wondered, his eyes scanning the pearl sky as if it too would reveal evidence of the glory of the past.

Cope, meanwhile, muttered into his chest, then burst out with his assessment. "There is hope, Mr. Sternberg. Do not despair. I trust that our labours shall uncover more than these shards, interesting though some of them appear. Yes, there is new life here. I can smell it."

He picked up a small pyramidal tooth, black as the stone, and suddenly popped it into his mouth.

At Sternberg's wide-eyed response, Cope laughed uproariously. The tooth bounced on his tongue as if it had fallen from his own plate. "I'm only tasting for the minerals, Mr. Sternberg. I've not gone insane. Not yet!" His laugh broke like crow caws down the slopes and died hundreds of feet below them.

The daylight passed in a blur of intense gazing and almost complete silence. Sternberg could believe he had left the earth, despite the fact that he was pressed so hard against it. Dusk came, and then a darkness to equal the shale. At last Cope announced an end to their labours. They scaled the slope to the ridgetop, found their horses by following their breathing, and unpicketed them. Then, without speaking, they contemplated the deep blackness in which, somewhere, food and rest lay waiting.

# 1916

STERNBERG STARED INTO HIS WIND-SCOURED, HEAVILY-
lined hands. Across from him, bathed in the fire glow, his resur-
rected daughter waited, her sallow face tilted expectantly. He
sighed heavily but gathered the strength to continue.

CHILD, WHAT MORE CAN I SAY OF THAT PLACE, THAT TIME?
With our packs full of the teeth and bone fragments of the great
reptiles—the first I had ever seen of the Lord's terrible lizards,
imagine!—we descended into that bleak valley. Such darkness,
Maud, I have never seen. Layers of it, each layer blacker than the
one preceding, and so dense it seemed we could cut it into slabs.
I was so awestruck by the hard evidence of the Creator's glory
that I did not even question the professor's decision to take the
horses into that perilous maze. How we survived the journey,
I do not know. It had to be the special design of Providence
that we made it back to camp. Of course, Professor Cope took
the lead. He encouraged his mount over the edge ahead of me
as if he was entering a meadow of wildflowers. I had no choice
but to follow. It was a frightening trip; we had to give ourselves
over to the instincts of our mounts, and I did not have great
faith in my recalcitrant mustang. But even in such darkness, the

professor would not surrender his will. At one point—how it gives me chills even now—his horse balked at a gap on the trail. Outraged, the professor immediately spurred the creature on, and it reared back, screaming. He kicked harder and the beast scrambled up stone chips as it plunged ahead and leaped into space. To my surprise, my own accursed mount did the same— one of the few times I did not have to coax or force it. The next morning, coming up that same trail, imagine my horror when I saw that the gap was at least ten feet across and that it opened onto a veritable chasm, nothing but air for hundreds of feet to the valley floor! That morning, I insisted on another route, and the professor, more to oblige me than out of fear for his safety, consented.

But I was speaking of the night before. Well, child, Providence brought us finally into camp, where Mr. Isaac had everything set up for our arrival. The cook, it is perhaps ungrateful of me to say, was terrible. Professor Cope had hired him on the basis of the man's great girth—he was no less than three hundred pounds and did not stand any taller than I. But while the food was ample, it was also indigestible. We sat around a fire of dried buffalo chips, hardly speaking. The night was silent but for the odd, hollow barking noises of owls on the hunt. Suddenly the professor announced that he'd spend only a few days in these gorges, as he wanted to try the region around Dog Creek on his own. And before that, he needed to trek back to Fort Benton to send a telegram! I was amazed. The man had such reserves of energy that he could not stand to be in one place for long. I felt, again, so small in the presence of his great vitality; it seemed he would cover every acre of badlands in the West before he was done.

After our meal, we held, as was to be our custom, a brief service, Professor Cope leading the worship. How that man could praise, Maud. I believe, even now, that his celebration of the Creator could have been equally well-served in the pulpit as in the bone fields and lecture halls. To see his strong, proud face in the fire glow, to hear the words of scripture flow from his mouth and fill the surrounding darkness! I often felt that I had been transported back to the time of Christ, that I was listening to the orations of one of the great prophets. The professor, I am not too humble to admit, was pleased by my attention.

But Maud, how can I really convey to you the divine force of that man's presence? He made of any wilderness a field of lilies into which he bid the Lord to come. If not for him, I would not …

Yet he was not more than mortal, I know it. I knew it then. How much he suffered! The terrible headaches that brought the red veins vividly to the whites of his eyes. And his love of creation so great that, after a day of futile searching in the field, he smouldered like a fire waiting to erupt into flame again. And then there was the affliction I learned about that first night.

Sternberg shuddered in the encroaching shadow. He did not want to speak of the past anymore, yet something more than Maud's interest compelled him.

# 1876

SEVERAL HOURS AFTER FALLING ASLEEP, HE WAS AWAK-
ened by screams. At first he thought it was the continuation of
a dream he'd had several times over the past months, in which
the boy, Jakob, was indeed being scalped, the bloodied, matted
triangle lifted off with a harsh ripping, a faceless savage raising
it on the end of a stick.

But the screams did not fade as he came fully awake and
knew where he was. His imagination pursued its logical ends.
The camp was being attacked by Indians. The professor had
erred—Sitting Bull and his braves were heading north earlier
than expected!

Sternberg leapt up and, clad only in his woollen under-
clothes, plunged through the dark towards the screams. At the
edge of his sight, another figure appeared. It moved closer.
Sternberg's body clenched. He prepared to defend himself.

"Charles." The voice spoke more calmly than circumstances
demanded. He recognized the speaker as Isaac. "I seen you running. No need, son. Don't wancha breakin' a limb for nothin'."

Breathing heavily, Sternberg stood rooted to the ground.

Isaac came closer. Soon, Sternberg saw the narrow face of
the older man. It looked weary but amused.

"It's Cope," Isaac explained matter-of-factly.

Sternberg fought to catch his breath. "What's wrong with him? Is he ill? Is he in pain?"

Isaac grinned. From a ways off, between the screams, the cook shouted for the racket to stop. "Sure, but he don't know it."

At Sternberg's mute, blinking confusion, Isaac pointed towards the source of the screams—they sounded like those of a man in mortal peril.

"I told Cookie already, and he just rolled over. So I leave you to wake the professor, Charles. I got enough of it in New Mexico."

Isaac yawned and rubbed his eyes. "Just be certain, when he's roused, he don't figure you fer one of them old critters. Or, even worse, fer one of Marsh's fellers." He chuckled and turned away into the thicker dark.

Puzzled and only partly comforted, Sternberg moved towards the screams. At the entrance to Cope's tent, he waited, too anxious to crawl inside. But the cook shouted another curse and Sternberg plunged in.

The interior was dimly lit with a flickering oil lamp. A makeshift table of fossil crates was nearby, covered over with books and papers. In the opposite corner, the professor lay face-up on his cot. Every twenty seconds, he let out another piercing scream, twisted violently to one side and back again, putting his arms out as if to defend himself. His face contorted with terror, but at no point did his screaming break into words. A few times, though, between screams, he mumbled long phrases, some of which Sternberg recognized as the Latin names of dinosaur species. What strangeness was this now, he wondered, bending nervously to wake his employer.

Surprisingly, it took little effort to do so. At first touch, Cope released a quick shout and lunged upward. Sternberg jumped to one side, barely avoiding a collision.

"Professor, it's me, Charles Sternberg!"

Cope landed on his feet, arms raised in a fighting posture. His breath came in gasps. His mouth was twisted savagely, his eyes had become two fiery points of light. Sternberg was certain that the professor, like an owl, could see in the dark.

A few seconds passed. Finally the professor's calm voice flowed into the air.

"The beasts, Mr. Sternberg," he explained with a sigh. "How they plague me. Whatever we find in the day comes alive for me at night to trample me, kick me, flip me up, stomp on my poor bones. It has always been thus in the field."

Sternberg didn't know what to say. While he had often imagined extinct life in its living form, his imagination had never gone to such dramatic lengths. But then, he did not have the knowledge of the great reptiles that the professor had. He waited in the silence for Cope to speak again.

"My apologies for jumping at you. You must understand, I have trained myself, with sound reason, to be prepared for Marsh at all times. There is no devilish trick that that charlatan is not capable of. It is not for the savages or highwaymen, Mr. Sternberg, that I carry a weapon." His voice shook with indignation. "He left me to die at Bridger Basin, in the grip of ague. And if I had died, he would have sent his men back in a month to claim my bones."

Cope stepped closer. His breath gave off a mineral smell, as if he were stone that had been endowed with life. The fury in his voice did not diminish.

"And he would have described my bones as antiquities! For

the man is a simpleton, a thief and a coward!" He lowered his voice. "I see you don't carry a weapon, Mr. Sternberg. That's very noble of thee. My own faith, of course, requires no such material safeguards either. Aye, but even the great man, George Fox himself, did not have such a villain as Marsh to deal with. If you are going to continue in this work—and I see you have a gift for it—then you should protect thyself. Marsh's devils respect no faith but their master's great greed. Be warned!

"And now, Mr. Sternberg," Cope concluded wearily, "we best retire. Another full day in the field awaits us. There's little rest for a bone sharp, if he's a worthy one. Good night to thee."

Sternberg emerged again into starlight. The camp was still. He smelled the burnt embers of the fire, heard a nighthawk cry in the distance. Was there anything about Cope that did not surprise? His genius. Yes, Sternberg decided as he returned to his bedroll, that at least he had foreseen.

The next morning, in pink light that gave the appearance of a dying fire, the bone hunters separated again. As if in deference to Mr. Isaac's fears, Cope gave him the job of surveying the area closest to camp. Or perhaps, as Sternberg gradually realized, he saw Isaac's value more in the sheer physical labour of transporting the wagon, team and fossils than in the act of finding bones. Hours later, the professor admitted as much, adding that a man was little use scouring the ground for bone if he could not keep his scalp from tingling.

"Hunting demands our full attention," he said. "And the real sharps forget everything, their aches and pains, the past, the future, everything, once the prospect of a specimen is at hand."

Sternberg understood this well, had experienced it in Kansas, and it pleased him to know that the professor appeared to sense this gift for focus in him. The excitement of the day surged in his veins again.

Soon he and Cope were travelling along the great level stretches that skirted the badlands. The prairie was covered with thick bunches of grass, and often had been rooted up for acres by grizzlies in search of wild artichokes—a sweet morsel they loved, as Cope explained. Often, the two men saw herds of deer, elk and antelope, moving always at the edges of their vision. Silently Sternberg again praised the Creator, grateful that he had been chosen to hunt what could not be killed but only brought to life once more.

They kept to a route among the foothills of the Judith River Mountains to the south, and eventually emerged again onto the open plain. Amazingly, Cope seemed to have some exact location in mind, though he did not mention it.

It grew hot. The sun shrunk to a bead and the sky around it turned pale yellow. Cope spoke only to point out some natural splendour or to curse his mount for stubbornness. Sternberg thought it best to allow the professor his moods, whatever they were. Besides, he was equally content to gaze in wonder at the scenery.

Cope had stopped his horse, so Sternberg did the same.

"Montana!" the professor enthused. "Was ever a place so aptly named?"

They found themselves in a great amphitheatre, a hundred miles across. To the west, the Rockies rose in lofty grandeur, their sides scarred deeply with canyons in whose recesses the white snow gleamed and sparkled. To the south, east and north, the Judith River Mountains, the Little Rockies, Medicine Bow and the Sweet Grass Mountains on the borderline of Assiniboia completed the circle of stone. Yet Sternberg felt no sense of entrapment. Rather, his spirit rose in exhilaration to meet the spectacle. And they were alone, likely the first white men to touch this land! Never had he felt such richness in solitude, at least not since that mossy haven he and Esme had made their ...

Cope spurred his horse on and quickened the pace, as if, in the brief pause, he had reflected again on his rivalry with Professor Marsh. Sternberg was content. It was bones they had come for, after all.

Hours later, they again entered the badlands, picketed the horses, climbed halfway up a steep ravine and clung there like flies, crawling inexorably upward, eyes locked on the shale. Swarms of black gnats plagued them. In vain they smeared cold bacon grease on their exposed skin to keep off the pests.

More hours passed. The light dimmed. Sternberg's eyes swam in the blackness of the shale and the gnats.

Suddenly Cope cried out with joy.

"Mr. Sternberg, the Lord has chosen to smile on us!"

Sternberg scrambled over, eyes widening as they took in the exposed portion of skull. It showed a small horn over one orbit. A horned dinosaur. Sternberg swallowed dryly.

"The first ever found in America," Cope grinned, his eyes ablaze. "Let's see. What shall I call it?" He bowed his head, his left hand touching the exposed horn. "Yes. *Monoclonius*. That will serve nicely."

"*Monoclonius*," Sternberg repeated, astonished by how easily the professor settled on a name for what had not been known to exist until that moment. He reeled with the daring and confidence of it.

232

Cope settled in to the dig. He removed chisel, brush and awl from his pack and threw himself face-down to the shale, his eyes inches from the skull, so close that Sternberg feared their glow would combust the bone.

Poised to help in whatever way required, Sternberg instead felt his attention drawn away. The back of his neck prickled. He sensed a flow of blood nearby. Slowly he raised his eyes to the ridgetop.

"Professor," he said quietly. "Professor Cope."

# 1916

THEY WERE TOLD TO GO DOWN THE LADDER. SCOTT LEANED
over and peered into the dark. He knew that if he hesitated too
long, Wheeler would push past him, volunteering. So he turned
to face the length of the narrow sap they'd just walked down,
and, grabbing the top rung, gently swung his body over. He had
no idea what they were being led into, but the hushed voices
disturbed him; he had a feeling that he and Wheeler had been
unluckily chosen at random.

It was a cold night, close to freezing. Breath was visible and
the ladder was slippery, either from the recent rains or evening
dew. Scott was surprised to find, once he'd descended two dozen
feet and stood again on solid ground, that it was warm. He could
no longer hear the intermittent rifle fire and shell bursts. Flickers of yellowish light played off the walls of the confined space.
Oil lanterns, Scott noted, flinching at the shadows, his body still
tense from days of sentry duty. He'd spent much of the previous
night crouched in a tiny listening post in no man's land, imagining Germans crawling towards him, bombs in hand, bayonets
fixed. The tension felt permanent now, as if his body had forgotten what its natural state was. A huge, grappling shadow lunged

towards him. Jumping back, he bumped into Wheeler coming down. The shadow shrank away.

As ordered, Scott and Wheeler did not speak. An Imperial officer with a fox-like face appeared and directed them to remove their packs and greatcoats. He held a finger to his lips. Then, in a whisper, he instructed them to tie some empty sandbags over their boots and gave them rope for that purpose.

A narrow tunnel, barely three-feet wide and four-feet high, led away from the lit central space around the ladder. A man emerged from the tunnel on all fours, his taut face dripping sweat. The officer nodded at him and vanished up the ladder.

"Kendrick," the man introduced himself. "Come wi' me. Do as I show you, lads, but no talk once we get there, alright." He had a dark, heavy face, as if he'd been underground all his life. Even his words seemed to move on all fours.

A low creaking began to one side of the ladder. For the first time, Scott noticed the narrow steel tracks on the chalk floor, and the small wooden trolley sitting astride them. The creaking, though, came from a winch cable slowly raising a broad bucket, the size of a packing case, to the surface. Looking up, Scott saw only darkness and a thin circle of slightly paler darkness, which he took for the night sky. As the bucket rose to chest level, Scott saw that it was filled with whitish chunks.

"Follow me," Kendrick ordered, and slipped into the tunnel-opening on all fours.

Once inside, he proceeded in a crouch, his hands out to each side as if to stop the walls from closing in. Scott and Wheeler followed. The air was dark, stifling. As they proceeded deeper and farther into the earth, the air grew sharper, strangely potent. The smell seemed familiar to Scott, but he was too preoccupied with the narrowness of their passage to spend time in reflection.

Somewhere behind them, a man spoke and was rapidly cursed into silence.

Kendrick had stopped at the sound. Very dimly, the same yellow light came down the tunnel towards him. He looked like a statue from some lost, buried civilization caught there in the flickers. Scott turned to look over his shoulder but couldn't revolve enough to see into the long dark. Who was back there? Had the whole unit followed? He noticed that the steel tracks hadn't gone very far into the tunnel, and that the walls were closer to his shoulders. Every few seconds, his helmet nicked the roof, but silently. He struggled to walk at an even level. It was difficult, the sandbags shifted under his boots, making a whispering sound that echoed far back of him, except, he realized, those weren't echoes but rather the painfully slow progression of other men.

The tunnel widened again. Eventually, Kendrick, Scott and Wheeler reached a broad face of chalk. It had been roughly cut, into what must have been blocks, for the holes were that shape and descended, at places, unevenly, like a staircase. Kendrick gave Scott a bone-handled butcher's knife and pointed at the chalk. Then, when Scott moved forward, he grabbed his elbow. There was a wooden tub off to one side. Beside it sat a spray bottle. Kendrick dipped it into the liquid in the tub, then sprayed the chalk face where Scott was about to carve. The sharp smell filled the tunnel. Scott recognized it now; it was vinegar.

Kendrick gestured him forward. The whispery sound had ceased behind them. Scott heard nothing except his own pulse and breathing, then the quiet scrape of his knife. If the vinegar had been sage, he realized, he could have expected to look up and find a huge sky clotted with stars. The familiar work calmed him, though the tension never left his body. It was strange. Kendrick sat to one side, spray bottle beside him, rifle held firmly in his hands. Each time Scott was about to remove a chunk, Kendrick crouched beside him, coiled, knuckles white on the barrel. Then, once Scott had turned and given the chunk to Wheeler, for him to then hand back along the line until the last man placed it in the trolley, Kendrick relaxed again.

The work went on for hours, without variation. Twice, Kendrick grabbed Scott's arm, then pressed his own ear to the chalk face. Satisfied, he nodded for Scott to resume.

Scott could not believe what Kendrick's actions foretold. It seemed so much more likely that he would strike into a fossil than a tunnel filled with Germans. The silence told him this, and the repeated motion, which soon brought out a blister on his thumb. Sometimes, looking at Kendrick's profile, he almost recognized one of the Sternbergs, but the image quickly faded and he turned back with another chunk of the deep earth in his hands. It occurred to him that he was no longer in France, no longer at the war; countries must have borders in all directions, and he was digging himself out of everything human. Yet the odd sensation did not ease him. He expected to pull out a chunk and find himself … where? Around a campfire in Dead Lodge Canyon? In a Cretaceous swamp? Certainly it was humid enough. Sweat poured off his face; he had to rub his slick hands dry on the chalk floor. The knife scraped. Kendrick tightened and relaxed his fingers on the rifle. The men passed each chunk back as if it were a swaddled babe, back into the long dark. Hours passed.

He was thirsty. His hand ached. His thumb throbbed. He began to see the shadows as fire flicker, then as figures dancing around a flame. He would go below them, to the deeper, ancient layers. Surf pounded on the shore. Something screamed in the chalk. The man gripped the bone on his lap as if he would fight to the death before giving it up. But Scott was lower than that. He drove the blade in. The chalk was wet. It had gone back to the sea. The shadows loomed larger, the bones had gone into them, the bone on the lap as well. There were no walls, no roof. He bore the heavy stars on his aching shoulder blades. A black shadow lunged.

"Easy, mate," Kendrick hissed as Scott scrambled away from him.

Scott shook his head, blinked. Sweat fell off him like a spray of the vinegar. The tunnel walls closed in, the earth thickened above, its surface crawling with soldiers. And he was one of them, his clothes clotted with blood and smoke.

A figure rushed towards him, open-mouthed, wide-eyed. The walls collapsed inward. Someone screamed. Scott plunged his bayonet into the enemy, just above the groin. A wet sound. He couldn't pull the blade out. Bone-clenched, it turned him around. He tried to scream, but his mouth cracked with dryness. He could hear each crack, loud, distinct. Wildly, he spun back.

"Easy, easy," Kendrick said, hushed. He held up his wrist and tapped it. Then he nodded back in the direction they had come. Their shift was over.

Scott rubbed at his eyes, shook his head, upset by the horror of his trance.

Crouching again, his right arm dragging, he followed the others into the flickering dark.

# 1975

LILY CHANGED BUSES AT CALGARY. THEY ARRIVED IN THE
city mid-morning. The sunlight, which had been mostly cathe-
dral shafts through the mountains, had flooded the foothills and
now flashed off the sides of the few downtown skyscrapers in the
burgeoning oil town. It was warm behind the bus window. Lily
dozed off and on, having slept poorly through the night. Eventually, she gave up on sleep. Her eyes were too sore for reading,
so instead of turning to the letters for solace, she removed the
tissue-wrapped skull from beneath them.

She didn't dare to lift the skull out of its nest, for fear that
someone else would see it and ask questions. But she didn't
need to take it out. After sixty years, she was amazed at how
familiar the sensation of it was, and how powerful. It was like
receiving an injection of her young blood, as if the girl that
still walked in her memory had briefly reclaimed her flesh and
heart and veins. Her eyes as well. That was the most wonderful
thing. And it persisted, even after the brief vigour in her body
had given way to the usual aches and numbnesses of age. She
continued to look out through the eyes of the young woman
she had been, at the time when she had used every ounce of
her strength and intelligence to secure the skull from the earth,

when she had first held the letters from France and breathed rapidly through the words, her hands shaking, her blood fluttering, as if eyelids were opening over her whole body.

She had to wait an hour for the bus to Brooks, so she bought a cup of tea at the depot restaurant and settled into a booth. Two men in suits, grey-templed, fleshy-jowled, sat in the neighbouring booth and talked business.

"So I told the fuckin' s.o.b. to go fuck himself if that was the best he could do."

Lily closed her eyes. The men's voices buzzed like flies, and she waved quickly at her ears to rid herself of the sound. But the tone of their conversation remained. Harsh, aggressive. How cold the world had become. She thought of Mr. Sternberg's tenderness, his decorum, his love of knowledge. Of course, he had hated the war, once confiding to her, alone at the campfire, that he had had many dealings over the years with German scientists and the curators of German museums, and that they had always treated him fairly, with great respect.

"They did not hold my lack of schooling against me," he had said, gratitude dancing in his large, black eyes. "They understood my contribution. Yes, fair men, good men. It's a shame, a terrible shame. How destructive we are, Lily!" And his sigh was like an expiration from an earth tired of being fought over.

On the bus to Brooks, Calgary dwindling rapidly in the west, Lily felt the dead of her badlands youth returning to life. She sensed that she would find them all there, as they had been, serious, impassioned searchers, rabid with knowledge and wonder. Had she ever looked at the night sky and not seen the passion of those men reflected there, Scott foremost among them?

"Just think, Lily. We don't have any idea of what mysteries surround us. Any day, any rainfall, here or in a million other

242

places on the planet, anywhere, anywhere, another mystery can appear! How can anyone not be moved by that?"

His voice was so clear and alive that she looked beside her, startled. But the seat was empty. Foolish woman, she smiled, his voice would be old now too, not young and trembling with excitement.

She tried to steady herself by reading one of the letters. But the urgency and excitement she found there was contagious, the words as stirring as they had been when she'd first read them.

*Dear Lily,*

*How are you? Well, I hope, and enjoying your work. All is much the same here. Cold and wet. But as long as I keep myself busy, this life is bearable.*

*Thank you for the sweater. How did you find the time to knit it? Did you tell Mr. Sternberg that you were making a special protective garment for a duckbill skull?*

*I've been having some pleasant conversation with one of our unit's older men. His name is Macpherson (we call him "Mac") and he's from Nova Scotia. Have I mentioned him before? Well, he has a daughter almost your age, believe it or not. And she just loves horses. Mac is very, very fond of her, and when he gets his next leave, he wants to go to London and buy her a real English saddle. He has his heart set on buying her a fine one. Do you happen to know of a good brand, not too expensive, suitable for a young lady? I know you have little time for riding yourself, and the Sternbergs won't even let you hold the reins of one of their old plough horses when they're dragging a specimen out of the rock (you, a blacksmith's daughter!). But I told Mac, I know just the young lady to ask. If she doesn't know, I don't know who would.*

*And Lily, just for fun, and if you think of it, could you write*

*down one of Mr. Sternberg's stories about eohippus, one of those*
*Professor Cope told him? I think Mac's daughter would find it*
*interesting. It's funny: all of us hardened soldiers have a soft spot*
*for the girl and are always thinking up things for Mac to put into*
*his letters to her. It's a nice diversion for us. We all love to hear*
*him read her letters aloud. And you should hear how we kid him*
*when she signs off "Your little gopher." He always blushes a deep*
*scarlet, which is something to see in a man nearly fifty years old.*

*I'll write again soon. Thank you for your last letter. I'm*
*happy to hear that the work is going well on George's chasmo-*
*saur, and that you're enjoying being his helper. With any luck,*
*I'll be back for the next field season.*

Reading his letters didn't tire her now. Strangely, the sore-
ness had gone from her eyes. She felt wide awake, refreshed,
and the optimism in his words invigorated her even more.

Lily gently folded the letter back in its envelope. It was an
earlier letter, before he started signing "Love" at the bottom,
before he began to admit how much he missed her, before his
intimations that he wanted her to be with him once the war was
over.

She smiled. Had she written to him a story about eohippus?
She must have—when did she not do the little he asked of her?

She looked out the window at the flat, gold-brown countryside. Ranch country. Plenty of horses around. She leaned back,
wondering if that young woman ever received her real English
saddle. She hoped so. She hoped, even, that the young woman
was still alive, remembering her father and the gift he had sent
her from the war. She hoped he had made it back to her.

By the time the bus pulled into the depot at Brooks, Lily
could hear the ringing of the badlands stone calling to the skull

in her purse. She could feel the earth falling away to either side of her. Now the old letters had the same indestructible fragility as the ancient bone. She carried the fossil and the letters off the bus. The clean air gently stroked her cheek as she walked a short distance away from the depot and stopped.

Dazed in the midday sun, her senses heightened, she stood in the wide, deserted street and turned her shining eyes to the east.

# 1876

THE INDIAN AND HORSE WERE NOT SILHOUETTED ON THE ridgetop—it was too late in the day for any striking contrast of flesh and sky—but somehow Sternberg saw everything so clearly that he might have been standing only a few feet away. But this impression, he realized, was instinct and memory. He and Cope were hundreds of feet below, clinging to the black slope of a gorge. Yet even at this distance, the Indian's stillness and lack of colour were powerfully apparent. He wore no vivid war bonnet, for instance, a fact that should have been reassuring, given the recent troubles between the Indians and the army. Sternberg wasn't reassured, though. The presence of a stranger in such a desolate place was one thing—it startled if it did not necessarily alarm. But that was his reaction, and he knew, had known for some years, that he could trust himself not to panic in most situations the Creator placed him in.

The trouble was how others reacted. In this case, after he had alerted the professor to the horse and rider, Sternberg wasn't sure what Cope's reaction meant.

Squinting into the dimming horizon, the great man bristled and emitted what sounded like a low growl.

Sternberg's pulse quickened. "He might just keep going," he said. "He might not come down."

Cope, never taking his eyes off the ridgetop, calmly placed his awl and knife into his pack. "We'll mark this spot and go down, just in case. Level ground will make for a level chance."

Such talk alarmed Sternberg more than the Indian did. A level chance? It was well to take precautions, he realized that, but something in the professor's tone seemed to anticipate violence. Or was this just another example of the man's astonishing confidence? After all, they were in the field collecting, scant weeks after the Sioux had killed Custer. Few men of science would have taken the risk. And the whole time they'd been in the region, Cope acted as if he'd been there several times before, that the Judith badlands were akin to his own backyard in Philadelphia. And now, too, he acted as if he'd encountered this very Indian before. Action for him seemed nothing more than a constant triggering of memory. But perhaps the professor did know the Indian; it was unlikely but possible. For, Sternberg thought quickly, don't I know him? He had no time to pursue the question.

He followed Cope down to the floor of the canyon, five hundred feet below the ridgetop. Here, on the scrub and cactus, the canyon walls rose like the sides of night itself, with only a few scattering pines capping the summits. The light of day weakened further. A strange, early dusk set in. They might have descended into the remnants of the previous night. Already, Sternberg felt the boundaries of time and place beginning to shimmer. And it did not surprise him, for now he knew that he'd encountered the Indian before.

Cope began to collect lignite out of the side of a small rock. He prepared a fire, lit it with satisfaction.

"Since the man is coming," he said, grinning, "we might as well offer him a guiding light."

Sternberg swallowed dryly. He looked up at the bare ridges. Something was very wrong. He could not determine what it was, though. After all, the professor prepared for almost every encounter as if it were the climax of some hope or dream he'd long harboured; the quality made him attractive, brought the most ordinary experience vividly alive. But dangerous? Sternberg didn't believe so. Cope was volatile of temper, but was also a Quaker, strongly averse to violence.

No, it was something about what was descending to them, something about the Indian. A chill ran the length of Sternberg's neck. The lignite fire might as well have been ice. He scanned the ridges, but knew the Indian had gone from them.

Cope spoke suddenly, almost directly into Sternberg's good ear, making him flinch.

"It feels like a time for prayer, Mr. Sternberg. I will not say this man's a hired killer, but Marsh stands on no ceremony where the ethics of his employees are concerned. Under the circumstances, prayer is particular wisdom. Besides, we have time."

Sternberg did not protest; no moment was inappropriate for prayer. Yet he could not shake the disturbing sense of an unease that had nothing to do with the fear of another man. He knew Cope had the wrong idea and wanted to tell him so, but he couldn't speak. A different order of fear was present. He could not name it, though it seemed like a herald of some greater, darker loss. Even so, he was relieved when the professor did not pull out a Bible or recite Scripture from memory. Instead, without consulting a text, Cope stood in the arising red of the fire glow, his head immobile, his eyes fixed on the flame and sparkling back its light. Sternberg's relief, however, soon dissolved at what Cope orated. The text was strange, and the great man's voice took up the strangeness, trembling with it but never breaking. The air of the canyon darkened further, though the fire remained faint, a shadow of some greater fire burning far below the earth.

"And I had a vision about the time that I was in this travail and sufferings, that I was walking in the fields, and many Friends were with me, and I bid them dig in the earth, and they did and I went down. And there was a mighty vault top-full of people kept under the earth, rocks and stones. So I bid them break open the earth and let all the people out, and they did, and all the people came forth to liberty; and it was a mighty place.

"And when they had done I went on and bid them dig again. They did, and there was a mighty vault full of people, and I bid them throw it down and let all the people out, and so they did.

"And I went on again, and bid them dig again, and Friends said unto me, 'Edward, thou finds out all things', and so there they digged, and I went down, and went along the vault; and there sat a woman in white looking at time how it passed away. And there followed me a woman down in the vault, in which vault was the treasure; and so she laid her hand on the treasure on my left hand and then time whisked on apace; but I clapped my hand upon her, and said, 'Touch not the treasure'.

"And then time passed not so swift."

Cope said nothing for several moments after he'd finished. He remained motionless, eyes blazing, fixed on the flame.

Sternberg kept looking towards the gap in the rocks where the Indian would be likely to emerge. He did not know what Cope meant by his vision, but it sent the chill down his neck again. Beneath the strange echo of the words, to grasp onto something solid, he mouthed his own simple prayer: "Lord, let this meeting be and end in peace." He shut his eyes. The fire burned almost soundlessly. He saw the faint red as if printed on his mind's black.

Cope suddenly broke the silence. "Doth thee not feel it, Mr. Sternberg? The power? What can a man not do, chosen by the Creator to lead the Way? Marsh is too late this time. The field is mine. Yea, I have not been passed over." He chuckled, grabbed his pack by its strap and stepped away from the fire.

"Professor," Sternberg began, "this is not what you ..." But he realized he wasn't speaking loudly enough. His voice trailed away. Like Cope, he trained his eyes on the gap in the rocks.

WHEN THE INDIAN APPEARED, HE WAS MOTIONLESS, HIS head and chest level. The horse moved slowly, like a vapour. Sternberg felt that if he should blink, the horse and rider would vanish. But they came on, the Indian expressionless, his skin as pale as firelight in the full sun. Unpainted as before, garbed only in a buckskin cloth, he carried no weapon. Sternberg instinctively looked for one, but his attention was quickly drawn to the mosasaur limb hanging on a leather strap around the Indian's neck. He was stunned to see it. Bones were fragile when exposed; out of the earth, unprotected, they generally crumbled. And no matter how intelligent this strange Indian was, he would not know how to preserve and extend the life of a fossil. Yet there it hung, its tan colour smeared with what looked like dried blood. Sternberg wondered where it had travelled since the Kansas Chalk. And for what purpose?

The horse came on. Sternberg gasped. The Indian's arms were criss-crossed with dozens of vivid red cuts, his bony chest sported two violent purplish welts near the nipples. Even more

frightening, the Indian acted as if he did not see the bone hunters, though now the horse was only feet away. The man's thin
face and sharp features were even paler than Sternberg remembered, and his black eyes looked farther and farther in the distance. No doubt he'd taken part in the recent violence, perhaps
had killed some soldiers and settlers himself. Yet violence was
not the energy emanating from him. Bewildered, Sternberg
turned to Cope.

The professor stood with his arms crossed, his tiny pistol dangling casually from one hand. When he noticed Sternberg looking at him, he raised the gun to his lips. His eyes made a plea for
silence. Then they took in the mosasaur limb, and widened.

The Indian swayed a little as the horse stopped, then turned
away from the lignite fire. His eyes were open and filling fast
with the coming darkness. The limb dangled as if pointing at
something in the earth. Trembling, Sternberg saw the bright
ochre outline of a hand on the horse's flank. Looking back up,
he met the Indian's blank gaze. Only it wasn't blank. It was seeing something, just not the fire or the two men beside it. Yet
Sternberg felt the look enter him, as if to search, and then pass
through and rise to the star spaces. Sternberg felt the chill, then
the strange sensation of falling, though the Indian never moved
and there was no sound of rushing air.

When the Indian spoke to him, his lips not moving, the
words flowed straight into Sternberg's good ear, softly. You will
see her again. They were sad beyond any words he'd ever heard,
aching with sorrow. Yet they were a kind of gift too. Sternberg
leaned towards them. You will see her again.

Cope's voice yanked him back.

"Fasting for visions," he said quietly. "It is their way. Self-mu-
tilation."

The horse and rider had gone by. Sternberg felt as if the clothes had been flayed from his body. The words … he couldn't shake the feeling their darkness was his too. He couldn't swallow. Who? Who would he see?

"But the *Clidastes velox* paddle," Cope went on. "A fine specimen. Did thee note it? Like one of those you sent me from the Niobra chalk. Strange."

Sternberg nodded. He opened his mouth to tell the story, but Cope had turned back to the steep black slopes.

"I fear we have lost the light, Mr. Sternberg. We must wait for dawn."

Sternberg looked to the top of the ridge. Stars were faintly showing, the black between them like the black of the Indian's gaze.

"A reprieve from the thieves of Yale," Cope grinned coldly. "But it cannot last. If the Lord had but given us eyes for seeing at night. Come, Mr. Sternberg, we are some distance yet from camp."

Sternberg helped to gather up their tools. He looked once in the direction the Indian had gone, but saw only stone. And the Indian's words scratching out an epitaph behind him and before him, though he could not be certain of the names recorded there.

# 1916

EVEN BEFORE SHE AND GEORGE REACHED CAMP, LILY sensed that something unusual was about to happen. A sliver of sky to the west pulsed vividly, though the day had been dark, building to a storm, rainbursts coming and going since the mid afternoon. Now leopard prints of wet walked the bare rock, then vanished under the rising, scouring wind. Huge black clouds shunted heavily.

Lily could hardly raise her head to look at them. She was exhausted, walked without feeling the sensation of walking. Her eyes were sore, crusted with the blowing grit. All she wanted was a few hours of sleep, enough to give her the strength to rise again after dark and finish the excavation of the skull. It was so close to being removed that it had begun to glow for her, and she could not understand why the Sternbergs and Kim-Lu and everyone in Steveville did not rush to investigate the radiance.

They came down past a row of hoodoos. Lightning cracked and the thick gloam lifted for a few seconds, replaced by a pallid shimmer that brought the hoodoos into stark relief—they seemed to be walking away from camp. Lily watched them collapse back into the early evening's dullness, and felt a quick stab of anxiety. The rolling thunder seemed to come from inside her. She sniffed at the metallic air, then looked at the vivid red on the horizon. All at once she knew that the skull had to be removed as soon as possible. But could she wait for the Sternbergs to retire first? Could she sleep even just a few hours to give her the wakefulness necessary for the final, delicate moments of excavation?

Their arrival at camp quickly answered her questions.

At the cook tent, Kim-Lu stood, angrily dishing out plates of food for Charlie and Levi. The smell of pork and beans overpowered the faint metallic taste in the air.

"Your father still not come yet," Kim said with a scowl. His small, owl-alert face seemed poised to strike at something. "He should be back."

Charlie, still as stone, did not even turn to face the cook's worry. "You know what he's like, Kim," he said calmly. "As long as there's any daylight …"

Kim smashed his wooden spoon against the side of the pot. Lily jumped back.

"You not stupid! Why you not understand? Your father very sick! He should not be alone."

Charlie turned his broad, intelligent face to George. Though he did not wink, it was clear to Lily that Charlie was mostly amused by the cook's concern. After all, Kim-Lu's fierce attachment to Mr. Sternberg was often a source of humour in camp. For Lily, however, the cook's loyalty had been only a source of guilt of late. For Mr. Sternberg, as far as she knew, had never nursed Kim back to health from the brink of death.

She looked at the three brothers. They stood together now, in profile, waiting for Kim to hand over the full plates of food. Lily saw their exhaustion. Another long day spent blasting and then heaving massive rocks into the valley to clear space around

256

the matrix of a specimen, followed by the tedious backbreak of plastering, no doubt made concern for their father a vague subject. Lily often noted George's hands, scraped and bloody with the task of applying plaster to the undersides of rock. How like their father the sons all were in the quality of patience. She looked at them again, and an image came to her of another day, another lineup of profiles, when she had stood beside the brothers as a young man carrying a book approached over the floodplain with Mr. Sternberg. A young man with blue eyes.

She looked over her shoulder at the slowly fading hoodoos.

Lightning raised them out of the gloom again, and caused Kim-Lu's voice to tremble.

"And a big storm coming. You know your father come back before now if he alright. You know it! Why you stand here?"

Charlie sighed as he extended his hand. "Alright, Kim. Just let us have something to eat and we'll talk this over. I suspect by the time we're finished, he'll be back, probably with a map sketched out showing a couple of complete skeletons new to science." George and Levi laughed, and the three brothers soon rode that sound to the fireside.

Lily followed. The wind gusted several broad cottonwood leaves in her path and she felt that same quick leaping in her blood. A big storm? Then there wouldn't be time for sleep. She'd have to go sooner than that. After the meal, perhaps. She could excuse herself, head for her tent, then sneak away.

She sat with the brothers at the fire.

"A good day?" Charlie asked George, stretching his legs towards the warmth.

George grunted. "We can take it out tomorrow. If we can get the horse and wagon down."

"Why not? How's the road?"

"Narrow. But maybe just wide enough."

Kim emerged out of the dusk and stood, hands on hips, between the speakers.

Charlie bent to his food again, spooned in several mouthfuls quickly.

"Well?" Kim finally said.

Charlie laughed. He'd always enjoyed the cook's over-protectiveness of their father, because, as he said, it was so unnecessary.

"All right, Kim. We'll talk about it, if it'll make you happy."

"Talk? Look at the sky! Your father not here yet and you want to talk?"

Still jovial, Charlie played along. "What do you want us to do? You know Father doesn't like us going into the badlands at night."

This was too much for Kim. "Then I go alone!" he snapped. "I get my lantern!"

An even louder roll of thunder followed the cook's departure. Some large splats of rain fell, turning the smell of the earth even heavier. Lily looked up. All the light had gone in the west. There were no stars. The dark flowed like a river.

"Maybe he's right," Charlie said, chewing another spoonful. "Father's not been himself, we know that."

Levi nodded. "He ought to be back by now. We'd better go."

Lily's eyes darted from one brother to the next. Was she to be included in the search?

"George," Charlie said, rising, "why don't you and Levi follow the river? I'll walk up a ways higher, head towards the quest site. He likes it there."

258

Lily made no sound at all, yet the eldest brother still turned his eyes on her. "You can come with me, if you like. I suppose you've had enough of George by now."

His smile was slight, the humour almost a reflex. Lily could not tell, she never could tell, what any of the Sternbergs were really thinking or feeling. As Scott had said to her once, they were so intent on their work that they had become part stone. But Lily did not remember that he had meant this as a criticism.

She regarded the three brothers closely. Perhaps Charlie would be the easiest to slip away from. His humour, at least, made him less intimidating than the other two. And George certainly had had the most opportunity to read her mind, if he had ever been interested in doing so. No, she didn't think slipping away from Charlie would be difficult. Only ... if Mr. Sternberg really was in trouble, if he had fallen or become disoriented ... Another pang of guilt cut through her, because she did not doubt what she was going to do.

The rain stopped. Now only the wind touched the surface of the earth. Kim's lantern bobbed towards them as if drifting on water.

Charlie explained to the cook that he had convinced them.

Kim grunted with satisfaction and handed a small bag to Charlie. "Take this. When you find him, he need to eat."

"Give some to George too then. He and Levi are going along the river."

The cook hurried back to his tent.

Charlie spoke matter-of-factly to his brothers. "You might as well follow him. You're going that way." Then he smiled. "Come on, Lily. No rest for the wicked."

The wind tore at the clouds. Somewhere the stars swam in

great curves. Lily's heart beat faster as she kept to Charlie's heels, following quickly through the hoodoos. She could already see her hands raising the skull.

# 1916

AT DAYLIGHT, A THICK, CLINGING MIST OBSCURED EVERY-thing. Scott watched it rise from the broken earth of no man's land, convinced it was smoke from some shell he hadn't heard fall. That was possible, even likely. The battlefield was a quagmire. It had rained heavily for three days, almost without cease. Scott's unit might well have been in the one trench in the whole salient that had any ground to it. Scott was numb, exhausted. He could barely feel his limbs. Hunger defined him even more than terror. His uniform was sodden flesh, his rifle a bone that he'd pulled from his pack, free of the blue-clay bones he still struggled to preserve. Rain tapped his steel helmet, sluiced off its brim. He peered out through the blurred interstices at the mist, then turned slowly to the sea of mud at the rear.

The ground seethed. It was like a tilted saucepan of burning oil; every drop of rain hissed and added to the creeping mist. But Scott could make out some faint heaps and mounds among the craters. He turned to Wheeler.

"I'm going to have a look. Maybe I can salvage something for us."

Wheeler, all the colour drained from his face, just nodded.

Scott's words seemed to rouse him from sleep or another prayer; it was impossible now to tell the difference.

There were no officers around. The sergeant in charge of the platoon hadn't been seen in several hours. Scott acted on his own initiative.

After the night's heavy shelling, after slogging over wasted ground, avoiding rifle fire, trying to establish new trench positions, again and again, ignoring the cries of the wounded, their own and the Germans, Scott found the morning's relative quiet especially unnerving. He could not believe it signalled the end of something; it had all the character of a horrible pause. It ticked like the watch on that dead soldier's wrist that he couldn't put out of his mind. When had that been? An hour ago? Three days? He couldn't feel his own wrists. But he felt the ticking of the dead in his skin. He shook all over to rid himself of the sensation. If he moved, it would be better.

So he scrambled through the mist and mud. The dim shapes turned out to be a number of dead South Wales Borderers. Scott discovered that they had full packs. He looked in their mess tins and found MacConachie rations, a tin of jam and, in one pack, a full loaf of bread. Unfortunately, the canteens were empty. No matter; there was water enough for tea, once you boiled the hell out of it. He shuddered, remembering how, after using water from one shell crater for a day, he'd watched a dead German float up to the surface.

He gathered what he had found in his arms and scrambled back to the trench.

In a few moments, Wheeler, Macpherson, a tall fellow named Meggert, and a skinny, grinning Cree Indian from the Far North nicknamed "Eagle Eye" for his great talents as a sniper, had gathered around. Somebody had a tommy cooker, so they boiled water for tea and heated the meat rations. In the meantime, they cut away the green mould from the outside of the bread and ate the centre. It wasn't much food, but they were happy to get it.

They ate in silence. The light came on, grey, watery, and the rain kept falling. Meggert looked over the parapet and saw a dead officer.

"Look at them boots," he sighed pleasurably. Then he scowled at his own torn, flapping excuses for footwear. "He won't need them anymore, those beauties."

"Don't! Don't!" Wheeler grabbed at his shoulder. "It's bad luck, robbing the dead."

"Bad luck?" The tall man frowned, as if the very idea of luck had long ago been killed in him. He pulled away and climbed over the trench. The others watched him twist and wrench the boots off the corpse. A minute later, he returned with them and pulled them on, grinning savagely.

They drank their tea in silence, rain burbling in their cups. They squatted around the cooker as if it was a campfire.

Scott looked at the worn, unshaven faces. "Poor Mac," he thought, and hoped again that the army would somehow take pity on him for his advanced years. He'd fought well, and long enough. Let him go home to his family, to his daughter.

The shelling resumed.

"You see!" Wheeler glared at Meggert. "I warned you, didn't I?"

The tall soldier's face darkened guiltily. He looked down at the boots for a few seconds, then shrugged. "What's done is done. Can't put 'em back on."

The shelling began as it had ended an hour before, sporadically, but with the persistence of water torture. Often, the shells landed in so much mud that the explosion was mostly a loud splash and a kind of fiercer rainstorm pelting.

Scott saw that there was nowhere to go and nothing to do. He remained hunched around the cooker, waiting for the meat to heat through. He had long since given up any belief in the grand purpose of the war. The fighting just had to be endured until, somehow, it would end. If it would end. Of late, he'd met soldiers whose gloomy belief in the permanence of the war was no longer unspoken. One, a bespectacled stretcher-bearer nick-named "Professor" because he was always at a book when not on army duty, simply floated the idea one night that the future might always be like this, that there'd never be peace.

"Not until all the fighting men are killed," he said with a grimace. "But then I suppose they'll start drafting the women." He laughed, and everyone preferred to believe that he was joking, even though his words, given the reality of trench life, seemed a fair enough prophecy.

"Did you know," he went on, "that a fellow could walk from the North Sea to the Alps and never once stick his head above ground?"

Macpherson, no doubt depressed by the possibility of never being a civilian again, had had enough. "Now who'd want to do a damned fool thing like that!" he flashed, as if the Professor was seriously contemplating it.

Scott tried to picture the stretcher-bearer's sardonic expression, but it was gone like so many others in the rictus of agony. The Professor had been riddled with bullets one night while taking a wounded man out of a shelled pillbox. Now his body lay in the mud under a wooden cross hung with his identification disk. Christ, when was that?

Another whump and a long tremble in the earth, as if the ground were a bedsheet being shaken out. Mud splattered down, but no bodies, no half-crazed shepherd boys. Scott wondered if he'd made it back to his regiment all right. He'd had time, at least, about an hour without shelling. Scott had had to peel him off. But the boy was sensible enough, more sensible than many much older, and he understood as well as any veteran that a man's best chance lay with sticking to his regiment. He had run off along the trench as if in pursuit of one of his uncounted flock.

The shelling grew heavier, but the individual sounds could still be picked out. We'll wait for an officer, Scott plotted. Stay together, wait for orders. He knew that was the only sensible plan, but, as always, sense was a rare commodity in a time of tension.

Meggert, the tall soldier, suddenly shouted. "We're sitting ducks! For fuck's sake!" He bolted to the rear, heading for a small ruined building off to the east.

"What's he doing now?" Wheeler groaned. "Doesn't he know?"

"I guess not," Scott interrupted, hating to hear the obvious. If a man didn't know that the Germans, and their own artillery, needed targets to aim for …

A few moments later, the ruin took a direct hit.

Cursing, the remaining soldiers scrambled towards the smoking rubble, only about thirty yards away.

"Forget it," Mac said, and hurried back.

Scott had to agree; there wouldn't be any remains.

"I warned him about those boots," Wheeler said peevishly.

Then they were all in the trench again.

Eagle Eye complained that this kind of fight wasted his talents. "I just need to get a bead on one of them spiky helmets. Not even a bead. But nothin' I can do crouched here." He grumbled mostly to himself.

The others ignored him. Snipers, on either side, made most men uncomfortable. But they weren't looked down upon as much as the artillery; at least the snipers knew what it was to be at the front. They didn't get any luxuries. And, Scott believed, it couldn't be pleasant to kill the way they did, no matter how much they seemed to enjoy it.

Having shared the food and finished their tea, the soldiers took their former positions along the trench. Eagle Eye lingered a while behind Mac, to bum a cigarette.

Scott heard the crack of the high-velocity gun and yelled "Watch it!" as he pressed into the trench wall. The shell buried soundlessly just in front of the trench, throwing an avalanche of mud over the parapet.

Everything fell silent. Scott could not move. He was buried in the mud, but fortunately his rifle had landed pointing straight up, the bayonet creating a narrow shaft. Air flowed along it to where Scott's head rested at the butt of the rifle. All was dark. So he kept his eyes closed.

Then he heard voices.

They sounded at once very far away and as if they were coming out of Scott's own mouth. But he didn't even dare to move his lips. Any movement might cave in the thin tube of air the rifle and bayonet had formed.

The sound of digging came faintly to him. Scott's mind reeled. What if they found Eagle Eye first and he was dead? They might not dig any further. Their position, too, was precarious.

It was torture not to be able to move or shout. He lay stiffly, breathing in the wet earth. The digging became a grim clockwork. Again, he felt the blood pound in his wrists. It threatened to burst his skin.

Other voices broke through. He heard Wheeler's name shouted. Then Wheeler's voice screamed "Scott! Scott!" The digging scraped and squelched louder.

I might die like this, Scott realized, and panic tightened down on his bones. Not this way, not like this! He imagined that he'd already stopped breathing, that he'd never even know if the men had found him. He had to keep himself from shaking, try not to gasp, be calm …

A spade struck his boot. He wiggled a toe, heard someone shout "Here! One of them's here!" Then the digging resumed, slower, more carefully.

Finally, arms pulled him free of his clutching grave. Scott shook the earth and mud from his limbs, then, shakily, sat down. No one spoke to him, not even Wheeler. The digging resumed.

Scott shivered the whole length of his body. Though chilled, he felt sweat run off his brow; his face was slick with it. He was on the verge of vomiting.

They brought Eagle Eye up. He was limp, his mouth dribbling mud. They lifted the body gently over the parados and covered the face with an empty sandbag.

Wheeler came over and sat beside Scott. His face was mud-splotched, resembled a mahogany globe. He didn't say anything except "Poor Eagle Eye," and shuddered, looking towards the corpse.

The shelling kept on. After a few moments, Scott stood and walked over to where Mac crouched below the parapet.

"I'm starting back," he said.

Mac just nodded. Wheeler, who had followed closely, said, "Come on, Mac, we'll all go."

The others had disappeared along the trench. No relief had come, no runner with a message.

Scott moved off, his head lowered into the grey light. As he hurried forward, he thought he heard the old bones clack in his kit. It was, strangely, a sound of promise, as if they said, "We will not be buried again." He carried them as if they were the bones of his own child and it was his responsibility to survive long enough to join them to their living flesh.

# 1916

THE FLOOR OF THE MINE SHAFT WAS A FINE, SOFT BLACK. Sternberg, shocked awake by a rolling clap of thunder, sat against the wall, breathing heavily, running the dust through his fingers. The light of day crept only a few inches into his shelter. He looked sadly towards the dimness. Maud had gone from him again. And there'd been no kiss, no goodbye of any kind. Just as it had been twenty years before.

With difficulty, he stood and limped to the mine entrance. Before him, the badlands lay in shadows. The river was a thin strip of rippling buffalo fur. A great black thunderhead hung in the western half of the sky. Sternberg could taste the brassy shiver in the air. He needed to get back to camp, but he felt no urgency. The day had been wasted.

Another roll of thunder. Or was it George still at work, blasting stone?

Sternberg heard a shifting behind him and turned.

It was Cope. His blue eyes were brighter and more piercing than Sternberg remembered. The great man's jaw was fixed hard, his nostrils flaring. Behind him on wall-length dark shelves, the black eye-sockets of two dozen skulls seemed to glare in support of the man who had described them for science. Time dissolved again. It was the end of the last century. Sternberg, twenty years younger than he was in the Red Deer, a mature, experienced bone sharp of forty-seven, a father of four, nonetheless stood nervously fingering the brim of his hat, trying to be strong. But already he felt his will weakening, even though he had prepared long for this resistance, had mounted sound arguments against it.

"I tell thee," Cope said, his voice low but bristling with suppressed energy, "there is a stratum rich in fossils between the Permian and Triassic. And it will yield fauna not known before."

Sternberg swallowed. "Professor, I went over the territory with the utmost care in the summer of '82. It was barren …"

"To the northwest! Can thee not hear now with thy sound ear, man? To the northwest, I say!"

It was no use. It had never been any use. Sternberg sighed. Cope's eyes, though living, became as the black holes beyond him, which held that immense, silent eternity of the western night that Sternberg knew he'd soon be leaving for again. It was as if the eyes of the beasts and the eyes of the greatest scientist in America had blended at the command of the same god into an incomprehensible and wearying distance.

Cope did not move, he did not blink. Sternberg watched the wall of the study darken to the western night, until suddenly he was there, the denuded red clay bluffs of the Texas badlands arrayed around him like the breathing, fire-lit forms of the extinct creatures whose bones they held.

# 1975

"STEVEVILLE?" THE CAB DRIVER REPEATED THE WORD dully. He turned his middle-aged, unshaven face towards her.

Lily nodded, resolved not to offer any explanations.

The man dropped his hands from the steering wheel. Slowly, kindly, he spoke. "I'm sorry, Ma'am. But there's no such place anymore. I mean, I know where Steveville used to be, but there's nothing there now. No buildings. Just rock."

"Ah yes," Lily replied calmly. The information meant little to her, for Steveville was not where she needed to go; she thought only that the name would give the driver a general sense of direction.

"I can take you to Patricia. Would that be okay?"

The poor man, Lily considered, he looks so distraught. How could she make this easier for him?

She smiled, turned slightly to meet his wet brown eyes. He had yet to put the cab in gear. Outside the windshield, a few farm trucks whirled up dust along the road. The afternoon sun, small and blazing, had begun the second half of its journey across the sky. Scattered black clouds hung low in the west. A breeze rippled the flag above a used car dealership.

"I once lived in Steveville," she began. "Many, many years

ago. I didn't know it was gone. But it's fine. What I really want to see again is the badlands. I don't suppose they're gone as well?"

He laughed, obviously relieved. "No, Ma'am, they're still there. I can drive you right into the park, if you like. There's a road now. You won't even have to get out if you don't care to."

"Oh no, I care to," she replied, rather more irritably than she'd intended. "I plan to walk around. You see …" She paused, considering. "When you reach my age, there's a lot of remembering you wish to do."

The driver widened his soft eyes at her. He really was a pleasant man. Lily made a mental note to tip him generously.

"Yes, I suppose there is," he said. "We'd better get started then."

Fortunately, the man was perceptive as well as pleasant. He must have sensed the importance of the trip for her, because he did not plague her with questions once he started to drive. Just to be careful, Lily kept her head turned slightly to the right to discourage conversation.

The gold-brown fields rolled by. Houses. Ranch buildings. Barbed wire. Every few miles, a herd of cows. Beef, not dairy, as she was used to seeing in the fields back home. The area hadn't changed much. The roads were improved. Had there even been a road into the badlands? No, only what the Sternbergs blasted out of the rock and laid down. Maybe a wagon trail over the prairie. It was so long ago. But she thought she recognized a few old houses. Mile by mile, time was being shed from her eyes. A vagueness crept over the land, a haze where there had once been such clarity. The haze, strangely, did not obscure what she saw, but acted as a sort of chemical into which the old images were dipped and then lifted, ready to emerge into clear shape again.

Twenty minutes later, the cab was moving swiftly over a gravel road that lay like a basking bull snake in the full sun. Now the buildings were gone. A large, official-looking sign loomed ahead. Lily just managed to read part of it before they sped past: "Dinosaur Provincial Park." That was also new.

"Almost there," the driver said quietly.

Lily felt the change in the land before she saw it. She sat straighter, leaned forward, looked beyond the short grass of the prairie. On the horizon, she saw the bare stone, the beginning and the end of everything. Then the earth gave up all pretense of softness, and even as the valley dropped shockingly away, the striated stone thrust itself heavenward. A great falling and a valiant, undefeatable rising. Lily understood what the vision was saying. Light of heart, almost floating, she made no protest when the driver took a small, slightly rising side road, and said, "There's a nice view of the whole valley from up here."

He stopped the cab on the crest and got out when she did. The wind had picked up and there was nothing to stop it now. Lily felt the surprising chill of it and tightened the cardigan at her throat. When the driver started to walk with her to the very edge of the bald rock, she stopped him.

"If you don't mind, I'd like to be alone."

He hesitated, coughed deep in his chest. His jacket flapped wildly. "Well, okay. But watch your step. There's no railing."

She left him, too entranced now by the metallic heat of the stone and the aroma of sage flowing out of the crevices to be polite.

In a few minutes, she came to the vision-quest site, the rough circle of whitish stone the Indians had used for spiritual purposes. The site was marked by an official park sign explaining its meaning, but she did not read the words. She did not need to, for she understood the energy that had brought her to the place.

The wind flung her hair out lengthwise, tugged at her purse strap. Lily looked up from the thin strands of grass fluttering over the circle of whitish stone.

Far below, half the badlands were in shade, the other half blazing. Even farther down, the river glistened silver and thin, its bankside cottonwoods adding a streak of greenery to the surrounding muted tones—grey, brown, olive, tan, ochre. Slopes, jags, towers, sheer faces. Snake-skinny trails beside the tottering, wind-gnawed hoodoos. Heat rising in waves off the fragments and scrub, rising to die in the depths of the sky's blue, which itself appeared deathless, though only hours and it too would be killed.

Lily searched the valley. She could find the place, she was sure of it, given enough time and freedom to wander. And once she'd found it, she'd simply have to wait.

She returned to the driver, asked him to drive her as far into the badlands as possible.

He looked long at her, but said nothing. The cab regained the main road and plunged deeper, winding all the way right up against the buttes and hoodoos, finally coming out to a flat area of picnic tables and firepits. To the right, the road ended abruptly at the foot of a sheer cliff. The driver stopped close to a picnic table and shut off the engine.

"If you want to walk the trails a little, I'll come with you. I promise I won't talk. But you really shouldn't go in there alone. Nobody should. But especially not at …"

Lily smiled to reassure him. "At my age? Young man, it is exactly because of my age that I intend to do just that. And alone."

"I really don't think that's …"

She narrowed her eyes and scowled at him until he looked down. Then she opened her purse, removed some bills and gave them to him.

"Thank you for your services," she said.

"I beg your pardon, Ma'am?"

"That's all I need you for. You may go now."

"Go?"

Really, had the man suddenly become dull-witted? He'd seemed so bright only moments before. She decided to appease his worrying, simply to be free of him.

"I have a lot to remember, so I'll need to be here a while. If you like, you may return for me at sunset."

A look of confusion crossed his face. "If I like? But how else would you get back?"

She sighed and snapped her purse shut. "Of course you're right. If you could please return for me at sunset, I'd be more than happy to pay you for your time both ways."

The driver blew air through his pursed lips. Finally, with a shrug, he stuffed the bills into his front pants pocket. "Do you at least have a warm jacket, Ma'am, in your suitcase? Let me get it out for you."

"Oh yes, that's kind of you, thank you." Lily had forgotten about her luggage. But she would be happy for the extra warmth. It could be surprisingly cold in the badlands once the heat of the afternoon began to fade.

The driver was clearly reluctant to leave her. She could see the struggle on his face—he was likely wondering if he should insist on waiting for her until she was ready to leave. But also, likely, he was realizing that he had a job to do and was considering whether he should force her to return with him now.

But Lily saw clearly that he was not the insistent type. To help him along, she offered a promise of caution.

"I won't go far. And I'll keep to the trails. I suspect I'll just sit here at this table most of the time."

"Well," he said slowly, "I suppose that's okay."

As soon as he smiled, Lily knew she had won.

Ten minutes later, when she was certain he had gone, she stood up from the table where she'd been resting and headed for the nearest trail.

It was approaching four o'clock in the afternoon, the summer of her eightieth year. Her bones were so young that they floated like seed off the spring grasses. Soon, very soon, the letters in her purse could turn to dust. And the skull? The skull could again be the flower it was always meant to be.

# 1896

IT WAS MID-WINTER, AN EARLY TIME FOR COLLECTING.
He'd already been here for weeks, in the northwest corner of
Texas, not far from the Oklahoma border, working the heads of
several creeks feeding into the Big Wichita River. Like all of his
work sites, the region was at once fantastic and desolate. Thousands of acres of weather-gnawed bluffs of red clay, whorled
into crumbling towers and giant beehives, spilled away to the
horizons. The rains were torrential. And when it didn't rain, the
temperature dropped and it snowed instead.

Shivering with fever, Sternberg forced himself into the
field each morning, and returned each night, empty-handed,
despondent, berating himself for not having resisted the professor's will. There was no productive bed to the northwest of
the old sites—he'd spent almost a month in fruitless labour,
tramping through the heavy, blood-coloured gumbo of the
clay, each step carrying an extra fifteen pounds of weight. To
make matters worse, his strength was already diminished by a
depressing combination of futility and fever. For once, Cope
had been wrong: there was no treasure here, only misery. It was
the loneliest and most defeated Sternberg had ever been in the
field. And all because Cope had insisted! Never one to believe

gossip, Sternberg nonetheless could not help thinking of the rumours surrounding the professor's financial affairs. Several acquaintances in the bone-hunting business claimed that Cope had squandered his entire private fortune in speculative mining ventures, ventures he'd made in order to keep besting Professor Marsh in the always fiercer hunt for the finest specimens. One source, a generally reliable man, even suggested that Cope would soon be selling off much of his personal fossil collection, which he stored, apparently to the rafters, in two Philadelphia houses. Sternberg, thinking of the eyes in the skulls massed behind Cope's indomitable will, shivered deeper in his flesh. Who could ever own such gazes after the great man himself had owned them? Truly, the dead beasts seemed like living allies. Perhaps they were, perhaps they whispered information to Cope about where to find their extinct brethren?

Sternberg tramped on wearily, eyes scanning the bluffs, and tried hard to shake off his doubts. The professor had always been right before. Unfortunately, that meant nothing to Sternberg's hired man, Harkins, a reed-thin, inveterate complainer with no interest in science and one rheumy eye that gave his wasted, grizzled face the appearance of a running canvas. Each day, Harkins attempted to start an argument, doubtless hoping Sternberg would give him an excuse to leave. After weeks of the man's relentless mutterings, Sternberg could hardly bring himself to care, nor could he really blame him. After all, two weeks before, he'd written a despondent letter to Cope, begging to be released early from his contract. Maybe Cope's response would come today or tomorrow, and relieve his suffering. Or maybe Harkins wouldn't even return from the nearest town, thirty miles distant, with the mail. Either event was likely and unlikely in equal amounts.

Sternberg struggled across the apparently boneless wastes. The heavy rain threatened to pull him under. It was like walking in a giant wound slowly turning gangrenous (for there were green concretions in the clay). He came to the sloppy remnants of a trail and followed it over a slight rise. Blinking away the rain and feverish sweat, he looked out on a natural amphitheatre, perhaps three-acres across, carved out of a mountainside and entirely denuded of soil. Eager to escape the gripping, slippery clay, he descended the side of the amphitheatre and, upon reaching the bottom, immediately stopped, all senses sharpened. After two decades working as a bone sharp, he didn't even need to see the fossils; he felt their presence all around him. It was as if a cloud was peeling back off the earth to reveal a sky brilliant with stars, some in perfect constellations and others broken and scattered.

Scant moments later, he had picked up several skulls, ranging from less than an inch to over eight inches in length. Even better, he had never seen such skulls before. Eagerly, he began to fill his canvas collecting bag, trying not to hurry, reminding himself of the long stretches of God's time during which these treasures had been lying here. The rain continued to pelt down, but Sternberg had passed beyond the simple physical facts of existence. His hands were touching origins. Time died. The canvas bag bulged. He did not hear the howl of the wind down the sides of the amphitheatre, nor the voice of the man hailing him.

At last, his bag crammed with seventy-five pounds of skulls, Sternberg turned and staggered back the way he had come. A switch had been turned on in his spirit. No man, he thought rapturously, can realize the glory of this march! Not Nebuchadnezzar, when his chariot headed the army that was carrying away the treasures of the Lord's house from Jerusalem, with the King of Judah, blinded and bound in shackles of brass, in his train. To find such a bountiful harvest in the very heart of the old fields—the great gift of the Creator, the great genius of Cope! He beamed into Harkins's bewildered face, its fluid eye, the endless weeping of the ordinary world for which Sternberg now could feel only a boundless compassion.

Harkins, perhaps sensing something of the value of the bag's contents, offered to relieve Sternberg of his burden.

Sternberg jumped back as if struck.

"Don't touch this bag! It is worth more than an equal weight in gold and I will protect it with my life!"

Harkins's good eye widened like a moon beside the rippling tide of his sick eye.

"Found somethin' good then," he muttered. "About time, I'd say."

Something good? Something good? Twelve million years, another earth! Sternberg's broadening smile was stopped only when Harkins pulled a piece of paper from his coat pocket and held it out in the rain.

"Looks like you got word from that perfesser in the east."

Of course, of course, Sternberg thought, it is in the will of the Creator to draw continually a direct line between His glory and Cope's sensitivity to it. No doubt the letter would urge persistence, faith, courage. No doubt Cope, with his uncanny attendance to the subtlest communications of Heaven, would have foreseen this moment.

But Harkins did not pass him a letter; it was a telegram.

Sternberg read it quickly. Then, his jaw unhinged, he turned and looked behind him.

"A letter come too," Harkins said, and pulled it from his coat. "That same perfesser, looks like."

280

Maybe there'd been a mistake. Maybe, somehow, the letter was written after the telegram and would cancel the awful summons. Sternberg couldn't think clearly. The bone field dazzled his blood with promises of glory unseen by man. His eyes devoured the words on the wet page:

*Your letter is very blue but you must remember that bad weather is not your fault; neither is it your fault if you find nothing when following my directions. In fact you have no occasion to be blue as to yourself, for you fill an important place in the mechanism of the development of human knowledge. Very few men pursue a more useful life than yourself ...*

Sternberg's eyes roamed down the page.

*I have personally the highest respect for your devotion to science.*

Respect. Devotion to science. The respect of America's greatest scientist. For him, Charles Sternberg, who'd never gone to college. For his devotion to science.

Sternberg raised his eyes to the red earth stretching away for miles. He swallowed hard. It wouldn't take long to get the finest specimens out. Even just another day. If he didn't do so now, who knew when he would get back and what he might lose, what the world might lose of God's greatness, in the meantime.

The telegram dampened in one hand, the letter in the other. He stood before the weeping eye of the world and tried to weigh the unweighable.

Maud, he whispered, and suddenly everything went black. He was standing in the entrance of the mine shaft, in the very pupil of that weeping eye. He leaned against the cold rock for support. Time was whirling now, faster and faster. He could barely keep his weight against the rock as he gazed into the wrack of the storm.

Maud.

Again there came a slight rustling behind him. This time, when he turned, Sternberg was not even surprised; he knew he was in the past again.

IT WAS A HOT JULY DAY IN 1897, THE DAY OF COPE'S funeral. Several men were seated around a coffin in the great man's Philadelphia study. Sternberg, now forty-eight, with grief added to grief, stepped into the scene.

Head bowed, he took his chair between Henry Fairfield Osborn and Persifor Frazer. The coffin was laid across two large study tables and covered with a dark cloth. In the centre of the cloth rested a spray of white magnolia blossoms and green leaves.

Sternberg looked around the room, curious despite himself. He had never been in Cope's residence (only his office at the Institute), though the address, 2102 Pine Street, Philadelphia, was as well known to him as his own address.

Fossils lay everywhere: on tables, windowsills, the floor, in plank crates that looked as if they'd never been opened. Skulls of various sizes, leg bones, teeth, claws—Sternberg noticed what looked remarkably like the skeleton of a horse, only in a greatly reduced size. The hallway leading out of the study was half blocked with bones, as if it were a trench leading off directly into some Western badlands. The room even smelled faintly of sage beneath the dust and shellac.

Where there weren't bones, there were books, hundreds of them, several held open with fossils for paperweights. A sturdy desk in one corner threatened to collapse under the weight of massive, leather-bound tomes. Sternberg saw it must have been where Cope did the most amazing part of his work, naming and describing thousands of species of animals, often from nothing but fragments of remains. A chair was pushed back, angled towards a large glass vivarium in one corner. Before Sternberg could see what was in it, something brushed his leg. He looked down.

A huge land tortoise, no doubt one of Cope's pets, was silently patrolling the room. Sternberg took its slow, almost respectful progress as a kind of pallbearing tribute to everything the professor had taught the world about man's fellow creatures. It even seemed to lift its eyes to the coffin from time to time.

The room was still except for the tortoise. The perfect Quaker silence stretched on. From outside came a faint rumbling. The air was muggy. Sternberg wiped his brow and fought off the urge to clear his throat. He looked back to the tank.

Some kind of reptile, sere as an autumn leaf, was circling it slowly, then rising on its forelimbs to gaze out at the desk. Every minute or so, it completed a circuit, rising again and falling back.

"*Heloderma suspectum*," Osborn whispered in his ear. "A gila monster. Many times I saw the professor get up from his desk and scratch the top of the creature's head." He sighed deeply. "Perhaps he is still looking for that friendly hand." He paused, his eyes wet. "I've had enough silence. The spirit is meant to move someone. But I have been here nearly an hour and the spirit has moved no one except the reptiles." Osborn pointed his long, aristocratic nose first in the direction of the tortoise, then the gila monster.

He cleared his throat and stood. From the pocket of his vest, he removed a small black Bible, opened it and began to read in a deep, sonorous voice.

"Where wast thou when I laid the foundations of the earth? Declare, if thou hast understanding. Who hath laid the measures thereof, if thou knowest? Or who hath stretched the line upon it?"

The air was close, soporific. Sternberg listened with his eyes half-shut. He still could not believe Cope was gone. Only fifty-six. So much work yet ahead of him, so much for his genius to do. A gust of wind dimmed the lights briefly and spattered a few drops of rain against the room's lone window. Sternberg opened his eyes. The tortoise dragged like a shield across an empty battlefield. The gila monster rose in the corner of its glass tank, as if taking the verses from Job as a sign of Cope's return.

"Whereupon are the foundations thereof fastened? Or who laid the corner stone thereof? When the morning stars sang together, and all the sons of God shouted for joy?"

Osborn closed the Bible quietly. He trained his small, intense eyes on each mourner in turn, then said, almost defiantly, "These are the problems to which our friend devoted his life."

He bowed his head for a few seconds over the coffin. Then, moving nearly as slowly as the tortoise, he left the room.

One by one, as the minutes ticked away, the other mourners followed until only Sternberg remained with Cope's body.

The wind blew stronger. The lights flickered. Sternberg wanted to pray, but felt his words would dilute the lingering tribute of Osborn's reading. Instead, he kept his head bowed and tried desperately not to think of his terrible grief of the previous summer. It was all he could do, in homage, to remember it was Cope and not Maud who lay in the coffin.

He watched the gila monster complete five more circuits.

Finally, almost overcome by the warmth, he joined the other mourners in a smaller room, a kind of parlour, heavily draped and free of bones and books.

Osborn took several long strides towards him, as if he'd been awaiting the opportunity.

"Mr. Sternberg, I believe? Henry Osborn."

Sternberg shook the extended hand, amazed by the length and thinness of the fingers. Osborn was as regal and intimidating as his reputation. One of Cope's fiercest supporters, many said he was destined to be the next great American naturalist.

"May I offer my sympathies for your own recent bereavement. Professor Cope often spoke with me of your admirable attachment to your children."

"Thank you," Sternberg said quietly. The reference to Maud's death surprised and disturbed him, given that he'd been trying so hard not to dwell on it.

"The professor thought very highly of you, in general. He would be gratified by your attendance here today." Osborn grimaced. A muscle twitched in his neck. "Few seem to fully appreciate the magnitude of this loss to science. I was almost on my own in the final days." His look darkened further. "The pain was terrible. Only someone of the professor's courage could have borne it so long. But when I heard, Mr. Sternberg, that he was self-injecting formalin to find some respite from his ordeal, I begged him to stop. Morphia and belladona, yes. But not poison."

Sternberg was stunned by these details. What he knew of Cope's latter years was general: that he'd become estranged from his wife and had lost much of his family fortune. As for the much-publicized, scandalous battle with Professor Marsh, in which each had attacked the other's reputation through the press—Sternberg had refused to read the accounts. In any case, he'd been too busy in the field, working for Cope as he had done for decades.

"Self-injections?" he asked finally. "But what illness so tortured him?"

Osborn's upper lip curled. His voice rose slightly. He seemed to be addressing the other scientists. "I will not traffic, sir, in abominable gossip. Uraemic poisoning and an enlarged prostate. That is the end of it."

Sternberg nodded. Clearly, Osborn assumed he had heard the gossip. He narrowed his gaze accusingly, and spoke in a fierce hush.

"To suggest that such a man would ever be reduced to injecting his own testes to treat a syphilitic condition. Marsh and his unending spite is behind this, sir. He has unscrupulous friends in the press. But, mark me, he will not have a clear field now that the professor has retired from it. I make that solemn vow. Ah, we must follow the hearse."

Staggered, Sternberg walked out of the house and down the front stairs. The day was damp and redolent of lilac, the sky soot-grey and torn by black clouds. Two carriages waited at the curb. The horses stood quietly, their heads lowered. At a long, rolling rumble of thunder, they looked up, huffing nervously. As he descended the stone walk, Sternberg recalled his first carriage ride with Cope, across the great western plains towards the towering mountain peaks, when the professor had taken up the reins himself from the drunken driver. Such vitality and confidence Sternberg had never known before or since. Now a carriage was taking the body of the great man to his grave.

Before Sternberg could reflect on the idea, before he had even reached the carriages, the heavens opened. Rain gushed down. He limped hurriedly out of the deluge and took a seat by the black-curtained glass. The carriage lurched forward. Rain drummed the roof. Black and wet and violence conducted Cope out of the world.

# 1916

STERNBERG STOOD AGAIN AT THE ENTRANCE TO THE MINE
shaft and watched the storm break over the badlands. Torrential
rain darkened the valley's formations in a matter of seconds,
as if a great axe had split the stone and the stone was bleeding.
Water poured over the entrance to the mine, obscuring his view.
Yet he was warm and dry, carriaged, alive, while the bones of
Maud, his parents, Uncle Wilhelm, Cope, Marsh—so many others—lay in the earth, prey to the elements, as vulnerable as the
bones of the great beasts he'd spent his life tracking.

What did any of it come to, all that energy and ambition? He
saw Cope again pulling himself up a skinny pillar by rope, hand
over hand, fifty feet in the air, to secure the grinning skull of a
sabre-tooth tiger perched mockingly on the narrow top. He saw
him jump his horse over a black crevasse in the Judith River badlands. He saw him pop stones into his mouth to taste for minerals. He saw him on his knees in a sooty railway car madly writing
a monograph for the government on dinosauria. He heard him
curse Professor Marsh, saw his eyes blaze as he read the Quaker
passage over the lignite fire, woke again to his screams as the
great lizards came to life and trampled him in the night. And
then he saw him at his desk, reaching out to scratch the head

of a gila monster, opening a telegram, putting his hand to his brow, then leaping to his feet.

My god, Sternberg cried, whirling around. My god in Heaven! It was not Cope who had delayed, Cope was not the villain. His hunger for glory was not greater than his love. And she was not even his own child. Oh Lord, forgive me … Maud! Maud!

Tears in his eyes, Sternberg saw the Indian pass by again, his words clear as the waters of Otsego Lake in Sternberg's deaf ear as well as his sound one. But they weren't words of an earthly kind; they spoke of things beyond, of darkness too vast to be heard or spoken. They promised nothing else.

He had to explain. If she was still there, as she had been there for days now, he could beg her forgiveness. That was what she had meant by God's compassion. All this was not meant to torment him, but to redeem him. Breathing rapidly, Sternberg hovered briefly before the storm, then plunged through the curtain of water.

The badlands were being scoured again. The bones rising like froth. Water rushing, carving the stone. Crack of lightning. The valley like a great pigeonholed desk of water smashed by a glittering axe. Sternberg slipped and slid, grabbed hold, fought to get his footing again. On level ground, in a flash of lightning, as he rounded a hoodoo blue as a wasp's nest, he saw her.

"Maud!"

She was running, head down, the storm trying to tear her back.

"Maud!"

He struggled to reach her, his eyes blinded with tears and rain. She was a scarf of smoke. He fought past the aching in his leg, the Indian murmuring in his ears. It was his last chance. He had to explain, to tell her why. The stone was a sheet of yellow paper on which the rain was typing the message that had come in time, the summons he had not heeded right away.

THE HEADS OF THE MEN TURNED AS ONE, AND STAYED turned as the raised cross loomed closer. No one spoke of it, though. Not even to curse it. The two carpenters, black-garbed and bareheaded, laboured on in the rain. The cross was lowered. One man began to hammer at it again. Yet the blows were just audible over the rumble of heavy guns up the line—a dull pock-pock-pock.

The company slowed as it came opposite the work yard. Scott saw a sergeant confer in whispers with a lieutenant. Then the order came to halt. The men still trained their heavy gazes on the two dark figures by the shelled house. Rain hung in beads off their steel helmets. Scott removed his helmet, shook it, placed it back on. He was past believing in such omens, though he knew the majority readily placed their fates in them. But how could this cross mean anything? Which man did it belong to? No one. Every one.

He watched the sergeant approach the carpenters. A conversation of gestures ensued. One of the Frenchmen raised his arms, palms up, in a shrug, and pointed in the direction of the farmyard. Scott followed the sergeant's gaze through a gap in the rubble, but could see nothing. Still no one spoke. The rain tapped the helmets, taking up the hammer blows that had briefly ceased.

Grim-faced, the sergeant hurried back, spoke with the lieutenant. The order was shouted to march again. Like a muddy chain, the company dragged past the farmhouse. Pock-pock-pock.

Along with everyone else, Scott kept his eyes to the right. The carpenters, like men clinging to a sinking mast, fell away. But what the one Frenchman had pointed to suddenly appeared in the open farmyard as they marched past. Scott felt the bodies tense all around him. His own, at the sight, shrank inwardly.

Hundreds of fresh crosses lay on the flattened earth, stacked haphazardly, forming a mound of broken angles. To one side, neatly stacked, were the beams out of which the crosses were fashioned. The stack was head-high.

The order came to quick-march. But Scott knew that was pointless. The message had already been received. Scott could hear the thoughts of those around him as if they had been shouted: "Must be a big push coming. We're in for it this time." And the thoughts and the words entered the heavy rain, and kept echoing with their bootsteps at each burst drop.

WHEN WAS THAT? IT MIGHT HAVE BEEN YESTERDAY, TWO days ago. In any case, the rain and the dullness hadn't let up. By now, the company knew it was in the lowlands, and to a man they knew what that meant. No stacks of fresh crosses were necessary to deepen the gloom. In the oppressive overcast, the soldiers reached a wooden plank road and halted, numbed by the sight. Battle formation, came the shouted order, which meant they'd proceed in platoons, single file, about a hundred yards between platoons.

On each side of the road, as far as Scott could see, stretched nothing but a swamp of shell holes, most of them brimmed with black water; there was not an inch of ground that had not been turned over. All along the roadsides as they progressed lay dead mules, their carcasses in various stages of decay, some green, some black, some with the eighteen-pound shells in their packs half burying them in the mud. The stench was indescribable, made worse by the implication that the corpses of men lay nearby as well.

Scott looked farther. About a mile to the northeast rose the jagged black outline of a town. It stood in the blear like the blood-clotted wing of some wounded hawk. Scott had never been anywhere with such an absence of colour. The mud here seemed black with blood, and the sky was the colour of decayed flesh. But the stench—many hands had come up to the faces of men who'd been breathing foulness for months. Some new drafts retched on the roadside.

They pushed on, grateful for the low cloud cover, which kept the shelling down. But it felt as if the Germans would open up at any time. And where could cover be found?

Finally, they reached slightly higher ground and looked out on nothing but a churned sea of mud. After a hundred more yards, they reached a sacking-curtained entrance to a resting place entirely below ground, thirty or forty feet into the earth. The steps down were concrete, slippery with the mud of previous occupants, and current ones, for it appeared that the whole battalion had sought refuge inside. The place smelled dank and musty and Scott could hear the pumps working away to keep out the water. He descended, breathing easier with each step.

Now it was night, or at least he believed so. Men slept fitfully around him, groaning, sometimes crying out. The pumps kept going, a sloshing rhythmic sound, like a heart beating in a pool of its own blood. The soldiers slept on the bare ground—a few candles threw shadows against the earth walls.

Scott dozed off and on. Waking, he kept taking letters out of their envelopes and staring at them, though it was too dark to read. He peered at each page, trying to feel the words into his consciousness. He knew the tone, if not the exact words. It was impossible not to think of never seeing home again. And though he fought the instinct, he could not keep Lily's image from his thoughts. What was she doing now? It hurt him that he could not share his suffering with her, but, like the others, he would die before telling the truth of these experiences to loved ones.

He looked beside him to where Wheeler lay, snoring softly. His once round face was much leaner and the vivid red had drained from it. For days, he'd not been himself, spoke in short bursts. Just an hour before, he'd given Scott his precious Bible, claiming "Take it. I won't need it anymore." And when Scott had demanded to know what he meant, Wheeler paled and said he knew he wasn't going to make it this time. Over Scott's protests, he pressed, urging him to write to his mother, to lie to her about the manner of his death. "Make it quick and painless, even if it isn't," he pleaded, his eyes wide.

Scott had reassured him he would, but felt hollow as he did so. Wheeler? But why should anyone be able to resist the oppressive atmosphere forever? He'd held up better than most, and for longer. Yet the young man's sudden fatalism was more ominous to Scott than any sight of fresh crosses or dead mules. He'd calmly placed the Bible into his pack, where it rested among the letters and bones.

Now he closed his eyes. Soon they would try to take a ridge, some point of ground lower than even the smallest hill in the badlands. A man screamed in his sleep. Scott saw blood flowing through the hoodoos, beating against the bases of them. A nighthawk circling, vast-winged, bodies floating in mud and sinking, the earth falling away in front of him, a red morning breaking over silence, then nothing but black.

THERE WERE NO COMMUNICATION TRENCHES, SO ADVANC-
ing to the battle area was over open ground, in darkness. The
rain fell harder. Slipping, gasping, Scott kept up with the platoon. Eventually they reached the front trench, which wasn't a
trench at all, but a series of shallow, connected shell holes.

Dawn broke. Scott peered into no man's land. A few yards
away, on the muddy mound on which he too lay, a pair of boots
stuck up. Just beyond them, another partly buried booted foot
and a shattered Lewis gun completed the mound's refuse. He
raised his head slightly. The dead lay everywhere, mostly Canadians. The pink dawn light touched the dead coldly. Suddenly a
bullet swished overhead. Scott ducked. It must have come from
the shattered wood beyond the corpses. He'd seen it briefly, a
dense blackness, but no longer of trees—they were all behead-
ed. The trunks, little more than rags of dark, ranged from a few
feet to ten-feet high. But that was cover enough for snipers.

Faintly, some groans drifted out of the corpses. The living
on their way to slow death. For once, the sniping proved a blessing—Scott did not want to look out at the carnage. It was torture
enough to breathe it in.

The morning was cool, autumnal. The trees had shed their
leaves. Despite himself, Scott smiled at the black humour, but
he had no desire to share the joke with anyone. He crouched
in the narrow trench and grimaced as the desultory shelling
intensified. Most of the shells pitched about thirty or forty yards
behind him, rumbling as they went over. Vivid bursts of red
streaked the pink horizon. Gradually, the range shortened and
the shells began to burst closer, splashing up geysers of mud,
spraying burning chunks of metal in all directions.

As the barrage pounded, the men began chain-smoking.

There was no other way to ease the tension. Instinctively, the soldiers moved closer together, until they were touching, as the trench hole was deeper in one corner. Wheeler, right in that spot, was the only one who could comfortably stretch out. Next to him was Macpherson, then Scott, then a corporal, another man, a new draft who'd hardly spoken a word since his arrival the week before.

All the faces were tight. Spirals of smoke climbed as if their mouths were on fire. Wheeler was madly writing on a scrap of paper—was it his will, Scott wondered. Perhaps a letter to his mother. The corporal asked him to move so that he could stretch his legs in the corner. He had to shout the request. Wheeler shouted back, nodding.

"Okay, just another minute!"

The sky shrieked. Only a split second of sound. There came a blinding flash. Scott felt a blow on his shoulder, found himself buried up to his armpits. His first thought was a kind of wild joy—"I'm alive, and I've probably got a blighty. I'm out of it!"

But he was soon dug out and discovered that he'd caught a bit of shrapnel in his arm—it hardly even drew any blood. Nearby, the corporal, bloody faced, was screaming so loudly that Scott felt certain the Germans could hear him. Macpherson was okay, sat trembling to one side of a fresh mound of earth. The quiet one lay dead with a head wound—he looked almost the same as he had in life. The other man, too, lay still. But it was soon discovered that he was unconscious and could be taken out with the corporal.

Scott shouted at Macpherson. "Where's Vic!"

Open-mouthed, Macpherson pointed to the corporal. He still lay where the impact had thrown him, partly covered by the same fresh mound of earth, screaming through the blood for someone to help him out.

"No! Wheeler! Vic!"

Macpherson nodded dumbly, pointed again at the mound.

Some men from another platoon scrambled over to help. The Germans kept taking occasional potshots. The mound was dug into. Scott turned up a completely flattened helmet. It turned out to be Wheeler's. His head, severed from the trunk, rolled up with another man's shovel blade. The man staggered, looked as if he would pass out. But the digging had to continue. Somehow the corporal's legs had been tangled around Wheeler's body, which was shredded and bloody. Scott managed to disentangle the wounded man, careful not to touch the torn trunk of his friend. His adrenalin surged.

With help, he pushed the quiet soldier over the back of the trench. It was hard to believe that he and Wheeler were the same: dead. Then, Scott helped throw a scattering of earth over Wheeler's head and body. There was nothing else to be done. The last Scott saw of his friend's mortal remains, the head lay face-down near the hip, like a trophy.

The shelling intensified. The men threw themselves to the earth, clutching at it with their fingers, then clenching their fists until the flesh broke. All day, Scott tightened his leg muscles, jaw muscles, anything to keep control. He didn't think of Wheeler lying in the ground nearby, or of home. Only the interminable rumble and flash, the swishing of snipers' bullets, the fear of another direct hit, reached him. He managed at some point to wash down a bit of biscuit with some gasoline-flavoured water, but that was all.

When the dark began to rise from the earth, he heard it tearing off the fresh corpses. And the cries of the wounded and slowly dying? If they were lucky, and he knew many of them wouldn't be, it would be the last change of sky they'd have to endure.

He lay, tensing, as the black closed around him like stone.

LILY CAUGHT HER BREATH. A FEW FEET IN FRONT OF HER, Charlie clung like a fly in a web of rain, his body pressed tight to a sandstone slope. Then, slowly, he began to move, spray spiraling off his shoulders. Lily lowered her head like his and plunged forward until they had both reached the scant shelter of an overhang. The lantern light, which had lengthened like a flickering sunbeam, resolved itself into a dim lump of yellow. Below them, Lily thought she could hear the current raging at the banks of the river. And that same current was tearing the skull out of her hands.

Water gushed off the overhanging rock.

Soberly, Charlie said they'd better not wait it out.

The wind quickly smothered his words. Just then, the sky tore open with a long ripping roll and a terrific clap that brought Charlie's shoulders down a foot.

"We'll climb towards the quest site!" he shouted, not even looking at her as he swung his body and the lantern into the elements.

Lily followed, half-running in a crouch. The rain clawed at her skin. A cliff rose up like a black gate. As soon as the shivering yellow lamplight vanished around it, she turned and, kicking across the cherty fragments, vanished amongst the hoodoos in the opposite direction.

ZERO HOUR AND HEAVIER RAIN. SCOTT HEARD THE SHRILL whistle and pushed up off his belly. In the slanting half-dark, the dead appeared, each a knife-gash in the flesh of the earth. He picked his way slowly through them, eyes doggedly searching out a route. At the edges of his vision, bodies collapsed without sound, as if deciding to swim away on the deluge. He imagined that they were clawing at him, trying to drag him down before they gave up and slipped free.

But he could not hear their cries, even if they came. The horizon behind him had burst into fire as thousands of guns began the barrage. It was as though the dawn had been reversed, violently, the sun flaring and cracking as it forced its new path up in the west. New, except the war had been on for years.

Scott winced at the piercing whine of the thousands of shells passing over in the slag sky. A few seconds later, the earth erupted in shreds, and he started his slow walk over the churned-up ground, between bodies, where he could manage it. He reached a flooded shell hole glaring at him like a sick eye. He went around it. Strangely, the day lightened, though the rain kept pelting. Slipping, yet staying on his feet, he reached a narrow trench filled to the brim with dead Germans. How much neater they were at collecting their dead, he thought, jumping over them, chemical smoke in his mouth like a barbed bit.

It was a creeping barrage, lifting about twenty to thirty yards a minute. The plan was to reach the German lines before they could reorganize, which meant risking being shelled by your own artillery. Shell fragments splashed in the marshy ground all around Scott, but none hit him. All of a sudden, he realized he was alone. At least he couldn't see any others. The rain fell harder; it was strange not to hear it. What he could hear, or thought he could, was the clack of the bones in his pack.

Reaching the black wood, he realized the sound was machine-gun fire. Already! His solitude ended as quickly as it had begun. With others, he followed a sunken farm road and reached an enemy dugout. Two men collapsed from shots fired out of the entrance. Bombs were hurled at it. A Lewis machine-gunner emptied a whole magazine down the dugout steps.

The Germans poured out, hands raised. From the far bank of the road where he'd crouched, Scott watched them come, grey, thick as stunned wasps. They appeared weaponless.

Then some of the drafts began shooting. One after another, grey figures collapsed until the vets put a stop to it. The prisoners were led back, straight into their own counter-barrage.

That shelling stopped. The Germans would not shell their own positions; they had to wait to estimate the depth of the advance. But far above, the swishes and shrieks of countless shells continued. They were invisible, moving too fast. Scott rose, walked on through the wood, weird, jagged shapes blacker than the rain, smoke rising from them as if they breathed.

The crackle of machine guns stopped him. Bullets clotted the air, rivalled the raindrops for numbers. More bodies collapsed around him. But he kept on, seeing no option.

His lungs burned, as though his blood had heated and had begun to press against his insides. The stunted, smoking trees blurred. He saw a shallow shell hole and ran for it, diving in as a bullet ripped into his pack, almost swinging him around.

With his entrenching tool, he tried to throw up some more cover, but instead dug into the grey uniform of a dead German seething with maggots. He pressed flat. It was difficult to look around as bullets were flopping into the earth at the back of the shell hole and the machine-gun fire maintained its relentless pace.

But once the sharp crack-crack had fallen to a lower tone, he peered out. He lay on the edge of the wood, the ground sloping down towards the Germans and open country, a flooded marshy area of dark blobs, which he supposed were concrete pillboxes. No Canadians were in sight. No Germans either. It was easy to believe that everyone was dead, the whole human race, all life. Yet the shells screamed overhead and the machine guns spattered sporadically. A few bullets smacked into his pack. Did they smash the bones? He nestled lower, surprised that he no longer cared. He could see no way out, except to run the gauntlet of the machine guns. But that was suicide.

Some time later, a green flare shot up to his right, then another. The machine gun fire slacked off. The flares died. He took the chance, rose out of his cramped position and sprinted down the slope at the wood's edge.

THE LAND DRANK THE STORM LIKE A THIRSTING MAN. Long weeks of dryness, relentless heat, made for wild excess. Water coursed through every channel, carved new ones, until it seemed the ancient Cretaceous Ocean must return, turning back millions of years in fifteen minutes. The river's surge seemed a hunger urged on by the mineral formations and grotesque shapes surrounding it. What wasn't badlands now? What wouldn't be stripped to its essence and flooded with tropical tides? The clocks of the sleeping ranchers whirled backwards, the watches exploded on the side tables. Rock to water to mud to boundlessness. Huge bodies with black-red eyes the size of a man's skull rolled by, drifting, sinking lower. Towering redwoods and cypresses reared up on the shore. A terrible hungering scream. A shriek and a plummet out of the sky. Blood and flesh in the teeth. In the claws. Swamp grass fibrillating like part of a great gill. Half of the earth breathing in its own bloody water. And silence pounding and pounding the night-void. The terrible-boned before-God, invisible everywhere, clawing down the limits of the limitless stars. And water the hush, and water the cradle, and water the source, and water the way back. Gone the golden plains, the grass-fat beast, the red stalk of the scheming appetite, gone the white smoke of the new ravage. And water always the way back.

Lily scrambled down the slope in the ankle-deep waters, sometimes putting her hand to the sliding fragments underneath to stay upright. It was like thrusting her bones into a black mirror. Each time, she drew a sharp breath but kept going, quickening her pace as much as possible.

Scott ran, head down, the mud alive beneath him, a grey mass, slippery, churned. His gas mask flailed. He gritted his teeth against the machine-gun fire, thick as the rain. His heart thrashed. He was running with the contours of the land, as if on the slow rolling waves of some hidden ocean, running with the black coming down in dust over his shoulders and the earth swelling with its stored heat, running as if his bones were flickers of fire.

Lily touched the hoodoo's side. It was rough, warm. She traced out the name, but the stone did not take the letters. In all directions, the cenotaphs rose blank around her, as if the deaths had been forgotten. I've come, she whispered, her eyes on the wilderness of stone. I'm here.

Sternberg froze. He looked into his hands. They had done so many wonderful things, for God, for man, for science. They had given him an honoured place in the world. It was all he had wanted, all Cope had wanted for him. He looked for his daughter through the pelting storm. My god, my god! His hands covered his eyes. Then he dropped them, and looked for her again.

She reached the site. It was underwater. The skull, if it remained, would be clinging like a starfish to the rock. She dropped to her knees and thrust her hands into the flowing black.

Maud was on her knees, searching for something, just as he had searched in the Texas badlands, just as he had gone on searching.

He shouted her name.

Her distraught face turned towards him. Her hands were empty, palms up, as if in a prayer that the storm had broken apart.

Scott fell, mud in his open mouth, mud thick, sloppy as entrails. Hitting ground, his eyes open, streaming earth and blood. To his shock, he passed through, mud flailing off him like rain, and suddenly stood upright on solid stone, an evening of sage-scent cooling his bloodless brow.

He walked on, his hands out, open, over the ash-grey deposits, past the fluted sandstone towers, downward, to where the woman knelt, her head bowed over a small hole in the cracked clay, her hands also open, around the hole, as if to be warmed. The weight of his pack had gone. He drifted down, his hands open to give or receive.

Lily watched him approach through the blank monuments. She felt the skull dissolve to a fine powder as he took her hand and lifted her to face him.

Flesh rotting. Bones sinking.

Sternberg fingered the cold dark air, forced himself up, his legs weak.

Fire. Earth break. The bones sinking.

Something or someone was raising him to his life. Child, he murmured, and looked to the sky.

Cloud low and black and fast. Buffalo herd shadow.

Lightning. Sky fossil.

And the eyes of the dead and the eyes of the living.

Sixty million buffalo. Heads turning as one, like a storm.

Breastworks of stars.

A hundred buffalo.

The Western Front.

Cataclysm.

Silence.

Since the Red Morning of Time.

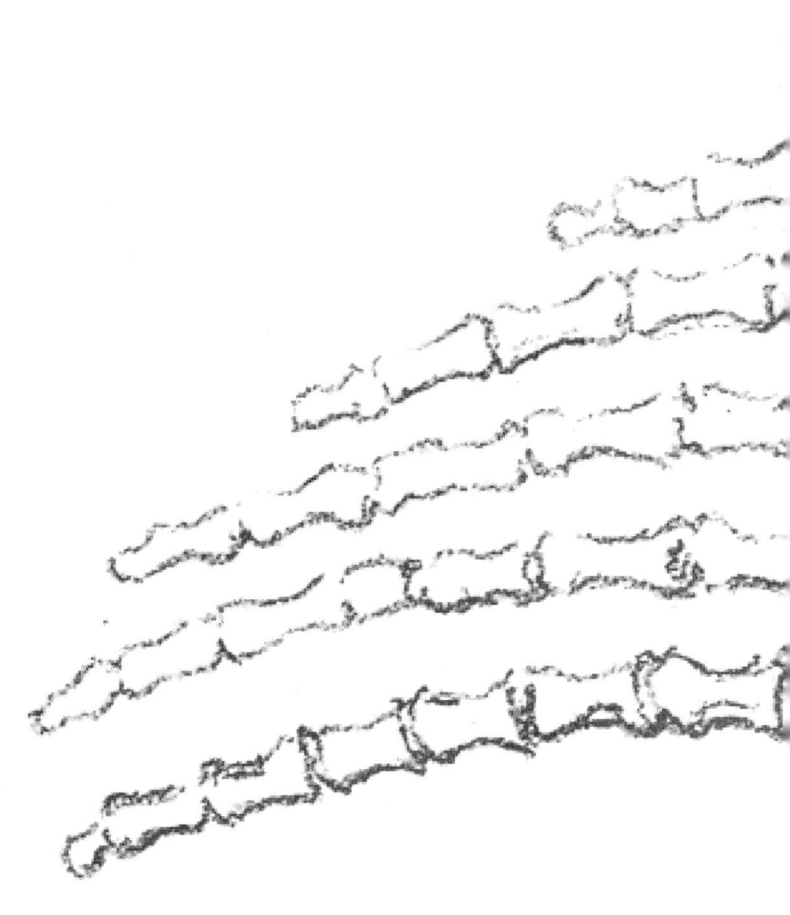

ACKNOWLEDGEMENTS

A slightly different version of the opening chapter of *The Bone Sharps* first appeared in *AlbertaViews Magazine*; thank you to the editors and publisher. Thank you as well to the Edmonton Artists' Trust Fund and to Kathryn Mulders for their early support of the novel, and to Jacqueline Baker for the literary insights, shared laughs and prairie grouses.

Gaspereau Press acknowledges the support of the Canada
Council for the Arts, the Nova Scotia Department of Tourism,
Culture & Heritage and the Government of Canada through
the Book Publishing Industry Development Program.

This is a work of fiction.

Typeset in a digital version of Baskerville by
Andrew Steeves & printed offset at Gaspereau
Press under the direction of Gary Dunfield.

7  6  5  4  3  2  1

*Library & Archives Canada Cataloguing in Publication*

Bowling, Tim, 1964–
The bone sharps / Tim Bowling.
ISBN 978-1-55447-035-8
1. Sternberg, Charles Hazelius, 1850–1943 — Fiction.  I. Title.
PS8553.O9044B65 2007    C813'.54    C2006-906950-6

GASPEREAU PRESS LIMITED
*Gary Dunfield & Andrew Steeves · Printers & Publishers*
47 Church Avenue, Kentville, Nova Scotia
Canada B4N 2M7   www.gaspereau.com